Beach Cove Home

Book 1

Nellie Brooks

Copyright © 2021 Nellie Brooks

All rights reserved

The characters and events portrayed in this book are fictitious. Any similarity to real persons, living or dead, is coincidental and not intended by the author.

No part of this book may be reproduced, or stored in a retrieval system, or transmitted in any form or by any means, electronic, mechanical, photocopying, recording, or otherwise, without express written permission of the publisher.

ISBN-13: 9798532255227

Cover design by: Nellie Brooks
Library of Congress Control Number: 2018675309
Printed in the United States of America

Contents

Title Page	1
Copyright	2
Chapter 1	7
Chapter 2	22
Chapter 3	31
Chapter 4	45
Chapter 5	52
Chapter 6	61
Chapter 7	75
Chapter 8	82
Chapter 9	92
Chapter 10	101
Chapter 11	118
Chapter 12	125
Chapter 13	138
Chapter 14	148

Chapter 15	163
Chapter 16	170
Chapter 17	181
Chapter 18	188
Chapter 19	198
Chapter 20	207
Chapter 21	223
Chapter 22	234
Chapter 23	240
Chapter 24	247
Chapter 25	257
Chapter 26	269
Chapter 27	276
Chapter 28	284
Chapter 29	290
Chapter 30	303
Chapter 31	313
Chapter 32	322
Note to the Reader	329
Books By This Author	331

Chapter 1

The sea sent her great rushing waters into the bay; the bay settled the surge and channeled it into the cove. The cove, calm and sapphirine, comforted what remained of the Atlantic's temper so that the waves lapped at the sandy beaches like kittens drinking milk.

Maisie rounded the last curve in the road as the sun settled into the highest branches of the pine trees. She slowed the white Acura to the speed of windswept houses, crying gulls, and rambling gardens.

For ten long years, she'd avoided the oyster-shaped cove that carved itself—warmer than it had any right to be—into Maine's rugged shoreline. She'd avoided the small town of Beach Cove that sat like a pearl at the tip of the cove, avoided picturing the sandy beaches that gave the cove its name, the fishing boats and lobster vessels bobbing in the harbor, the quaint shops sprinkled throughout the few streets like nuggets of sea glass.

She had more important things to do than drown in memories, so she'd avoided all of it.

Until she couldn't. Until the call of duty came, and she had to return.

Only for a brief time, though. Two days, maybe three. No more. She'd do what she had to do, give the interview, point out the places, answer the same old questions, and if she was lucky, some new ones.

She wasn't there to visit. She would not get in touch with anyone or check to see what remained of the town she'd moved to as a young bride, eager to start a family and be happy. She was simply going to slip in and out.

Her place was in New York City. Besides offering the infrastructure she needed, the Big Apple was a conglomerate of glittering distractions. Sleepy little Beach Cove, with its lazy morning mists and endless afternoons, was not.

But Maisie needed the noise of the City to drown out her thoughts. There were ringing phones to answer, deadlines to meet, desperate people to talk to, and stacks of documents covering her desk. So much work; important work. It forced her mind into a narrow one-way street. It kept her from straying into the dark.

Slowing to a crawl, Maisie entered the historic village. It was the heart of Beach Cove, as important to the town as a diamond to an engagement ring. Maisie stole glances left and right as she passed by the shop windows she used to browse and the doors she used to walk through.

Everything seemed the same...only a little *off*. Like an acquaintance Maisie couldn't place. Familiar, but out of context. In her head, she'd changed the place into something that didn't altogether match reality. Now, the village pulled on her mind, pushing it back into a shape it hadn't taken in a long time.

When she reached the far side of the village, Maisie released a pent-up breath and turned into the narrow road that led toward the house. There were the same gray Cape-Cod style houses still... The front yard hydrangeas were coming into their May greenery, the young leaves waving as Maisie passed.

It wasn't long until houses became sparse and finally trickled away. Sand started to replace soil. Gardens gave way to a different sort of beauty as native plants claimed their place. Tufts of yellow beach heather widened into swaths, their tiny flowers coaxed into bloom by the mild spring. Here and there, tussocks of little bluestem and pinweed interrupted the blooming sprawl of heather. Adding its tribute to the cove's beauty, the sinking sun streaked the evening sky in matching shades of lavender and lilac.

By the time Maisie pulled into the gravel driveway, climbed out of the car, and took her first deep breath of the salty air, everything had snapped back into place. She knew Beach Cove again. She knew it intimately, like an old friend she'd missed all along.

Maisie closed her eyes to shut out the feeling, but losing the images only awakened her other senses. The sea breeze lifted the hair off her shoulders and brushed her hands with the tenderness of a lover. The dry kelp flavoring the air, the melodies of breaking waves and rustling seagrass, the red-winged blackbird trilling its evening song...

Maisie blinked. That had done no good at all. Wiping a hair out of her face, she eyed the tall brick house at the end of the driveway, gathering courage. It seemed to her that the light of a happier past must shine behind the closed shutters.

But of course, it was all dark inside. Beach House had stood empty for ten years.

Maisie pulled her suitcase from the trunk and walked to the house. The key with the silver whale pendant was tarnished from neglect, but it unlocked the front door without complaint.

Maisie touched a fingertip to the wood. She'd painted it herself. Silk Sophistication in Carmine Excitement. The girls had giggled over the outlandish name, but it'd been the shade both she and Robert had liked best. Red because soon after they'd bought the house, Maisie had found in a magazine that a red door was an olden-day signal for weary travelers to rest the horse and stay the night.

She'd stay only a couple of nights. No longer.

Maisie pushed the door open and stepped inside. A sigh of dry rosewood and dusty marble brushed past, escaping into the night. Maisie waited until it was gone before she closed the door behind her. She set down her suitcase and flicked on the light.

Everything was the same. There was the dent in the floorboard where Alex had dropped his skates. There was the chandelier, dripping with crystals and too high to be dusted properly. The mahogany board and mirror on the wall, the green cast-iron coat tree nobody ever used. Maisie turned to the arched floor-to-ceiling windows that framed the central staircase on the far side. Beyond the windows, the overgrown lawn swept toward the beach and finally the sea.

The sea.

Maisie walked across for a better view.

The sea, always hungry, was busy swallowing the sun, and the fading light tinted the sand an unlikely anthracite. Beach grass smudged into sand, sand into sea. The only spots of color came from the white-crested waves far out, where the bay washed through craggy cliffs into the cove.

May was early yet for Maine. But in the cove, spring, this reluctant transition from barren winter to the tourist-luring glory of summer, had long started to whisper across the water and kiss the coast.

Maisie loved spring. She'd loved all the seasons here.

The first jellyfish of spring, the summer heat that brought guests and open-air concerts, the heartachingly gorgeous fall when the tourists finally left and the small town settled back on its heels to take a breath. Then winter, beautiful and lonely and never-ending, bringing out the grit in those that stayed after the charm of wood fires and hot tea had worn thin.

Maisie had loved it all.

Until.

Slackening one finger at a time, Maisie pulled off her leather gloves. They helped with the pain in the joints of her hands after typing too many emails too many days in a row, and she'd needed them for the long drive. But they wouldn't be good here where the air vibrated with salt and sand and the whispering mist snuck between the fibers of wool and leather.

She probably still had some nylon gloves in the basement closet, though it was unlikely she'd need them. Last evening's forecast had predicted a freak heatwave for Maine, so Maisie hadn't packed much. Certainly nothing warm enough for a breezy beach walk, should the forecast turn out to be wrong.

Maisie shook her head once at the window, telling the view to stop tempting her. She wasn't planning on beach walks, even though she used to love them. Especially in the early morning, before the family woke. Letting the clear water tickle her toes and her heels sink into the sand. Admiring what treasure the sea had brought her.

But the sea also took what it wanted.

Maisie cut that train of thought and returned to her suitcase. Her job was to keep her head and to stay focused. Families relied on her clear thinking when their world dove into a whirlpool of panic. Most of all, Alex needed her. Not brooding or taking anguished beach walks, but acting calm, efficient, and —

Her cell phone rang, the shrill sound startling Maisie into a hasty pat-down of her coat pockets. "Hello?"

"Mrs. Jameson?" The voice was male.

"Yes, speaking."

"It's Jim Andersen. From the Lost Souls podcast?"

Jim always sounded apologetic, as if he was afraid Maisie thought he was exploiting her heartbreak for his own purpose.

In a way, he was.

But the deal ran two ways.

Maisie clutched the phone tighter. The connection was breaking up. Beach Cove liked to swallow radio waves. "Jim. How are you?"

"Yeah, good." Jim cleared his throat in an embarrassed staccato. Maybe he thought he had no business being good when talking to her. "Is it too late to talk?"

"It's barely evening. Go ahead." Maisie shimmied out of her navy trench coat and tossed it onto the walnut chair Robert had inherited from an aunt in France. While Jim spun polite introductory wool, Maisie also kicked off her sneakers and made her way into the kitchen.

Here, too, nothing seemed to have changed. Other than being a little dustier and a lot tidier than when Maisie had kept house. She opened a cabinet.

Robert had left Maisie plenty of fancy wine, even though he hadn't managed to leave her a note. She searched until she found a cabernet; the label told her nothing beyond that. Her husband had been the connoisseur, not she. She'd simply enjoyed what he'd poured.

She'd never paid enough attention to anything.

Not even the wine labels.

"Mm-hmm." Maisie rummaged on until she found a corkscrew and a glass that she dusted with the sleeve of her button-down shirt.

"Anyway." Jim had worked his way to the actual purpose of his call. "I could have the team in Beach Cove, like, tomorrow?"

"Fine." Holding the phone between cheek and shoulder, Maisie jerked the cork out of the bottle neck. "How many are you, exactly?"

"Like, five." Jim coughed. "Is there a motel or something?"

Maisie poured herself a glass. He wanted to come tomorrow and hadn't yet looked up places to stay? Hopefully, he'd turn out to be a better sleuth than that promised... His email had said he was an investigative reporter, but there'd been no official header or footer that showed he came from a reputable news outlet.

Not that it mattered. She'd take whoever she could get. Whoever wanted to help. Jim was fine. He had a platform.

"We don't have hotels or even motels near Beach Cove. There used to be a few inns a couple of towns over, but as far as I know, they're closed this time of year. So are the B&Bs." Maisie lifted the glass to her lips and swallowed.

Sour!

She spat the wine into the sink, frowning at the burgundy rivulets of vinegar. "You can stay with me if you bring sleeping bags. The house is big enough to be an inn, but I don't know what the linen situation is. If there are any, they're dusty. Or moldy."

"Well no, we don't want to bother you. I didn't mean to fish for an invitation and—"

"Nonsense." Maisie stepped on the trash can pedal and tossed her glass in. It hit the metal, the long stem snapping with a satisfying crunch. She sighed. Nothing about being in Beach House was going to be easy, least of all controlling her emotions. "Don't be silly; there's nowhere else to stay. You can help out and make breakfast."

Jim hemmed, but when she didn't respond, he eventually said, "Okay. Thank you, Mrs. Jameson, that sounds great. We'll bring eggs and bacon."

"I'm too old for bacon."

"Oh, sure. Do you like bagels and cream cheese?"

"Coffee would be good." Eating had become strictly functional. At fifty-two, Maisie finally was that skinny stick who could wear anything off the rack. But it wasn't worth it by a long shot. If she could, she'd take back her pleasure in food. And her curves.

"Coffee. Got it." Jim sounded conciliatory. "We'll see you tomorrow morning then?"

"Don't be very late, if you can. I don't want to be here, least of all on my own. Just me and this place—that doesn't work so well."

"I understand. I'll make sure we'll get there early, Mrs. Jameson. Thanks for the invitation. Take care."

"You, too." Maisie ended the call.

A whole night ahead of her, quiet, and dark, and

quiet. No flashing lights, no drunken yelling in the street, no midnight-laughter or honking to break the silence.

Maisie picked her phone back up. She had audiobooks to keep her company and she used them all the time, even if she wasn't in the mood for a book. She tapped, and an authoritative narrator picked up mid-sentence, reading from a daily news digest.

Tucking her phone into the pocket of her jeans, Maisie got her suitcase and carried it upstairs. Time to catch up on email.

The mahogany steps creaked in all the same places.

She'd meant to stay in one of the guestrooms. But if Jim was going to bring four or five people with who-knew-what sleeping arrangements, they'd need the guestrooms to spread out.

So it was the master bedroom for her after all.

Maisie padded down the high hall—Beach House had been built back in the day when heating bills must've been considered fun and dusting kept you elastic—and stepped into the old bedroom.

Her and Robert's old bedroom.

She opened the door with a quick push and looked inside. The curtains on the window moved as if someone had brushed against them, dust motes rising from the hand-laced batiste into the dim light.

It was only the door that had moved the air.

Maisie set her suitcase down.

There was the carved rosewood bed, the slim

vase of blue Spode on her nightstand. Robert had put a new flower in it every night.

From the day of her wedding to the day their son disappeared.

She'd been happy here.

They all had been so happy here.

Back in the kitchen, Maisie switched on the recessed light over the sink, then off again. Darker was better. Night had fallen entirely, and bright light just made the empty kitchen feel cavernous.

The old gas range—top of the line thirty years ago but long since outdated by electronic devices so sharp they did all but the eating—hissed to life. Maisie let the flame burn for a moment, though she didn't have anything to cook. There was propane in the tank, then.

Thanks to Liz, Maisie had gas, electricity, and water. Maisie had hired the young woman to check on the house now and then. Liz kept an eye on the carpenter ants in the woodwork, made sure the roof didn't leak, and shut off the water when the temperatures dropped.

Maisie tried to peer through the French doors into the sunroom, but it was too dark to see anything other than her reflection. The garden was out there. Used to be, anyway. Liz watched the house, but she had kids and a proper job as an accountant.

She wouldn't have been able to take on the garden, even if Maisie had thought to ask.

But it hadn't even occurred to her. The garden wasn't a turn-on-the-sprinkler job. Every plant had an opinion about soil, pruning, watering, timing. Maintaining it took hours, and well-off as Robert had left Maisie, she didn't splurge on hiring a gardener. She only had to keep Beach House—old, rambling, and impossibly high-taxed as it was—until Alex found his way back there.

Tomorrow morning, she'd make herself a cup of coffee. She'd hold on to it as she surveyed the damage. Maybe not all was lost. Maybe at least the boxwood had survived the decade of neglect...and possibly the roses?

Maisie closed her eyes and breathed the pictures of the past away like a painful contraction.

Don't go there.

She had rules. Simple, but dearly paid for with experience.

Don't remember. Don't imagine. Don't speculate.

Those were the rules on top of the list; the most important ones. They were the hardest ones, too.

Maisie shook her hair out of her face. A single shoulder-length strand sailed through the air and landed on her sleeve. She picked it up and rolled it between her fingertips. When she'd left Beach Cove, she'd been blonde, courtesy of the sun and the salty air. Beach-bleach blond, Robert had called the color.

That was over. Now she was gray.

Maisie knew Robert wouldn't have liked it. Not

dying her hair felt like a benign act of revenge, even though it had nothing to do with him and everything with the fact that she couldn't be bothered.

Maisie tapped the trash can open and let the hair flutter inside. It settled on the shards.

She shouldn't have broken the glass—antique crystal, inherited by Robert from a rich European uncle or cousin. Maisie couldn't remember because she'd never met them; she'd never met anyone other than Robert's parents and sister. Once for the wedding, once for the funeral. The Jamesons weren't warm people by a long shot. Robert had grown up in boarding schools, the relationship with his parents summed up in a yearly settling of tuition and a monthly letter to practice penmanship and composition or some such.

Then again, Robert was gone and had left Maisie everything. It didn't matter if she broke all the glasses. The Jamesons sure didn't care.

She opened the cupboard and the fridge, taking stock. Liz had come through. Sort of. Tonight's dinner could be either a bowl of frosted flakes or ramen noodles.

Maisie fished out the hot pink pack of wheat noodles and weighed it in her hand. She didn't mind ramen, but she wanted enough calories to get through the night. If hunger woke her, she'd lie awake for hours. She'd have to fight hard to stick to her rules.

Suddenly starving, she squinted at the label, then put the pack back. It wasn't enough. She picked up her phone, found a restaurant she didn't recognize that delivered, and called.

"Beach Cove Corner Café, Tom here. How can I help you?"

The voice was familiar; the name matched. Ellie's son. Maisie closed her eyes. She'd called Tommy, of all people.

"Hello?"

"I'd like to order a cheese pizza for delivery, please. Large." It might as well last her a few meals. "A bottle of wine, too. Red, if you have any. I'm on Seashore Lane."

There was a small pause, filled with background clanging and distant voices. "Mrs. Jameson? Is that you, Mrs. Jameson?"

Maisie opened her eyes again. "Hello, Tommy. You work at a restaurant now?"

"Better, Mrs. Jameson. I own the restaurant. Are you back?"

"Only for a couple of days."

"In your house?" He sounded as if Alex had pulled out a coveted new video game, or Robert offered to take the boys sailing.

"I'm in my house," Maisie confirmed. "How are you, Tom? I had no idea—" He owned a café? But of course, he did. He'd grown up.

Tom skipped the small talk. "My mom will want to see you," he said, his voice warm with conviction. "Did you tell her you're back?"

"Uh." Maisie put a hand to her forehead. When she spoke, the words came out too hasty. "No, it's only a spur-of-the-moment thing, and I'm not staying. Tommy, can I order a pizza, please? I'm starving."

"Oh. You certainly can, Mrs. Jameson. What can I get you?"

Maisie repeated her order and ended the call.

All of twenty minutes in Beach Cove, and the town had found her out.

Chapter 2

"Mom, you'll never guess who just called."

Ellie, phone pressed between cheek and shoulder, lowered the lemon sole onto a layer of ice. It was a beautiful fish, a perfect, shimmering oval molded by the sea.

Even though Ellie had run the Beach Cove Fish for most of her adult life, it still surprised her when she had fish left over at the end of the day. Who wouldn't snap up this beauty while they could? It made no sense.

"Sweetheart, how would I know who called you. Dad?" It'd be newsworthy indeed if Dale had called. His own son, too.

Ellie picked up the second sole, as glossy and perfect as the first, and added it to the cooler bag. Hopefully, the lemons she'd bought last week were still good. Lemon juice, maybe a little peel, in a light cream sauce would be perfection. Had to be real lemon though, the stuff in that little yellow squirt thing was too acidic. Sole had such a delicate flavor.

"You know your friend from the brick house by the sea?" Tom's voice ebbed in and out, which meant he was kneading dough, phone pressed between cheek and shoulder. Like mother, like son.

Ellie looked up. The brick house. "*Maisie?*"

"Yep."

"Maisie called? You?" Ellie cleared her throat. "She called you? Are you serious?"

"Yes. I knew right away it was her. She's got that soft voice like she's—"

"Oh my." Ellie turned on the faucet to wash her hands. "Maisie, huh? What could she possibly want from you?"

Her son scoffed. "Thanks, Mom."

Ellie laughed. "I didn't mean it like *that*. I love you. Everybody loves you."

"Sure they do."

"Come on, spill. Don't leave me hanging." Ellie shut off the water and dried her hands. Tom was the same age as Alex, Maisie's son. The two of them had grown up together, been best friends. Was that why Maisie was calling Tom? Her thoughts began to whirr like an outboard motor spinning dry air.

"She didn't actually call *me*. She called the Café, and she didn't even say her name. But of course I know her voice and the address, so I asked if it was her."

"Are you kidding me," Ellie said again. So Maisie hadn't called Tom specifically, so that was…good? "What did she say?"

"She wanted a pizza."

"No!" Ellie slapped the counter. It stung, and she shook out her fingers. Then she ripped off a paper towel and rubbed the handprint away. "Tom, are you saying she *ordered* one? For here? She's in Beach Cove?"

"Yep," Tom said easily. "Anyway, gotta go."

Ellie ignored this. The kid was twenty-six, and he still couldn't resist teasing her. "She said she's at the house?"

"Yes, she's at her house. At least she ordered a pizza to be delivered to her house. In Beach Cove. The one with the garden."

"Yes, I know which house. Listen, I guess—" Ellie hesitated. Should she go see Maisie, uninvited and all? But then, why not? Maisie hadn't stood on common courtesy when she'd left Beach Cove, either.

They understood. It'd been too much to bear. Forget manners.

But even so, it'd been bewildering. Everyone had been reeling; there'd been too much loss in their small community already. And then suddenly, Maisie had been gone too. Just like that. One day she'd been there, the next she'd dropped out of sight like a cast iron anchor.

Tom made noises, but Ellie wasn't ready to let him go. There had to be more. "What sort of pizza did she order?" she demanded.

"What sort of pizza?" Tom paused. "Ma'am, I don't know if I'm allowed to give out that sort of privileged—"

"Tell me right now, Thomas."

"Oh, okay. Cheese. Plain ol' cheese pie."

"What?" Ellie frowned. "Cheese pie? No. Make the

Kalamata one with rosemary and goat cheese. Use the organic rosemary."

"Mom, I can't just change her order. What if she doesn't like goat cheese?"

"Maisie wanted to get a goat so she could have goat cheese every day."

"Oh yeah? Alex never said anything about goats. Why didn't they get one?"

"Um…" Ellie tried to remember. When she did, she smiled. "She thought about it for a few days, and then she said that she already *had* goat cheese whenever she wanted. She just bought it at the market."

"She didn't think the store-bought cheese was any good?"

"No, she loved it."

"Right."

"She probably never told Alex about the goat, so you didn't hear about it."

"Yeah." Her son's voice went quiet. "Probably."

"So use goat cheese," Ellie said gently. "And I'll deliver it."

"Mom. You already messed with her order. Think maybe you shouldn't just show up on her doorstep?"

Ellie sighed. "Why, are you worried about your reputation? Think she'll give you a bad review online?"

"I'm worried… I don't know that I'm *worried*. Seems pushy though."

Ellie shrugged. "I'm not letting her leave without seeing her."

"Think she changed?"

Ellie bit the inside corner of her mouth. It'd been a decade since she'd seen her best friend. It'd been a decade since any of them had really heard from Maisie. "I expect she has," she said, and now it was her own voice that was quiet.

"Yeah."

There was a moment of silence. Then background buzzing on Tom's end, the words muffled. "Shoot, I forgot to pour out that—Mom, I got to go, we're busy."

"I'll be down in twenty for the pizza."

"I'll have it ready." Tom hung up.

Ellie pushed the phone into the back pocket of her jeans.

Maisie was back in town.

When she'd left, life had gone on in Beach Cove. But for months, it'd been like living on a ship that had lost its figurehead in a storm. They'd all drifted, aimless, waters undeclared.

The girls still met now and then. Ran across each other at the market or the post office, but it wasn't the same. They'd all agonized when Alex went missing. They'd all frozen in horror when Robert took his own life. Shocked and frightened, they'd all turned to their own families.

Everyone had tried to make their marriage work a little better. Everyone still hugged their kids a little longer, a little tighter, a lot more often.

Ellie checked the time. Ten minutes until she had to leave to pick up the pizza.

Ten minutes was plenty of time for a couple of

calls. They should know what was going on. She let her finger hover over the speed dial.

Sam or Cate?

Sam could be stubborn. Cate was nice all around, poor thing. She'd be a better wrap-up, more likely to support Ellie's decision to go and see Maisie.

"Ellie?" Sam sounded as if she'd been sleeping.

"Did I wake you? Guess what. Maisie is back."

"Yep."

Yep? Sam should be dazed, not yepping the big news. Ellie narrowed her eyes. "Do you know something I don't, Samantha? I call you the minute I have information and you—"

"I know nothing." Sam blew air into Ellie's ear, making the line hum. "I just had a feeling."

"Oh for crying out loud, Sam, the woman's been gone for…since forever. Nine, ten years, and she hasn't called once." Ellie frowned. "Why aren't you surprised? I almost fell off my chair when I heard."

"I don't know." Sam cleared her throat. "Just seemed like it was time for her to come back, didn't it?"

Ellie shook her head. "What are you talking about? It didn't seem like that at all. There's no way I saw this coming."

Sam sighed. "Forget I said anything. You're right. There's no reason she should come back as far as we know."

"True." Ellie pressed her lips together. Right. Maisie would only come back if she had a reason. A reason other than her friends. "Do you think—something has changed?" Her heart hiccupped. Was there news?

"I think it must've," Sam murmured. "Yes, something must've happened. Have you talked to her? How do you know she's back? Did you see her?"

"She ordered food at the Café, to be delivered to Beach House. Tom told me. He said she didn't give her name right away."

"Oh boy, is she trying to hide?" Sam didn't sound sleepy anymore. "Ha. She's come to the wrong place for that. What exactly did she say to Tommy?"

Ellie nodded. This was more like it. "Only that she wanted a pizza delivered to her house. Cheese."

"Cheese? Hmm, strange. Is she alone?"

"I—don't know." It hadn't occurred to Ellie that Maisie could've brought someone with her. "It's possible. Could be she's married again and has kids, right?"

"Wouldn't that be so weird."

"I mean, good for her."

"Sure."

Ellie inhaled, breathing over the odd feeling curdling in her belly. "I'm going over there. I'm delivering her pizza."

Surprise thinned Sam's voice. "Really? You think that's a good idea?"

"I'm not sure I care." Ellie shrugged, aware Sam couldn't see.

"Did you say a *cheese* pizza?"

"I know. I told Tom to upgrade."

Sam hummed doubtfully. "What if she really wants a cheese pie? Maisie might've completely reinvented herself. She also wants to be left alone."

"I'm not giving Maisie that choice," Ellie said simply. "It's my son's restaurant, and it's goat cheese pizza. She doesn't have to eat it if she doesn't like it. And I'm delivering for the family business. Bam. Deal with it, everyone."

Sam chuckled. "Well, if that's how it is, good luck. I hope it goes well."

Ellie hesitated. "Do you want me to call when I get back?"

"No. No, that's your little adventure, Ells. If Maisie wants to get in touch with me, she's got my number."

"You're still mad. Ten years later."

Sam scoffed into the phone. "No, I'm not."

Ellie raised an eyebrow. Sam could be as stubborn as a limpet. "I'll let you know how it went."

"No, I—"

"And then we'll take it from there. We don't know how we feel yet."

"We do!"

"No," Ellie repeated firmly. "We *don't*. We never heard her side of the story."

"Whatever."

Ellie smiled. When Sam grumped like that, she was trying to protect her feelings. "It's okay to feel hurt, Samantha, but we don't let that stand in the way of communication and connection," Ellie said primly.

"Stop it."

"And *I* love *you*. So, I'll let you know," Ellie said. "And then we'll see."

"You do what you want."

"Yes," Ellie confirmed. "Sam?"

"What."

"Do you want a couple of lemon soles? They're perfect. Nicest pair of flatfish I've seen in years."

It was quiet on the other end. Then, Sam huffed. "Fine. I won't turn my phone off. And I don't want your lemon sole."

"I'll bring them over before I go," Ellie promised. "A nice, tender lemon sole with cream sauce will calm you right down, tiger."

"Funny," Sam muttered. But she did sound mollified, so Ellie figured she could let Sam go.

She had two more calls to make before Tom pulled the pizza out of the oven.

Chapter 3

The doorbell chimed.

The tune cut like a blade. Maisie pressed her palms against the cool soapstone of the kitchen island. Her heart constricted.

She'd listened for that chime so hard and long it was a wonder her eardrums hadn't burst. At the same time, she'd dreaded hearing it because it might not be Alex waiting outside the door but a couple of police officers. Faces pinched, eyes dark with pity, unsure how to tell her.

The doorbell rang again. An impatient doubling-ring this time that pulled her back; no police officer with sad news rang like that.

Maisie let go of the counter, closed her laptop, crossed the hall in socked feet, and opened the door.

Ellie tilted her head. "Hello, stranger."

The air left Maisie's lungs. Not in a quick gasp, but soft and low like an old balloon that passes from one state of being to another. Her shoulders sagged as if she was caving into herself, and Maisie grabbed the door for support. "Ellie."

"That's right. Ellie." Smiling sweetly, Ellie walked

past Maisie into the house. "I'm glad you remember my name – I wasn't sure you would."

She'd known they'd come to see her the minute she'd recognized Tom's voice. It wasn't a surprise, but it managed to be a shock.

Maisie glanced at the blue night outside. Two stars shone bright and clear, and a hint of lavender remained in the navy sky. She couldn't remember ever seeing stars over New York City. She'd never checked.

Maisie closed the door and faced her friend. "Ellie."

Ellie's chest heaved. She tossed her dark-brown hair back, eyes flashing, the smile gone.

Maisie waited. Ellie hadn't changed much. Maybe there were a few more wrinkles, but the eyes were still as big and blue as the bay.

"Thanks for nothing, Maisie." Ellie opened her hands, and the pizza box dropped onto the wood floor.

Maisie nodded, guilt stapling her heart to her ribs. She was lucky Ellie hadn't aimed the missile at her head. "I'm so sorry. I needed to get out."

"I understand." Ellie's lips pressed into a thin line. "We all did. But it didn't help, not after a year or so."

"Oh, my dear." Maisie knew that face. Ellie cried when she was angry.

"Don't *dear* me." Ellie's chin started to quiver. "I can't believe you. Ten years without a word, Maisie Jameson. If it weren't for Tom, I wouldn't even know you came back. You do that a lot?"

Maisie took a deep breath. "Do what?"

"Come to Beach Cove and not tell us?"

Maisie held her friend's gaze. "This is the first time I've been back. I promise. I haven't even looked into all the rooms in the house yet, and you already know I'm here." It wasn't a lie, but it was evasive. If she'd had her way, she'd not have let Ellie know. Or Sam. Or Cate.

"Hmm." Ellie's eyebrows rose. Not in a way that showed she believed Maisie, more…resigned.

Maisie hesitated. She should tell Ellie that she needed to work. She did; there were always kids going missing, desperate parents that needed the support Maisie provided. But she couldn't get the words out.

"Want some pizza, Ellie?" Maisie finally asked. "I haven't had anything all day. I was about to find something on TV and eat."

Ellie sighed. Her temper flared easily, but the storm burned bright and fast and settled as sudden as it had come. Maisie had often wished she could be like Ellie and have her feelings come and go the way clouds drift across the sky. But she was woven of a different fabric, sterner and unforgiving of the holes torn by time and fate.

"Ellie, I know I've hurt your feelings. I know. But I love you. You, Sam, and Cate. As much as always. So stay and have pizza with me, yes?"

Ellie nodded. "Okay. Yes."

"Good." Maisie squatted and closed the lid of the pizza box. The bottom had made amoeba-shaped grease spots on the antique pine boards, but it didn't matter.

Once, when Alex had been old enough to understand, Maisie had explained that from then on, he should wipe his feet on the doormat. He'd looked at her, unsure why she worried about the tidal mud that caked his toes together, then suddenly bolted into the house as if the request had just been too weird to handle.

Maisie had decided right then and there that she'd let that one go. Shiny floors weren't going to be her thing. Besides, she'd found that the nicks and marks on the soft boards were like entries in the journal she was too lazy to keep. The day the mover dropped the desk. The day Alex shot his first goal and wouldn't let her take his soccer cleats off. The day Ellie got so angry she almost threw a cheese pie at Maisie.

"I'll mop that up." Ellie pointed at the greasy smudge, shrugged off her parka, and tossed it on top of Maisie's trench coat. "I'm sorry."

"No, don't worry about it. It doesn't matter." Maisie stood and looked at Ellie. Ellie, who had bravely come to Beach House to confront her. She sure didn't have to apologize for a stain.

"Come here." Maisie wasn't a hugger, never had been, but now she opened her arms.

A small sound escaped Ellie's throat. She came and hugged Maisie, and the scent of her hair was warm and sweet and that of Maisie's best friend forever. Cross yourself and die.

"Girl," Ellie whispered, "you scared the living *daylights* out of us." She stepped back, wrapping her arms around herself.

"I texted you. You knew where I went, and you knew why." It'd been all she'd been able to give.

Ellie waved the text aside like a pesky fly and bent to pick up the pizza box. "We didn't know what was going on with you, Maisie. And after Robert and all… Next time, you come to my house, ring the door, look me in the eyes, and *tell me* you're leaving. No texts. Not good enough."

Maisie followed Ellie into the kitchen. She'd only switched on the dim lamp over the kitchen table so she could work. But with Ellie here, the lone light shone a little brighter. "What if I have to catch a train and don't have time to come to your house?" she tried to joke.

Maybe it wasn't the time for joking, but Maisie knew guilt. For a decade, guilt had been her daily bread, air, and water. She showered in guilt every morning, drank it, ate it, slept in it.

Ellie could scold all day long, heap on as much guilt as she liked. Maisie was already buried in it too deep to possibly tell the difference.

"There's no train station in Beach Cove." Ellie set the box onto the island. "Why is it so dark in here? Seriously, woman. Do you want to make yourself miserable?"

With a flick of her finger, Maisie switched on the kitchen lights. "Better?"

"Mm-hmm. I brought wine; it's still in the car. Do

you have glasses?"

"Yes, I do." Maisie opened the cabinet and pulled out two of the long-stemmed wine glasses. "I'll rinse them."

Ellie reappeared before the glasses were washed, a bottle of wine in each hand.

Maisie opened more drawers in search of a kitchen towel. "I asked Tom for one bottle only."

"The other one's mine," Ellie declared and squinted at the labels. "He gave me two different ones."

"Let's try them both and see which one's better." Maisie glanced at her friend as she dried the glasses. Wine with friends, dinners on the patio, picnics on the beach—that was in the past. Still, having Ellie in the kitchen felt good. But like driving through the village, it also felt off.

"Slice?" Ellie asked, putting the corkscrew back into the drawer and opening the pizza box.

"Sure." Maisie got out plates—the ones with the laurel leaves on the rim; she'd forgotten about them—and rinsed and dried them as well.

"Um, I thought we could do a little better than plain cheese, so I..." Ellie reached into the box, the crust tearing softly as she pulled slices off the pie.

The aroma of roasted rosemary and baked pear wafted into the air.

Maisie swallowed. She hadn't had good pizza in... She couldn't even remember. New York City had plenty of fine pizza, but Maisie had never taken the time to find a place she liked.

She pushed plates under the triangles. "I was going to watch TV," Maisie said, even though she'd meant to work, not watch TV. But now that Ellie was here—how deep would she have to delve back into the past if they talked?

"TV it is," Ellie said, not looking up.

Maybe Ellie didn't know how to tackle this thing, this reconciliation, this catching-up with a lost decade, either.

They carried their dinner into the living room where they sat on the couch, balancing the plates on their laps like teenagers. They settled on a cooking show and let chatter about garlic and butter and ways to peel a tomato fill the silence between them.

When the cooks started sampling the crawfish étouffée they'd prepared, assuring the audience that it was delicious, Ellie set her plate on the coffee table, grabbed the remote, and hit the mute button.

"I don't know how to do this, Maisie."

"I don't either." Maisie set her half-eaten slice back on the plate. It had goat cheese, which she loved, and she was hungry, but she couldn't enjoy it. "I don't know how to do anything anymore other than look for Alex. It's like a switch flipped and shut down all that was... I don't know. Me, I guess."

Ellie's eyebrows drew close in concern. "I understand, Maisie, I do. But falling out of touch like that —" She shook her head. "I've been worrying about you a good deal more than I think you'd care for. I'm forever thinking about what happened to you, how you are, where you are, what I'd say if I'd see you again. If you are set on not being in touch, I want to get those thoughts out of my head. I don't want to worry about you anymore."

Maisie nodded and looked down at her folded hands, wishing she could feel more than she did. But it was only more guilt, more things she should've done better. "All that grief was because of me, Ells. Be glad I left. I could barely live with myself. I certainly was a burden to everyone else."

Ellie rested her head against the back of the couch. "But you don't get to decide what I do with my burdens. I sure don't send them off to New York City when they're at their most fragile." She exhaled. "I've been so scared to get the news that you'd…like with Robert. That it'd gotten to be too much."

Maisie's hands twitched. "Oh, Ellie. No. I can't drop the ball the way Robert did. But I also couldn't stay in Beach Cove without being reminded of it. It's like my mind splintered into… I don't know. Shards. Fragments I couldn't put back together. I had to get away from Beach Cove to focus because I'm all Alex has. I have to find him. I can't give up. Ever."

Ellie's eyes were dark. "Thing is, I need to check up on my friends in person when, you know— they're *splintering* into *shards*. Or don't have enough strength left to say bye to their best friends. Or consider themselves a burden that has to take itself away."

With a groan, Maisie sank back into the couch. "Weren't you glad to be rid of me? Come on."

Ellie threw her a stern look. "No. I wasn't. Sam

wasn't glad. Cate wasn't glad. None of us were glad. Let me ask you this, Maisie."

Maisie lifted her chin to show she was listening.

"Were you glad to get rid of *us*? Did we weigh you down, maybe because we reminded you of what you had before Alex disappeared?"

Maisie inhaled through her nose, then slowly blew out the breath through pursed lips. "Maybe," she muttered. "No, not weigh me down. Keep me tethered to what was gone."

"And that's why we'd have appreciated a call. To make sure you tethered yourself to something new and wouldn't fly off entirely."

"Sorry."

"Your sorry is no good here." Ellie leaned forward and refilled their wine glasses, then handed Maisie's to her.

"Okay." Maisie took it and sipped meekly.

"Were you ever planning on getting in touch? I mean, if Tom wouldn't have let me know, would you've called me?"

Slowly, Maisie nodded. Somewhere deep down, she'd known she'd see everyone again. "I didn't have a plan. But yes. I was going to get in touch. Not now. But sometime."

Ellie sighed. "Your lack of enthusiasm isn't super flattering, but I guess we'll work with what we've got." She cleared her throat. "I told Sam and Cate that you're here."

There was no avoiding meeting them all. But now that the dice were cast, now that Ellie had set the ball in motion—Maisie touched her throat, felt the skin lift and fall with her heartbeat. Was she excited? "I'm glad." Her voice wavered, uncertain.

"Go on and sound even more doubtful than that," Ellie said. "You're lucky we're even talking to you after your ten-year stunt. But ..."

Maisie smiled. "But you love me too much?"

"Not that we should, mind you."

"Got it. I understand, Ellie. I'm asking for nothing. I just have to find my son." Maisie set her empty glass on the coffee table. Their peace seemed sturdier, the silence more honest. "Why didn't Sam and Cate come with you to throw pizza boxes at me?"

"They said I should go over first, check you out. See how much you can handle."

"Ah."

Ellie smiled back. "They'll be here tomorrow."

Something turned in Maisie's chest, like a cat settling in a sunny spot. "Well, tell them I can handle it, I guess."

"Since we settled that you didn't come to Beach Cove to relieve our worried souls—what did bring you back?" Ellie tried to make it sound breezy, but Maisie heard the tension in her voice.

The first cook had taken his crawfish dish off-screen. Now a woman pummeled dough. She looked like the type that would make a toddler eat asparagus.

"Always the same," Maisie muttered. "Looking for Alex."

Ellie shifted as if to take her hand but didn't. "No

news then?" she asked softly.

"No. Nothing. The closest I got was a sighting in Spain four years ago, but it turned out to be a different young man. Over the years all the other leads dried up. One after the other."

"What's happening in Beach Cove then?" Maisie felt Ellie's eyes drill into her. "Are you going to stay?"

"I can't stay long. I'm just here to try something new. Do you know podcasts?"

"Yes, I do know podcasts. Everyone knows podcasts. There isn't a room in my house that hasn't profited from them."

"What do you mean?"

"I listen to them when I'm cleaning. Once I start, I don't want to stop listening, so I don't stop cleaning, and on and on. You know."

"I don't… Okay." Maisie didn't have a big enough apartment for cleaning sprees. She cleared away what she used as soon as she was done, and it took all of five minutes to run the vacuum cleaner over the patch of carpet.

"Anyways. What about podcasts?" Ellie said encouragingly.

"There's this, I don't know, true-crime podcast. Do you know about those?"

"I do. It's a thing."

Maisie pressed her hands together and put them between her knees. "The guy who's doing the podcast has contacted me."

"No way. Which one?"

"It's called Lost Soul."

Ellie's eyes widened. "Lost Souls with Jim and Ashley Andersen?"

"Jim's the one who called me."

"Maisie, that's good. They're good. They sink their teeth in. I mean – they know what they're doing."

"I hope so." Maisie exhaled. "Have they ever actually found anyone?"

"Yes, I think so. They ask their audience to help look for people, maybe call in a tip they've kept to themselves, or do some internet sleuthing. And they have a large audience, thousands of people across the world. That's a lot of people that want to help. Tapping into that can be a great resource, Maisie." Ellie picked up her glass. "Are they coming here?"

"Yes, they are. Tomorrow. They want to see where it happened. I told them it won't make a difference, but they want to describe the beach and everything in their podcast."

"Let me know if I can help. I can come and cook or whatever you need."

A sudden rush of warmth filled Maisie. "Do you want to stay tonight?" Maisie asked, the words slipping from her lips before she could think.

Ellie opened her mouth, then closed it again.

"Sorry," Maisie said hastily. "Forget it." Of course Ellie didn't want to sleep in Beach House as if nothing at all had changed. It wasn't a good idea for Maisie, either. Slipping back into her old life was too easy. She couldn't afford to look back.

Ellie sounded apologetic when she said, "I'd love

to, but Dale and Tom are waiting for me. And this is just a little... A little..."

"I know. I'm sorry." Maisie stood and grabbed her plate and glass off the coffee table. "I'm going to do the dishes if you want to get going."

Ellie checked her phone, then uncurled as well. "I think so. I didn't realize how late it was. I should get home."

A few more polite words, a quick hug, and Ellie left.

Maisie stood alone in her kitchen, with only two plates and two glasses in the sink for company. She sat, flipped open her laptop, and settled her mind by counting to a hundred. Take a breath, release a breath.

She could still respond to a few emails so Angela wouldn't have to.

Angela was smart and educated, big-hearted and warm, and knew more about running Maisie's organization than Maisie herself. But Angela was also pushing seventy. She had a bad knee, five sons, and seventeen grandkids ranging from two to thirty-two.

Maisie clicked on the first email.

Ellie didn't need to go back home. If their situation was still the same, Ellie could've given Dale a quick call. Tommy was twenty-six. He didn't need his mom to get through the night, either.

Maisie closed her laptop and stood, then threw the empty box away and washed the plates and glasses. She switched off the lights, leaving only the one over the kitchen table, and went to bed.

Chapter 4

"Ellie? Did I wake you?" Cate stuffed Allen's pillow under her own; hers was as flat as a middle schooler's sense of humor, but he'd just ordered himself a nice new one.

"Cate? What's the time?"

Cate glanced at the clock on the nightstand. It showed past midnight. "Sorry! I thought you'd still be up."

"Those days are gone." Ellie yawned. "I barely make it past ten on a good day."

"Sorry," Cate repeated. "I didn't realize it was this late. I'll call tomorrow, go back to sleep."

"It's okay. What's going on?"

Cate hesitated. "It's just I can't stop thinking about Maisie. Is there any news?"

"No news about Alex, no." Ellie's down comforter rustled. Her bedroom door creaked open and shut with a click.

Cate felt her neck flush warm. It wasn't like her to be so inconsiderate. She'd messed up, calling this late. "I'm so sorry, Ellie. Is Dale home?"

"He's sleeping. I just went into the family room."

"Sorry."

Ellie yawned again. "Stop apologizing, Cate. I would've called too."

Cate swallowed the thought that in that case, Ellie might've sent a quick text before going to bed. But that was wrong. Cate should have texted herself instead of expecting Ellie to take care of her. And Cate shouldn't have forgotten the time.

"Cate?

Cate pulled herself together. "Yes. So how did it go? How does she look?"

"She's older, like the rest of us. But it suits her. Unlike the rest of us, she's gotten thinner. She probably doesn't eat enough. And her hair isn't blond anymore; it's silver. She pulls it off, though. It looks good."

"She's fifty-two, isn't she?" Cate felt a twinge of dread. She was fifty-one herself, and she wasn't thin or pulled her gray off.

"She's three years older than me, and I'm—yeah. She's fifty-two."

"We missed her big birthday."

"Hang on just a second. I'm thirsty." A fridge door plopped open.

Cate hadn't liked turning fifty, or fifty-one for that matter. Maisie was the oldest of them, their birthday trailblazer. Cate was next, followed by Ellie. Sam, at forty-five, was the spring chicken, though she often seemed older than the rest of them. It used to be so comforting that Maisie rounded milestones before it was Cate's turn. It used to give her the courage to turn older, too.

But Cate had turned the big corner without Maisie showing the way. And the way wasn't obvious; Cate couldn't see it. She wasn't graceful and posh like Maisie; she wasn't sparkly and sweet like Ellie. She was far from being strong and intuitive like Sam. She was just an aging high school teacher with a belly, whose best-kept secret was that she'd never made it out of the identity crisis of her teenage years. And at fifty-one, time was running out. She could *die* not being sure of herself. Drop at any moment.

Ellie was back. "Cate, *Maisie* missed her big birthday. Or at least she missed celebrating it with us. We'd have thrown her a party if she'd been around."

Cate pushed her duvet off and stepped into her slippers. The comfy ugly ones Allen couldn't stand.

But Allen was teaching relaxation techniques to stressed business types in Connecticut, and Cate was free to do whatever she liked. Eat chocolate despite the span of her hips, wear ugly slippers, toss and turn and snore at night. Allen always slept on his back, arms crossed over his chest like a stone mummy, and he'd told her plenty of times that she slept like a hog, claiming too much of the bed and waking him with her fidgeting.

"Are you alone, Cate?" Ellie asked. "Where's that no-good husband of yours?"

"Allen's a good husband. He's holding a workshop somewhere."

"How is his therapy going? He promised he'd go,

didn't he?"

Cate sat back on the bed. He'd yelled at her, all wound up after one of his workshops. The girls had heard everything, and so Cate had been forced to put her foot down, even though everyone was allowed to lose it once in a while. She'd gotten Allen to apologize and explain about his ever-increasing workload and figured that was the end of it. But the next day, he'd surprised her by apologizing again, more genuinely, and offering to see someone to deal with his stress.

"I think he's making progress." She could hear how unconvincing she sounded.

It's great. I'm getting ahead. She said I'm growing faster than anyone else she's been seeing, so I think things are good.

That's what Allen had said when Cate asked how therapy was going. But Cate's sensors were sharpened by scores of students claiming the cat ate their homework. The cat never did, and neither did the dog. So if Allen thought she was buying it, he was wrong. Not only did Cate not believe Allen was the fastest at therapy, she also didn't believe he ever went.

One time she'd come back from a shopping trip and found him reading in the living room. He'd said he'd just returned from therapy and needed a quiet moment to process what he'd learned. But when Cate had fetched the rest of the groceries from the trunk of her car, she'd put a hand on the hood of Allen's BMW. It'd been colder than the frozen broccoli in her bag.

"He's not going, is he," Ellie said.

"Of course not." Cate almost laughed. Ellie and Sam knew her—and Allen—better than was strictly comfortable. "He's lying about it. Oh well. Male fragility, am I right?"

Ellie muttered something under her breath, so Cate sat up again. The discussion had swerved off-topic, and she needed to bring it back on track. "Okay, so far, I know Maisie doesn't dye her hair. I like that. What else?"

"She apologized."

"For?"

"For taking off and never getting in touch."

Cate felt her eyes widen. "Tell me everything."

"Just like we said. She couldn't deal with the situation here anymore."

"She didn't want to be the only one left in that big house, huh?"

They'd sort of known it, but it was a relief to have it confirmed, and not carry that niggling doubt any longer.

"I guess not."

"Weird, isn't it?" Cate put a hand on her heart. "We've wondered for so long how she was, it's weird to finally know."

"Well, not really *weird*," Ellie said, unfeeling. "I didn't need her to say it to confirm it. It was obvious."

"Was it?"

"Yeah."

Cate smiled. Not only had Ellie harbored the same doubts as everyone else about Maisie's behavior, but she'd been the one that had worried most. Cate firmly believed in Maisie's good sense and mothering instincts, and for Sam, it'd been enough to feel like Maisie was okay. But Ellie hadn't trusted Maisie.

Cate propped her elbows on her knees. "Are you still mad at Maisie?"

There was a pause. "No. Maybe? I honestly don't know, Cate. I'm normal-mad she cut us off, but I love her. I understand. It was okay while I was with her in Beach House. So—I don't know. Like that."

Cate nodded. Of course it was all a mess. Three people ripped from the community—it affected them. But Maisie was the victim here; Cate for one was going to cut her all the slack she needed. "Did she say how long she was going to stay?"

"Only that it wasn't for long. If you want to see her, better do it soon. We should have breakfast with her, I don't think she's got much food in the house. And then you can ask her for details."

"Wouldn't that be—I think we should wait until she's ready to tell us herself."

"Cate, you make high school kids read Shakespeare and *like* it. You can ask Maisie Jameson how long she's planning to stay."

Cate shook her head. "I don't read Shakespeare with the kids, and I also don't see what one thing has to do with the other."

"You can do whatever you want, Cate." Ellie

yawned. "You just, you know...*have to do it.*"

"That's circular logic," Cate said. "I think." She wanted to talk more about Maisie, not herself.

"Cate, I gotta call it a night. I have to get up early for the Fish Market, or the competition is going to snap up all the good squid. I'll text you and Sam. We'll meet at Maisie's for breakfast."

"Good night, Ellie," Cate said obediently and ended the call.

She was tired too, but she couldn't fall asleep now. Hopefully, Maisie hadn't changed. Not too much. Cate had always liked Maisie the way she was.

Instead, she went into the kitchen. A glass of milk would settle her. Gently, so she wouldn't wake the girls, Cate rifled through the fridge, pulling out bread, mayonnaise, ham and salami, lettuce, the new brie she liked, and the old jar of olives that needed to be eaten.

Chapter 5

Rain prattled on roof tiles and against windowpanes, pulling Maisie from a hazy dream. She lay quietly, listening. She'd forgotten how comfortable the rosewood bed was, how sweet the seaside air coming in through the cracked window, how familiar the sounds of her old house. Sleep, deep sleep like this, was rare. It must've been the clean air that made her sleep like that.

But the night was over, and it was time to get up and get going. Maisie opened her eyes to the dim morning light. She felt calm. Like sleep, calm was precious. Carefully, as if haste might shake loose the feeling, Maisie folded her duvet over, savored the cool bedroom floor under her feet, and stood.

Every morning she stood, came hell or high water. Her instinct even now was to stay in bed, curl into the fetal position, and hope the day would pass without her. But one of the things she and Robert had promised each other after Alex had disappeared, was that they'd get up each morning. That they'd never stop searching but get up and do what they could.

She'd kept her promise, but Robert hadn't. Maisie understood. She understood very well. But one of them had to stay. One of them had to be there, in case there was a knock on the door or a call on her phone, the number carefully kept the same because it was the one Alex knew.

Robert had taken the easy way out. Adding his deadweight, quite literally, to a load that was too heavy already.

If she could divorce her dead husband, Maisie would. Still would.

Robert, with his keen sense for business and never-back-down attitude. In the end, when it counted, he'd simply left them hanging. Maisie was still angry, though the years had changed the shape of her anger. At first, his suicide had been like a gale blowing away everything else she'd felt for Robert. It took years for that wrath to wane, but eventually, her anger had morphed into a cold draught that only touched her now and then. Just often enough to remind her that Robert's death was still a door left open in her life. Heat getting lost, energy drained.

The only thing closing that door would be to properly grieve for her husband. But it was her son who needed every ounce of energy she had. Every second of time, every bit of effort needed to go to finding him.

And so, every morning, Maisie stood.

She went to the window and lifted the curtain. It'd been too dark to see much the night before.

Raindrops tapped against the glass, their streaky

tracks blurring the pewter sky. Spring in Beach Cove was full of wet mornings and sunny afternoons. Maybe the weather would clear later.

With sudden urgency, Maisie felt a desire to rush outside, check on the garden. She'd nurtured it for years, and every plant, every flower came with a story. Had the boxwoods dodged the blight? Had the roses dried up without fertilizer? The lavender must've gone woody without pruning... She'd grown the plants from seeds she'd smuggled back from a trip to Provence in France.

She smiled. That'd been a glorious vacation. Robert her rock, Alex safe. The trip had been sunny, fragrant, tinted in purple and gold.

Maisie craned her neck. Most of the garden stretched around the corner of the house, down to the sea. But the bit she could see was disheartening. Dried-out stalks, rampant weeds, sodden leaves piled a foot high. Regret nipped at her like a terrier, and she let the curtain swing back.

Didn't matter.

Abruptly, Maisie turned on her heel, scooped her toiletry bag from the top of the dresser, and padded into the bathroom.

When she turned on the faucet, the water came out rusty. After it cleared, Maisie washed her hands and her face, drying off with her pajama sleeve. A glance into the mirror—she'd washed the sleep out of her eyes. It was enough. Stress seemed to have eaten her scent; it'd been years since she'd needed to use deodorant. And Jim Andersen wasn't going to expect makeup and eyeliner.

Running the brush through her hair, Maisie looked around the bathroom. She'd left in a daze, only throwing in her bags what was already out by the sink and caught her eye. Toothbrush, hairbrush, Xanax.

A small tub of face cream still stood where she'd left it. Dried up, no doubt. She'd forgotten that she used to buy this brand.

There were no towels. Liz must've put them in the linen cabinet. The only thing hanging on the hook by the door was a navy blue bathrobe.

Robert's robe.

Maisie reached out and let her fingers trail over the plush fabric. Fleece with black piping, soft and yielding in her hand. Maisie hesitated, then she pressed her face into the material and breathed in.

Nothing.

There was no trace of his scent left, no reminder that yes, he'd worn this every morning.

Lifting the rope off its hook, Maisie slipped her arms into the sleeves and cinched the belt around her waist. She was tall enough for the robe not to puddle at her feet, and it'd be cold downstairs.

It *was* cold, and for a few minutes, Maisie fumbled with the thermostat beside the staircase. It'd be a wonder if the heating would simply come on... But something clonked deep in the belly of the house; hopefully, it was the furnace firing up and expanding, sending hot water into the pipes.

Maise gave the thermostat a small pat. Then she

went into the kitchen.

Not even seven. Had Jim mentioned when he'd show up, promised coffee in hand?

The doorbell chimed, the sound drilling into her bones. Maisie hurried to answer. On the way, she caught her reflection in the mirror. Pale, hair a mess, in a robe that badly needed washing. There'd been a time when she'd made sure she looked put together before opening the door. That was over. She yanked open the door, the vision of two police officers, eyes downcast and hats in hand, surfing her thoughts like a wave.

"Maisie Jameson! Hooray! She's still here."

Maisie clutched the door's brass knob. This, she had not expected. Not yet, not this early in the morning.

Ellie, peeping out from under the hood of a green parka, smiled and lifted two coffee cups in greeting.

Beside her stood Sam and Cate.

Sam was holding a red umbrella over herself; Cate was covering her head with a soggy magazine.

Maisie's stomach pulled in all sorts of directions; she pushed the door wider, waving her old friends inside. "Please. Come in." She cleared her throat but didn't try to say anything else. She needed a moment.

Ellie came in first, pressing one of the paper cups into Maisie's hand as she passed. "It's from the Cove Corner Café, and it's hot enough to burn your foot off if you drop it."

"Thank you," Maisie murmured. She hadn't seen

Sam and Cate in so long... Looking straight ahead, silent, both stepped into the house like ghosts of the past.

Her friends hadn't changed much. Maybe Cate looked a little heavier and more apologetic. Maybe Sam was even paler, her expression more enigmatic than Maisie remembered. The most notable difference by far was the distance Maisie had caused between them; that one was new. Stalling to catch her breath, she stared into the rain as if checking the weather.

"All right, turn and look at us," Sam's stern alto commanded. "We're not going to bite you. Much."

Maisie felt her face melt into a smile.

Cate, gentler, softer. "It's all good, Maisie. It's just us."

Maisie closed the door against the rain and turned, looking straight into three pairs of eyes the same color as her own.

None of them were related, but somehow, their irises were the same changeable shade of blue. Right now it was the blue of a hazy day at sea when sky and water blend into each other and become one.

Maisie pulled her robe tighter. "I'm so sorry, Samantha, Catherine," she started.

Cate set her coffee on the mahogany board. Without further ado, she reached for Maisie and pulled her into her arms.

Maisie stiffened, her grip tightening on her cup even though her fingertips burned. But Cate didn't let go, wasn't put off, and after a while, Maisie lost her rigid awkwardness and let herself soften and sink into the arms of her friend. Cate smelled so familiar, of the same lily-of-the-valley perfume they'd picked together a lifetime ago on a shopping trip to Boston.

"See? It's not so bad." At long last Cate released her, smiling as she took a step back.

Maisie took a moment to find her voice. Unlike the rest of them, Cate was never nervous to be kind. Cate knew that Maisie needed that hug. She knew that it was guilt and shame, not rejection, that caused the stiffness of her limbs. "I'm—"

"Okay, fine. Me too." Now Sam came forward and hugged Maisie. Her embrace was quick and firm, and she, too, smelled familiar. Of thin printed paper and the buckram covers crowding the shelves in her antique bookstore.

When Sam let go, Maisie nodded several times, her throat too tight to talk.

She was not going to cry. She never cried.

"We hugged yesterday, so we got that out of the way already." Ellie lightly elbowed Maisie's side and smiled encouragingly. She lifted a hand over her head like a tour guide, waving everybody to follow her into the kitchen and perched on a stool at the center island.

"Yeah?" Cate stepped beside Maisie and rubbed her arm. "Okay?"

"Yeah." Maisie managed a smile. Her stomach unknotted, slow and hesitant. They were all here, all three of them. This was what she'd been afraid of.

She needed to focus; not fall back into happy old patterns she couldn't allow herself anymore. Let alone the memories she felt rushing upon her like a swelling wave getting ready to break.

Sam and Cate seemed unaware of her apprehension. They pulled out stools as if it was just another day and joined Ellie.

Talk about the easy stuff. Be a hostess. "There isn't much I can offer for breakfast. I think I saw a box of breakfast cookies, but I could be wrong." Maisie started to open pantry doors and cabinets. Searching for food, even if it was random and haphazard, was something to do, something that kept the wave from breaking right now, right here.

But Cate stopped her quickly enough. She gestured for Maisie to join them. "We're old now. None of us can eat cookies for breakfast anymore. At least, we try not to." She patted her stomach.

It showed more than Maisie remembered, but she shook her head out of reflex. Cate was pretty enough on the outside, but her beauty came from inside. It shone in her warm eyes, on her kind face, in her generous smile. It was as real as a tiny waist and a lot more attractive. People gravitated toward Cate when she let them. Cate was the person everyone wanted to tell their story, instinctively knowing her compassion would lighten their burden.

All her friends were drop-dead gorgeous to Maisie. They always would be, no matter how many wrinkles and love handles and crooked hips they'd have between them. Because there is a point when friends turn into sisters, looks disappear, and all you can see anymore is the soul.

Maisie took her seat at the kitchen island; Cate had again managed to calm her down. "If I knew where the cookies were, I'd insist you have some. You look perfect."

"Careful," Sam muttered. "We've been trying to put Cate on a diet because of her cholesterol. It's high, and we don't mean to lose another one."

Cate's smile slipped, and she nodded solemnly. Ellie studied her hands. Sam could be blunt, even more than Ellie. And unlike Ellie, Sam's moods didn't settle easily.

"Sorry," Maisie murmured, aware that she'd just been chastised for not knowing what was going on. For not keeping in touch, for not caring. "I'm sorry."

"I understand why you had to leave, Maisie," Cate said. "I even sort of understand why you couldn't get in touch with us."

"Sam?" Ellie asked after a while.

Sam nodded but didn't look into Maisie's eyes. "I do too. Just—give me a bit."

"Thank you. Thank you for coming," Maisie said, unable to resist the wave. It was breaking right above her; she sensed the crest curl, white hooves rising to strike. She grabbed the counter, the knuckles of her fingers growing pale. "And thanks for bringing coffee. I thought I'd have to wake up without."

"Yeah, no," Ellie said and blew into her steaming cup. "That's crazy."

Chapter 6

They chatted.

Maisie didn't join in at first. She was trying to focus, stick to her rules, brace the walls as best she could. But also, she listened; it was impossible not to. There was so much she'd missed... Most of the banter went straight over her head.

It was okay, it was fine. She hadn't meant to see these women again. Not now, anyway. She couldn't be part of their lives.

Even so, the longer Ellie, Sam, and Cate talked, the brighter the kitchen seemed to become. Clouds covered the sky, but Maisie knew it was her friendship with the other women, not the sun, that lit the room and shone through the cracks in her resolve.

Sam looked at her. "I swear that's what he said. It made it even funnier. Maisie, you should've been there. We almost peed ourselves with laughter."

Maisie smiled dutifully. "I'm sure." Wrapped up in her thoughts, she'd missed most of the story and didn't know who Sam was talking about.

"I *did* pee myself." Ellie waved. "Tommy was born at ten pounds—"

"—eleven ounces." Cate held up a hand. "We know. If you're going to talk about that birth again, I'm going to cry. I still have post-traumatic stress disorder."

Maisie chuckled. Ellie's husband Dale had been out sailing when Ellie'd started having contractions. He'd tried to get back, but there'd been little wind and his tiny, emergency-only motor was nowhere as fast as Ellie's womb. In the end, it'd been Cate who'd rushed to her side, trying to get Ellie to the hospital. And it'd been Cate who'd delivered Tommy on a salt flat between Beach Cove and Merewif, the wind carrying Ellie's screams out to the sea, and, they'd all hoped, straight into Dale's soul.

"Got it." Ellie lifted her mug and cheered Cate. "It was a bloody scene, for sure."

Silence fell at the table, a sudden hush.

Surprised, Maisie looked up to see three pairs of blue eyes on her. Wide, afraid to have offended. "No —don't do that." She shook her head. "Let's not do that."

"We're not doing anything," Sam murmured. "Stop it, y'all."

"But it's so—" Cate laid her hands flat on the counter. "Let's get this over with, Maisie. Is there any news about Alex? What's been happening? We haven't heard anything even though we check online all the time."

"There's no news. I haven't found him. I know nothing more than I did ten years ago." The warmth slipped off Maisie's shoulders like a coat. "I'm doing everything I can to keep the spotlight on his disappearance and the public interested. But it's hard." White teenage male disappears—not exactly a feast for the media. People assumed boys his age could take care of themselves. "Mostly they think he ran away because his girlfriend broke up with him."

"Somebody must've seen something," Sam said. "I always feel like there's got to be something we've overlooked, even after all these years."

"That's why I'm here." Maisie cleared her throat. "Someone's interested in telling Alex's story in a podcast. He's an investigative reporter, and his wife is a social worker. They'll be getting here...well, they said this morning. But I don't know when." Maisie checked the time on her phone. "Oh. Almost nine?" Time had gone fast. She should be answering emails, not sitting and chatting with her friends like a self-indulgent teenager.

"How old are your podcasters?" Cate raised her eyebrows like a sage. "I always think podcasters sound so young."

"Twenties or thirties, I think."

"Emily's twenty-six, and she never even gets up before ten. I'm pretty sure she's picking her college classes so she can sleep in and stay up late."

The last time Maisie had seen Emily, she'd worn braces and hidden behind her hair. "What college classes?"

"Oh. Oh." Cate shook her head as if she was dizzy. "I forgot. Sheesh, Maise, how are we going to get you up to speed again?"

"Just answer her question for starters," Sam suggested.

"Emily's taking classes at the community college in Merewif," Cate replied obediently.

Maisie bit the corner of her lip, fighting a stab of senseless envy. To have a kid in college, to be able to see them grow... "What does she want to do?" What career would Alex have picked?

"Remember how Allen wanted her to try for Harvard?"

"Sure do. She wanted to be a doctor."

"Yeah. Well, that was a big fat no-go."

"She didn't get in?" Maisie had missed Emily's high school graduation. "Or did she change her mind about being a doctor after all?"

Ellie grinned, and Sam tilted her head expectantly.

Cate sighed. "Of course she got in. She made it all the way to residency. But after a year of that, she decided she couldn't deal with the stress. So she came back home to go to Merewif College and study theater instead."

Maisie blinked. "Whoa, that's...whoa. That's different."

"Allen's still furious with her. And Emily, poor baby, has a heap of debts and no hope of paying them off."

Maisie sat back, her mind struggling to bridge the gap between the teen she'd known and this. "She was in the drama club, wasn't she? Of course—she played Wendy."

Emily's little sister Claire had been crawling on all fours in a dog costume. Tommy had been Peter Pan. Alex... He'd had outstanding grades, but he couldn't act a penny's worth. "Alex was one of the lost boys." Maisie's thoughts tumbled out of her mouth before she could stop them.

Again, the women fell silent.

"He was, wasn't he?" Cate muttered finally and glanced at Sam. Not long, but long enough.

Maisie stood and tossed her empty coffee cup into the trash bin.

"Tell us about your podcast," Ellie said behind her. "I've listened to it before. I know these guys. Well, a guy and a girl. They're married, by the way. She's great. He is too, but she's funny."

"I've never listened to podcasts before, let alone crime ones. Is that a thing in their podcast, that they're married?" Maisie asked.

"It's not what it's *about,* but it's part of it, yeah. His wife's name is Ashley. The social worker?" Ellie looked at her as if she thought it'd jolt Maisie's memory.

Maisie nodded politely but was compelled to be truthful. "I don't know why their marriage should be important for a crime podcast, but whatever works, I guess."

"For sure." Ellie got up and tossed her cup as well. "The more listeners, the better."

Maisie caught another glance. Had she done something, said something out of place?

The doorbell chimed.

A tingling shot into the tips of Maisie's fingers and toes as if she'd touched an electric fence. "Married or not, here he is," she muttered. They'd have to go over everything. She'd talked about what happened often enough to create distance. But she hadn't seen the beach in a long time, hadn't stood where Alex had last stood.

"Are you going to answer the door?" Sam passed by, her words muffled, her voice underwater.

It took a hard clank and unfamiliar voices for Maisie to stir into action and hasten into the entrance hall. Sam was holding the door open, and a thirty-something man was lugging what looked like a large black metal coffer inside.

It banged onto the floor, and he cursed, then glanced at Sam. "Sorry, Mrs. Jameson."

"Never mind me. Look." Sam pointed at Maisie. "That's Mrs. Jameson."

The kid straightened and adjusted his glasses.

Maisie walked toward him. She shouldn't think of him as a kid. He was a man, a few years older than Alex would be now. *Was*. Was now. "Maisie," she said automatically. "Are you Jim? Nice to meet you." Against her will, hope raised its head. She held out her buzzing hand as if she was drowning, fingers splayed, grasping for the podcaster to save her. If they could just find *something*—

The young man took her hand and gave it an earnest shake. "I am. Nice to meet you, Maisie. What a wonderful house you have. It's beautiful." He glanced around the hall, taking it in.

Maisie nodded. Once upon a time, she'd been a very lucky woman to own a beautiful house. Now it hardly mattered. "Thank you. Where's the rest of your crew?"

"Here they are," Sam announced and opened the door wider.

The rain had ceased, and sunshine ushered in another three young people. Maybe the light pouring into the hall was a good omen.

"Hi everyone." Cate put an arm over Maisie's shoulders. "You okay?" she whispered. "You look pale."

"It's always nerve-wracking when a new investigation starts," Maisie whispered back. "It's what I want, of course. But..." She took a breath, allowing herself to dip down to the fear that lived in her belly. "What if this *changes* things, you know?" The emphasis was all she managed, leaving Cate to fill in the dreaded changes herself.

"Anything is better than not knowing," Cate muttered. "Don't you think?"

"I can't tell if that's the case." Yes, Maisie needed to know. She'd give everything to know. But knowing could be the end, too. As long as there was no news, as long as Alex had only disappeared, there was hope. Hope kept her going, and she didn't know what would happen if she lost it. She was unable to contemplate it.

Maisie clapped her hands, calling mostly herself to order. "If you wouldn't mind leaving your shoes down here, let me show you the house." She didn't care one bit about the shoes, but she remembered that she used to try and protect the upstairs rugs. It seemed a good, trivial thing to say. Normal, calm, we-can-do-this.

The talking and general busyness died down as everyone kicked off their shoes. The podcasters eagerly grabbed backpacks and electronic-looking aluminum cases, looking bright-eyed.

"Go you," Cate murmured and took her arm off Maisie's shoulders. "Do you want me to stay and help?"

Maisie smiled. Cate taught English at Beach High—go Sea Urchins—and had a trick or ten up her sleeve when it came to organizing young people. "No, I'm all right. Thanks. Cate—thank you."

Cate nodded. "We'll leave so you can settle them. But don't take off on us again. We need to know what's happening, too."

"I'll try," Maisie said, the numbness of her guilt surging, calming the buzz of her anxiety.

"You got this. Chin up." Cate looked straight into her eyes. Then she left to join the others.

Maisie heard her talk, telling them it was time to leave.

"Mrs. Jameson? Maisie? This is my wife, Ashley. She's co-hosting the podcast." Jim stepped aside so Maisie could see the pretty redhead behind him. While Jim was tall and gangly, with messy brown hair, round Harry Potter glasses, and the pensive air of an academic, his wife was short and curvy and had brown eyes that sparkled with energy.

"Hi Ashley," Maisie said, taking an instant liking to the young woman. "Thanks for taking me on." Even though she'd been introduced as 'the wife', Ashley very much looked like she stood on her own two feet.

"Hi, Mrs. Jameson." Ashley's voice was warm. "I'm so sorry for what you're going through. We want nothing more than to help find your son, and we can reach a few thousand people. Fingers crossed it'll help."

Maisie nodded. Unlike Jim's gentle, scared-to-offend manner, Ashley sounded like she was already rolling her sleeves up to get down and dirty with the facts. Nobody had tried harder to do that than Maisie herself, and she appreciated the determination in the young woman. "Well, come along inside." Maisie turned and led the way. "The bedrooms are upstairs."

The crew followed, the wooden steps creaking under their feet.

"We brought bagels," one of the yet unnamed crew called from the back of the line. "Should I leave them down here?"

"Sure," Maisie said and pointed. "Kitchen's to your right."

Upstairs, she turned left and opened the door at the end of the hallway, which led to a spacious guestroom. "This is the only room with a queen bed. Maybe for the married couple?"

"Great. Thanks." Ashley, a backpack slung over her shoulder and what looked like a cooler in each hand, shimmied past Maisie into the room. "Oh, how pretty."

Her husband followed, set down two duffel bags, and lifted the strap of his laptop bag over his head. "It's great. Beautiful."

"I'm glad you like it." Maisie cast a glance inside. This room had been one of the first she'd furnished, and it looked as simple and happy as her life back then. Charmed, cheerful, straight from a children's book about talking bunnies and slow-moving rivers. The applewood furniture glowed summer-warm, the leaf-green cotton rugs were clean and tidy. Maisie had sewn the curtains and bedspread herself shortly after they'd moved in, picking fabric with tiny white flowers. On the walls hung Robert's landscape aquarelles. Maisie had collected the frames over time from thrift stores. They were all different, save the fact that she'd liked each one the moment she'd spotted it.

On either side of the bed, windows gave a view of the garden. Maisie was used to her riot of flowers adding to the happy feel of the room, but that wasn't the case now. She stepped out of the room, leaving Jim and Ashley behind.

All the things she'd done, all that feathering of the nest, had been for nothing. Well no—not nothing. Alex had grown up in this house, sixteen long years. She'd given him some pretty things to look at. Beach House and the garden stopped mattering only after he left.

"This room and the next," she said, her voice mechanical, "have two full beds each and a lot of closet space. The rooms share a Jack and Jill bathroom between them." She opened the next door and went in. The Jack, fairly small and as cornflower blue as the Jill was lavender, looked out on the cove. Again, Maisie's eyes were drawn to the window as if the cove was calling her name. The beach was tawny after the morning's rain, but the sky over the cove was clear, and the last few clouds drifted quickly toward the open sea.

She blinked. How many kids still needed a bed? There was one girl and one boy left, but she felt like there'd been more before. "Is it only the two of you now?"

The two kids looked at each other. Or rather, again, young adults. Maisie guessed they too were in their mid-twenties, with the man sporting a beard down to his Adam's apple. "It's just us, Mrs. J," the beard said. "And we might not stay the entire time. Totally depends on what Jim and Ash want to do."

Maisie wondered what their function was or if they belonged together, but the beard didn't make any other statements. "Okay," she said. "You can take one or both rooms, whatever suits you."

"Thank you, Mrs. J." It was the girl that had wondered about where to put the bagels. Glossily dark-haired and skinny, she made her torn jeans and T-shirt look like high fashion. She threw the beard a look that was either warning or cue. "I'll take the Jill. Next door then?"

Maisie nodded and backed out into the corridor. "Call me Maisie." These two didn't seem to be a couple. "So what's your job in all this?"

"I'm the sound engineer," Beard answered. "I make sure the recordings sound good and that nobody chews into the microphone. You wouldn't believe how many people get mad when that happens."

"Oh. I wouldn't like that either."

He smiled. "My name's John. John Jay Mass."

"Glad you could make it, John Jay Mass." His name had rhythm; Maisie had to hand it to him. He could be on Broadway with a name like that.

"And I'm Amanda," Bagels said, reappearing in the door without her bags. "I'm the producer. I make sure things stay interesting." Her cheeks dimpled, soft and sweet like a baby's.

"You look awfully young for a producer." Maisie smiled to show it wasn't a criticism.

Amanda sighed, and the dimples disappeared. "I'm thirty-*four*."

Maisie had to grin. "Good for you, kid. Never mind me. When you're in your fifties, anyone under forty looks too young for their job."

Amanda grinned back. "I'm sure there's still lots to learn in the next sixteen years."

"Oh. That's not what I meant, but... Maybe." Maisie liked that the podcast women seemed quick and resilient, while both Jim and John Jay looked like they'd be meticulous and detail-driven. "Where'd you put those bagels in the end?" she asked. "I'm starving."

"Downstairs, on the table in the entrance room." Amanda pointed at the floor. "I didn't want to miss the tour."

"That makes sense, too."

Amanda shrugged the strap of her laptop bag off and set down the small suitcase she was carrying. "You go ahead, Mrs. J, we'll meet you in the kitchen in five."

Downstairs, the hall, kitchen, and living room were empty. Sam, Cate, and Ellie had left as unceremoniously as they'd appeared.

How little their lives seemed to have changed. And yet, how much; kids were always the measuring stick. It seemed like there was all the time in the world until you happened to look at them. And whoosh, there was the child, grown and changed so much it aged you, too.

Claire, Cate's youngest, must be... Maisie did a quick calculation in her head. Claire must be sixteen, the same age Alex was when the earth swallowed him. Tom and Emily were the same age as Alex. Only Sam didn't have kids—or did she?

Maisie had missed most of her friends' forties, those messy years when everyone struggled to stay afloat. Marriages, jobs, kids, the first tremors of midlife crises and changing hormones... The forties had it all when it came to trouble. A good time for an unexpected pregnancy.

But Sam would've mentioned a kid. Kids were huge.

Maisie should've asked more questions. Their chat had been superficial. She didn't even know who was still married with whom; she'd assumed that everything was as she'd left it. But for everyone else, time hadn't stood still. A lot could happen in ten years, and Maisie had caught only snippets of her friends' lives. She didn't know the half of it. Only that one kid was running a café, and another had caught the acting bug. Sam still had her bookstore, Ellie her fish market, Cate her teaching career.

"Mrs. J?" A voice—Amanda?—came from upstairs. "We'll be down in a mo. Okay if we record you?"

Maisie nodded.

"Mrs. J? Okay if we record you to get some tape?"

"Yes!" Maisie called back. "Record away." That's why she was in Beach Cove. Not because she missed her friends.

She glanced around the kitchen. Without them, the room looked a little scuffed, a little bare, a little cold.

Pulling an old sponge out from under the sink, Maisie started to wipe coffee rings off the counter.

Chapter 7

After their early morning visit to Beach House, Ellie had dropped Sam off at Beach Cove's minuscule harbor. Already halfway to the bookstore on Main, Sam climbed the last of Marina Alley when her purse buzzed. Without breaking stride, Sam rummaged in her hobo bag for the phone.

It was probably Cate, and opening the store a few minutes late hardly mattered—people weren't exactly running her doors in. Blindly groping the detritus of the past months, Sam stabbed the tip of a mechanical pencil under her fingernail. She sucked in a breath, got hold of the phone, and pulled it out to check the screen.

Her husband? Larry texted. He wouldn't call unless it was an emergency. Sam stepped off the sidewalk into the florist's doorway and answered the phone. "Larry?"

His voice sounded strained. "You don't have to sound so surprised."

Sam raised her eyebrows. Larry wasn't a morning person. "What's going on? Are you at the university?"

"Not yet. I'm still in Beach Cove."

"You are?" But it was Monday—even on a Sunday, Larry barely managed to stay away from his beloved university. "No lectures today?"

"Only Mobility and Identity in the Byzantine Empire at twelve forty-five."

"Right."

"Like every Monday. I wish you'd be able to keep track of my schedule, Sam."

Sam rolled her eyes at the sunflowers in the window. "Me too, Larry. But since it's changed two or three times a year, every year, for the last twenty years, I've sort of lost track. Forgive me."

"Stop being sarcastic."

"So why are you still in Beach Cove, and why are you calling me? What's up?" Sam hitched the strap of her purse higher. "Are you sick? Do you need Gatorade?" Larry liked to sip Gatorade when he wasn't feeling well. He claimed that he dehydrated easier than other people, which of course wasn't true. But indulging his whim was easy and kept him happy.

There was a pause. Sam frowned. "Hey, Larry. Are you okay? Talk to me."

Larry cleared his throat. "Yeah, I'm okay. I'd like to see you."

Sam shook her head. What was happening? "Are you at home?"

"I'm at the store."

"At my store?"

There was another pause. "Our store, yes."

It wasn't *their* store. It was Sam's store, and she had the papers to prove it. "I'm on my way." She was going to tell him to go on and wait inside, but she couldn't remember whether Larry had a key to get in. Did he? Sam had given spares to Ellie and Cate a long time ago. Maisie should still have one, too. But Larry? Probably. Right? She'd have given him one?

"Where are you? Says on the door the store opens at nine."

If he had a key, he forgot about it too. "I'm coming up Marina. I'd be at the store right now if you hadn't called."

"Where's your car?"

"At the store."

"That makes no sense."

"You being at my store makes no sense, Larry."

He chuckled. "Hey, Sam?"

"What?"

"Hurry, will you? I have to get going."

"I just said... Oh, I get it. Funny." Sam hung up. Tucking her phone back into her purse, she stepped out of the doorway.

"Hey."

Sam looked up, startled. She'd almost bumped into a woman in a hoody and denim overalls who was hastening along the narrow sidewalk. Eyes on her phone, the woman too had only looked up in time to avoid a collision.

Sam caught a look from eyes the translucent green of sea lettuce.

Bonnie Sagartati, the only female lobster-fisher

in town.

Without another word, Bonnie hurried on.

Sam moistened her lips and hitched her purse higher. What a strange morning. Maisie, Larry, Bonnie. She started walking again, soon turning onto Main Street.

Mother of Brandie Sagartati, the girl that had broken Alex's heart.

No wonder. Brandie had been as gorgeous as her mother, only with black hair instead of flaming copper. Brandie must've inherited her dark locks from her father, though nobody knew him. But Sagartati sounded Italian.

Two months after Alex had vanished, Brandie was gone as well. Thankfully, the girl wasn't missing. To protect her from the fallout of Alex's disappearance, Bonnie had sent Brandie to stay with her father. Sam knew this because Brandie had been friends with Cate's Emily, and the two had texted a few times before the contact fizzled out.

Ahead, the bookstore rose from the morning mist. There'd barely been any at the harbor, but up here, it looked like a fog machine had gone rogue. Sam wrapped her arms around herself, suddenly cold. Bonnie always spooked her. The woman's eyes were unnerving.

Pressing on, Sam dove into the fog. Just unlock the door and she'd be inside, safe and—

"Hello to you too?"

Sam jerked her head up. Larry leaned, arms crossed, against the door to her store. "Gosh, Larry.

I'm sorry. I didn't see you."

"I can't stay long, Sammy." Larry ran a hand through his hair. It had thinned in his fifties. Strangely afraid of people thinking he had a comb-over, Larry kept his hair short but still ran his fingers through the stubble as if it were the old luxurious mane. "I wanted to see you this morning. You were gone so early." His tone bobbed between accusation and whine.

Sam grinned. "Are you jealous?"

He frowned. "Of what? I meant to make coffee for you, is all. And I wanted to talk to you."

Sam pointed at the bookstore. "Let's go inside. I'm cold."

Larry threw the window display a twitchy look.

Sam liked to display her antique treasures: the more, the merrier. Some books splayed open to colorful illustrations; others were arranged into artistic chaos on ladders and pillows. Larry, on the other hand, preferred orderly stacks or clean rows with solid bookends to hold the books prisoner. There'd been some heartfelt discussions over the years. But different as their opinions on showcasing them were, they both loved books.

"It's getting late. I should go," he said. "Just a word."

Sam dropped her hand with the key in it. "What's going on?"

Larry's throat moved as if he wanted to say something, but then he only reached out and tucked one of her curls behind her ear.

It would never stay there since it was too short to be tucked away. They both knew that.

Sam tilted her head. Larry was starting to scare her. "Are you okay?"

Larry smiled. He had a charming smile, and it was hard to worry when he went to the trouble of using it. "Sure I'm okay," he said. "I just wanted to see you. Come here."

Public display of affection? Sam, too surprised to resist, let her husband pull her into his arms.

"Love you, Sammy," he whispered into her ear. "That's all I wanted to say."

"Uh, I love you too, Larry." Sam leaned back and squinted at him.

His brown eyes met hers. His smile deepened.

He was being too weird.

Sam was cold, she was late, she needed a cup of sugary hot tea, and people were just plain strange this morning.

Just to double-check that Larry wasn't being charming for the benefit of an audience, Sam glanced up and down the street. But there was no one there. Few shops opened before noon, and nobody was strolling past the dark windows. "Okay," Sam said and squirmed out of his arms. "Okay. Have a nice day, Larry."

Larry grabbed her hands and squeezed them. "You too. Hey—where's your wedding ring?"

Sam hadn't been wearing her wedding ring ever since a spot of eczema started underneath the gold band. She'd told him when it'd first started. "It's at home. In my jewelry box." Sam didn't own a jewelry box, but Larry didn't know that. The ring was at the bottom of a bowl that held hairpins and clips, only that didn't sound so good. She sighed. "Where's *yours*?"

"Right here." Larry held up his hand, showing the gold band. "Right here, baby."

"Good for you."

Larry laughed. "Good for you, too. Do you want to have a late lunch together? The seminar only lasts an hour."

"You want to come back early just so we can have lunch?"

"I think it would be nice. When's the last time we —"

"Approximately never, Larry. Not that I can remember. But fine. We'll have lunch. Is that it? Then go or the Byzantine Empire is going to identify without you. Love you."

"Love you, too."

For a moment, Sam thought he'd give her a goodbye kiss right there on the street. Instead, his shoulders dropped, guilty relief in the movement, and he turned. His car was parked at the curb. He got in, shut the door, and pulled away from the curb.

"You're being very strange, my friend," Sam muttered, pushing the key in to unlock her sanctum. "You're being very strange indeed."

Chapter 8

Judging by the clonking and creaking upstairs, the Lost Souls were getting ready for the day. Sitting at the kitchen table, Maisie opened Angela's email and scanned it.

Angela's favorite daughter-in-law had been due a week ago, refused to be induced, and was getting almost as frazzled as Angela herself. Maisie wrote a heartfelt note of commiseration. She pressed send just as the podcasters creaked downstairs and tumbled into the kitchen, eyes bright with plans and arms full of electronics.

Maisie closed her laptop and pointed out outlets while the kids chatted about visiting beaches and shops. When the last cable was plugged in, the crew applied themselves to making breakfast. They figured out Robert's complicated Italian coffee machine in under a minute, found pans, spatulas, pepper and salt, unwrapped cream cheese and sliced bagels, and politely ordered Maisie to relax and let them take care of things.

Maisie did as she was told, drummed her fingers on the table, and watched the youthful sprites work the kitchen like it was their job. Was Alex anything like them? Happy, capable, driven?

If he were, he'd have gotten in touch.

She quieted her nervous fingers. No whats, ifs, whens.

Rules to live by.

"You want sausages?" Jim, towel over his shoulder, stood in front of a splattering pan and craned his neck to see Maisie.

"I'll just have a bagel with cream cheese, please."

"One bagel with cream cheese coming up." Amanda sliced a toasted sesame bagel and slathered it in cream cheese, plopped it on a plate, added a small cluster of black grapes, and handed everything to Maisie. It was simple but looked and smelled lovely.

"Very nice. Thank you." Maisie wondered whether the podcasters would sit for the meal. John Jay Mass and Amanda were arguing about coffee filtration techniques, Ashley was filling coffee mugs, and Jim poked the sizzling contents of the pan. "Sausages and eggs are ready," he called.

Everyone filled their plates and found a spot at the kitchen table. Maisie, properly starved after the long morning, took a bite of her warm bagel. It was delicious. So was the coffee. Almost as good as Robert's brew.

"Okay." Amanda nodded at the bearded sound engineer. John Jay nodded back and, cramming half a bagel into his mouth in one go, hopped off his chair and deftly moved a few gadgets. He plopped headphones on, scrutinized a couple of black boxes he'd set on either side of his plate, and gave Jim the thumbs-up.

"Here we go." Jim put down his mug and pulled a piece of paper from the pocket of his shirt.

"Wait." John Jay looked up. "We need to let Mrs. J finish first."

"Oh. Right." Ashley giggled, and when Maisie looked up, she explained, "There's nothing listeners hate more than chewing noises."

"I don't make chewing noises," Maisie pointed out. "At least not that you can hear."

"Our microphones are very, very good," John Jay assured her, the look in his eyes smug.

"Fine." Maisie smiled and put the grapes down. "I'm done. I'm ready."

"Let's start with this, Mrs. Jameson," Jim said. "Would you describe for us what happened the day your son Alex didn't come home?" His voice was gentle, but it'd taken on a new, businesslike tone.

Maisie had said the words so often, she didn't even have to think. "The day was the twenty-first of September 2009. Alex was sixteen. School was out, and he and his girlfriend had gone straight from the school to the beach. They sat in the sand and had a snack they'd bought at the Cove Market on their way to the beach."

"Can you tell us his girlfriend's name?" Ashley asked.

"Sure. Brandie. It's Brandie."

"Okay."

Yeah, Brandie Sagartati. Maisie took another practiced breath, knowing it would carry her through to the next part. "Brandie was the last person to see Alex. They had their snack—"

Jim held up a hand. "Sorry. What did they eat?"

The interruption gave Maisie a mild start. Not because she didn't know what they'd had for a snack; she did. She'd clung to every detail she could get, whether or not there was a chance it'd be relevant to finding her son. But she'd never had an interviewer ask, not this early on. She cleared her throat. "Alex had a bag of chips. Brandie had a donut and an iced coffee."

Jim jotted down a note on a pad. "So then...?"

"Well, Brandie said—" *Said*, not claimed, because *claimed* biased people against Brandie when Maisie wanted them to keep track of the facts. "She said that they'd gotten into a fight about something Alex had said in school. She broke up with him over it."

"Do you know what he said to Brandie?"

"He said that she needed to try harder if she wanted to get ahead in life."

"Do you know what he meant by that?"

Maisie glanced at Jim. "He meant that she needed to try harder if she wanted to get ahead in life. Alex is straight and to the point. He doesn't play games."

"But try harder...what?"

Maisie shrugged. "Brandie didn't have particularly good grades in school. He must've thought she could do better for herself. To get into the college of her choice, maybe? College was definitely on his mind in those days."

"And Brandie was offended by that."

Maisie remembered the girl's voice rising as she'd told police about the argument. She'd taken it as patronizing, dismissing the fact that Alex had wanted to help. "Yes, I believe she was, judging from the way she told the story. I think he must've meant well and simply hit a tender spot, but I wasn't there. All of this comes from Brandie; nobody else heard them fight."

"Seems hardly a motive?"

"I didn't say it was." Naturally, Maisie had wondered herself. But it was an innocent enough comment, and she couldn't believe that Brandie had been so angry over it that she would've wanted Alex to disappear forever.

"Correct, you didn't say that. Okay, what happened after Brandie broke up with Alex?"

Maisie cleared her throat. "Brandie said that she was fed up and didn't want to date Alex anymore. She let him know, took her book bag, and left the beach to go home."

"Did she look back at him?"

"Yes."

"Was Alex upset?"

Maisie nodded. "Yes. He had pulled his knees to his chest and had put his forehead on them. He might've been crying, but Brandie wasn't sure."

Amanda and John Jay looked up.

"Oh no," Ashley murmured. "Poor baby."

"I know." Maisie pressed her lips together.

John Jay held up a hand to show they were still recording.

"And that's the last anyone saw of him?" Jim asked softly.

"Yes. As far as we know, that was the last time he was seen. Sitting on the beach."

"When did you notice he was missing?"

Maisie blinked. That bit was hard. It had started the end of her world. "We used to have dinner at six. I knew he didn't have practice that night, so he should've come home after school. He didn't, but I didn't think anything of it. He often hung out with his friends after school. Sometimes he forgot the time. So, just before six, I called his cell."

"He had a cell phone?"

"Robert—his dad—liked gadgets. He always got Alex the latest iPhone. For safety reasons." Maisie shook her head as the old disbelief at the irony washed over her. The phone had disappeared with Alex and done no good at all.

"Did Alex answer your call?"

"No. The call went straight to voicemail. I still didn't worry yet"—yes she had, she'd worried right away—"because back then, the kids weren't allowed to bring phones to school. If they did, they had to switch them off. The teachers were pretty strict about it. It wasn't a big deal because people weren't on their phones all the time the way they are now. And Alex often forgot to switch his phone back on after school. Probably because the only one who called that phone was me." Maisie smiled, remembering. "Not a great incentive for a sixteen-year-old boy to remember."

"No." Jim smiled back. "But it makes you wonder what happened to the phone."

The corners of Maisie's mouth dropped. "Everything makes you wonder."

"It does, of course. When did you call the police?"

"Well, first I called Brandie because I knew the two had been seeing each other. Not for long, I think you'd barely call it dating. She'd never even been to our house. But I called and asked whether she knew where he was. Brandie brushed me off, said she hadn't seen him after school."

"Do you know why she said that?"

Maisie saw Brandie before her inner eye, forever sixteen, staring at her with those rebellious bottle-green eyes. A textbook teenager, unaware of the seriousness of the situation. "Brandie told the police she lied because it was none of my business what was going on between Alex and her."

"Did she know Alex was missing?"

"Not until the police asked her to come to the station. Well, after I called her, I called all the other kids I could think of. Tommy Davidson was his best friend. Tom and everyone else said Alex had gone to the beach with Brandie. I went to the beach and looked, but he wasn't there. I drove to a couple of other places. The market, and the school. Nothing. I called the police when I got back home."

"How much later was that?"

"That was around seven that night. Sunset was

at six-thirty, and at seven I called to see if they'd heard of an accident. They hadn't, but they said I could report him as missing. I didn't have to wait twenty-four hours or anything like that."

"Did he have a car? Alex, I mean?"

"Oh. No. He'd only just turned sixteen. Nothing's far away in Beach Cove, and the kids pretty much walked or biked everywhere. Driving wasn't much of a topic, even though Robert had practiced with Alex a few times."

"And, sorry for asking, but I'm assuming drugs and alcohol and things like that weren't a topic either?"

Maisie shook her head. "Not as far as I know." She hesitated. There'd been the usual insinuations, anonymous, online, about secret raves and ecstasy, meth, cults, and freak sex. Sometimes Maisie addressed these issues straight on to get them out of the way, sometimes she didn't. But Jim and Ashley looked like they could handle whatever she threw at them.

"I know this sounds too goody-two-shoes, but none of his friends were into that stuff. They'd have told me. They were desperate to find him, too. I've known them all since they were babies. Robert and I forever walked in on Alex and his friends when they were hanging out in our den. The worst they did was throw their wrappers on the floor and play video games longer than they should've. You know." Maisie smiled. "Kid stuff. They were a fairly innocent bunch. Alex hadn't even had a girlfriend before

Brandie."

"So that breakup was the first one, huh?" Jim looked at her, his eyes brimming with concentration.

"His first one. As far as I know."

"What else can you tell us, Mrs. Jameson?"

Maisie thought. "Robert got into his car and checked the road out of Beach Cove. I went back to his friends' houses and talked again with them and their parents. The police searched with everyone they had, canvassing the village, the beach, the school grounds, backyards... Our neighbors and friends pitched in, even some tourists we didn't know..." Maisie swallowed. "Word spread quick. It was a warm night, so some of us searched until dawn."

"You found nothing at all?"

"Well, not entirely." Maisie frowned. "There was an empty family-size bag of chips in the trash can at the beach. The police took it and tested it for fingerprints. They matched Alex, the lady that still runs the market where they bought the snacks, and the kid that stocked the shelves. But no strangers. Nobody else."

"He got up after his girlfriend broke up with him, walked to the trash can, tossed his empty bag into it."

Maisie nodded. "They brought in dogs the next morning, and we also found footprints in the sand. He went to throw away the bag, then made his way down to the sea and walked into the water. The dogs followed his scent down to the waterline, but then they lost him."

Jim rubbed a hand over his mouth. "So he walked *into* the sea?"

The question always came, pregnant with implication. Maisie had tried to picture her son, distraught to the point of walking into the sea. Over the breakup with Brandie? Try as she might, she couldn't see it. "Only to get his feet wet the way people do when they're taking a walk on the beach. If he walked in the way you mean, they never found any evidence of it. The cove is so calm and protected and there's only that small opening to the bay... They know what to expect."

Ashley cleared her throat. "You mean, they knew where to look?"

"They definitely know where to look," Maisie confirmed. "And they did. Extensively."

"Do you think Alex would've been capable of it?"

Maisie leaned forward. "Alex would've never thought of suicide. He had everything to live for, and he was very much looking forward to it."

She sank back again.

What did you put in their heads, Robert.

Chapter 9

"I have three. Nice 'n big. Hard-shell, obviously." Bonnie pointed to the barnacle-encrusted bucket at her feet.

Shading her eyes against the noon sun that shone through the open door into her store, Ellie peeked into the bucket. The lobsters—all straight-tailed males—stared back, their eyes little black pearls full of confusion. They'd just crawled in the lovely blue sea, living their best lives, happy to have come across a juicy snack.

She'd be confused too. And it only got worse from the moment they were hurdled through the water and hauled above the surface. The next time they touched water, it was a boiling pit of death.

Ellie put a hand on her throat.

She was a fishmonger with taxes to pay, this was Maine, and in Maine, people ate lobsters. Lobsters brought in money, and Ellie needed money to keep her store running. Life was rough, and no one got a fair shake. No question about it.

"Thanks, Bonnie." She swallowed. "I'll take them."

Bonnie nodded as if there'd never been a question. "Got them marked just for you."

"Thanks. Um. They're *huge*. I don't think I've ever seen any this big. Where did you get them?"

Bonnie's eyebrow rose. "Where I always get them." There was a warning in her voice.

"Right. Of course." Lobster fishers were fiercely territorial in this neck of the woods. Even the hint of a suggestion that Bonnie might've put a trap into someone else's trapping grounds was an insult. Ellie smiled an apology at Bonnie, her eyes lingering just a moment before she tore her gaze away.

With those eyes and hair, and skin like the belly of a baby flounder, Bonnie should be in Hollywood. She'd be a star in the right roles. Roles that had few lines because the fisherwoman wasn't much of a talker.

But Bonnie didn't seem fussed about her Hollywood prospects. Her eyes were half-closed, hiding the green irises, and her glorious hair was stuffed under a salt-crusted hat that looked old enough to qualify for barnacles itself. Bonnie looked tough. She *was* tough. She had to be.

All the other fishermen in Beach Cove were male, and all bought into the old superstition that a woman aboard a ship was bad luck. Ellie had heard them mutter over their beers at the Fish Eye. Life wasn't easy for women fishers. And then, Bonnie had basically lost her daughter after Alex disappeared.

"You want I put them in the tank?" A flash of green, gone quick.

"Sure." Ellie stepped back. The lobsters weren't banded. Bonnie never tied the claws, and Ellie always wondered why her lobsters were so docile. They just sat quietly, waiting for what would happen next. It wasn't very lobster-like.

Bonnie grabbed the handle of the ten-gallon bucket. Saltwater splashed over the rim as she carried it to Ellie's keeping tank. Carried it as if it weighed nothing.

Ellie followed meekly. She wasn't weak, but Bonnie lifted that bucket like Ellie lifted an empty plastic bag. Maybe they should all return the expensive gym memberships they didn't want and weren't using and go fishing with Bonnie instead.

The woman set the bucket down with a splash and pushed back the sleeve of her sweater.

"Could we please..." Ellie turned to fish some bands from a drawer. "Here." She stepped next to Bonnie, who'd lifted one of the strapping lobsters.

He was gorgeous. His dark carapace shimmered garnet, deep reds fading to smoky black and back. His walking legs paddled for a hold, his tail curled and uncurled, the great claws gripped the air.

"He's perfect," Ellie muttered. "How do they get so perfect?" She didn't often get lobsters because she couldn't pay as much as the big restaurants in Merewif or Bay Port.

But whenever a fisherman—or woman—didn't have enough time or lobsters for a trip to Bay Port, they offered them to their local fishmonger.

Ellie looked up in time to catch Bonnie's gaze on her.

"Give them to me." Bonnie held out her palm.

Ellie set the rubber bands on it and watched as Bonnie slipped it over the claws as easily as if the monster lobster were a baby kitten. Her movements were practiced to the point of looking careless, her timing immaculate.

"I know you've banded a lot of lobsters," Ellie said, careful not to offend again. "But I've handled lobsters in this store ever since I was a kid, and I still prefer to use a bander when they're this big."

"I'm surprised you band lobsters much," Bonnie mumbled, dodging the implied question whether or not she was aware of it. "They're usually banded at catch point."

"That's true." Ellie wanted to talk more. This was one of the longest interactions she'd had with Bonnie. "But I've had bands snap. And then I've got to take them out of the tank and re-band them, so they don't hurt each other."

Another flash of green. "They can maim a finger real easy, the big ones," Bonnie said, and for a moment, she didn't seem as guarded as usual. The cadence of her voice waved like seagrass. "The claws aren't sharp, but they are powerful."

"That's why it takes me so long. I'm scared." Ellie laughed because it was nonsensical to be scared of lobsters. But laughing with Bonnie for an audience was like laughing at the ocean, so Ellie stopped and cleared her throat.

"Never be scared." Bonnie set the lobster, legs still paddling, into the tank. He whooshed away, and they watched until he settled on the bottom. There he sat, watching them back with his eye-pearls.

"I'll do the other two." With a few more easy movements, Bonnie banded the remaining lobsters and released them into the tank.

"I do like how you handle them," Ellie said, watching the animals swim to the bottom. One of them was another garnet, but the third shimmered in all the shades of green the sea could dream up. She should take photos.

"Now they're yours."

Ellie glanced at Bonnie. "Let me get the money." She went to count the bills from the register. The price they'd agreed on was high, but these lobsters would go like hotcakes and at a profit. Ellie held out the cash, and Bonnie took it.

Not a hint of a smile, no see-you. Bonnie simply picked up her heavy bucket, emptied it into the slop sink, and walked out the backdoor.

"Bye," Ellie said to the closed door. "And also, do you *have* to be so strange?" She shook her head and pushed the register drawer closed, then went back to the tank to admire her new pets. The lobsters stared back. Now and then one took a few steps until he bumped into the glass or the fake plants decorating the bottom of the tank. Ellie had tried to build a proper habitat before, but it made her clients nervous when the tank looked too nice.

Nobody wanted to be reminded that their food was a sentient being enjoying a cute habitat before they boiled it and spread it on a Kaiser roll.

The front door creaked open, and Ellie straightened her back. Early customers?

"Ellie? Where are—oh."

Surprised, Ellie smiled at her husband. There he stood, dark and handsome as ever. "Morning, Dale. Fancy seeing you here." Dale never came to the Fish Market. He couldn't stand the smell of fish. Though once fried, he liked eating it well enough.

"Good morning."

"You look nice." Ellie squinted at Dale's suit. It looked new and expensive; there wasn't a speck of lint, not a wrinkle anywhere. The day before, jeans and the blue sweater had been good enough.

"I have a presentation to give." Dale craned his neck as if the new suit was too tight at the neck.

"Which one?" Ellie tried to keep track of Dale's projects, but there were so many. Suits and projects both.

"A new development in, wait for it: Seaside Bay."

Ellie's heart sank. "Oh. Oh no. I love Seaside Bay."

Dale smirked, clearly annoyed by her reaction. "Everybody does, Ellie. That's why we're putting more houses in. People want to live there. Plus, it's a lot of money for us, so—hey. You're welcome."

"Will it look okay?" Like Beach Cove, the neighboring town, though miles away, was quaint and small. A large residential development could change a sleepy little coastal town forever.

"What can I say. I'm only designing it." Dale shrugged, the hitch of his shoulders offended. "How about giving me a little credit now and then."

"I'm sorry, I didn't mean it like that." For the second time this morning, Ellie had to smile an apology. "Cape Cod-style houses?" It'd been years since Dale had designed anything other than a Cape Cod. His were practical houses without bells or whistles, reasonably priced, and quickly built. Great for starter homes. Utterly without character, though Ellie made sure not to let that observation slip.

"Yeah." Dale's eyes shifted to the tank, and he pointed. "Can we have those for dinner? They look good."

Ellie exhaled. "I was going to sell them, actually. The store could use the cash."

The store could always use the cash; Dale knew that. It paid for itself most of the time, but there never seemed much left to set aside. Over the years, Dale had stepped in once or twice to keep the store afloat. Pay the rent. Ellie hated when that happened. She'd made sure to pay the money back into their common account. Still, ever since he'd subsidized her the first time, Dale liked to treat the fish market as his personal smorgasbord.

Now he winked at her. "Didn't I just tell you about Seaside Bay? Don't worry about the store, honey. Let's treat ourselves tonight. That's why I'm here in fact. I wanted to ask if I can take you out tonight."

"I'd love to go out, Dale. It's been a while since—"

"I was going to suggest a restaurant in Bay Port."

"Sounds lovely." Ellie hadn't been in Bay Port for a while. They could take a walk on the boardwa—

"But now that I've seen these succulent fellas..." Dale walked deeper into the store.

Ellie could see from the tight line of his lips that he was holding his breath. She made sure her store was sparkling clean, and her wares jumped out of the ocean straight into tanks or a luscious bed of ice. To her, the store simply smelled of the sea.

Dale, forced to take a breath, cupped a hand over his face. "Let's cook them and have a family meal with Tom instead," he said through his nose.

"Tom has to work," Ellie said, trying not to show her disappointment. So her husband preferred a family dinner over a date after all, provided she'd cook. "Your son's running a restaurant."

Dale held up his free hand. "Soo-rry." Throwing a last glance at the tank, he stepped back. "We'll eat them some other time. But for tonight, where would you like to go?"

Ellie turned on the faucet to wash her hands. "We could have Thai food."

Dale nodded, again craning his neck as if he was uncomfortable in his suit. "When, do you think?"

"I close at five, and I need an hour to get ready." Ellie knew she'd have to take a long, hot shower before Dale wouldn't complain of her smell.

"I'll be home at seven to pick you up." Dale took another step toward the counter, holding her eyes.

Ellie tilted her head. There was an obsidian glint

in her husband's dark eyes. Maybe it was a trick of the light, maybe the fact that he hadn't gotten the lobsters. "Seven it is. I'll make sure to wash my hair and put on something nice."

"Thank you." Dale looked grateful all of a sudden, the glint gone from his eyes. Maybe she'd imagined it.

Ellie smiled. "Love you, handsome," she said.

"I love you too, Ellie. So much." Dale's eyes flicked back to the tank. "I have to go. See you tonight."

Ellie watched as he walked out. Through the store window, she saw him close his eyes and take a breath that stretched his suit across the chest.

She sniffed the air.

Personally, Ellie couldn't smell a thing.

Chapter 10

The small golden bell over the door of Sam's Bookstore tinkled as Maisie walked in. She shut the door tight, careful not to let too much of the warm inside air escape. The store, at least when she'd lived here, had barely made a profit. A larger than usual heating bill had often enough tipped the balance, and Maisie didn't want to sour Sam's mood.

Sunlight filtered through the octogenarian windows, lighting the floating dust motes and casting a sepia glow over the bookshelves. Maisie almost sighed; she'd missed the bookstore. She'd missed everything about Beach Cove, but Sam's store had a special place in her heart. In here, one could almost believe in magic. Maybe it was because time had no meaning when it came to words.

Back in the day, Maisie used to bring flower bouquets from her garden for Sam's counter, just so she had a reason to visit. Often she'd kept Sam company for an hour, or two, or five, treating herself to old books and fragrant cappuccinos from the café a few doors down.

Maisie let her gaze wander. The dark wooden

shelves guarded their treasures proud and tall, like the conscientious keepers of secrets they were. Maisie resisted the urge to trail her fingers over the waving rows of spines. There might be valuable or rare copies among them, and touching wouldn't—

Suddenly, she smiled. Sam had sorted the books by the color of their bindings. Maybe that was the thing to do with antique books these days? But probably Sam had just gotten a feeling that she should rearrange the books. Those feelings came over Sam all the time. After a couple of glasses of wine and too much sun, Sam had once confided in Maisie that books got bored and cranky like toddlers, demanding things like new neighbors, or new spots on the shelves. The day after, she'd denied having said that, and Maisie had laughed and forgotten about it. But now that she looked at the books, the words came back to her like faint echoes. Had the books gotten bored again, asking to sit next to other covers of a color?

Maisie blinked, wondering whether she'd maybe had too much sun herself, and peeked into the next aisle. "Sam?"

The store seemed empty. No murmuring voices, no shuffling feet, no leafing through pages. Maisie checked her phone. There was no message from the podcasters, nothing that gave her a reason to leave and go back to the empty house she'd fled. The kids had taken off to visit the beach where Alex had sat with Brandie. They'd assured her that they didn't need her as a guide since they had GPS, Google, hotspots, whatnot. Maisie had gratefully accepted the get-out-of-jail card.

But after her years in the noisy city, the silence in the empty house had seemed oppressive. Maisie couldn't stomach checking in on her neglected garden.

And she still didn't know for sure whether Sam had a brand-new child. Since they'd all met again after all, Maisie felt she should know that much. And so, a short half hour after the podcasters had left her, Maisie had made a beeline for the village and Sam's store.

"Sam?" Maisie took another step. Over here, the books were blue.

Before Sam had inherited the store, it'd belonged to Sam's mother; before that, it'd been her grandmother's. And so on, and so on. Sam could trace her line, if not her bookstore, all the way back to a matriarch who'd fled the Salem witch trials. The story was that Sally Burrow arrived in Beach Cove with only the clothes on her back and a book in each hand.

Sally had preferred the dangers of the then-Maine wilderness and the risk of Indian attacks to that of getting sucked into the trials and burned at the stake. The trick was, as Sam liked to say, that Sally Burrow did believe she *was* a witch. She'd confessed it in a letter to a namesake great-granddaughter, who'd used the letter as a bookmark in her cookbook.

Sam still had the cookbook. And the letter.

Allegedly.

Maisie smiled. She'd never laid eyes on either. But it was a good story, especially when one owned something as unprofitable as a store for old books. Tourists that read the story in the town guide came to hear Sam tell more. Sam did, and she did it well enough to impress her visitors. They'd go on to browse the shelves for overlooked treasures until they fell in love with the velvet-feel of a vellum cover or a delicate illustration and ended up buying the book. Sipping cinnamon and cocoa-daubed cappuccinos, Maisie had watched more than one customer step out of the store just to stare at the new book in her hands with a bemused expression on the face.

"Sam?" Maisie called a third time.

Sam appeared at the door to her office. She pulled a pair of hot-pink earbuds out of her ears and stuffed them into her jeans pocket. "Hey. I didn't hear the bell."

"I have some time; I thought I'd come by and see if your store's still standing."

Sam nodded at the shelves. "Still kicking. Maybe not much longer though."

Maisie glanced at her friend. The bookstore hadn't done well for the last two hundred years, but the look in Sam's eyes said she wasn't joking. "Why not?" Maisie asked. "Business not going well?"

Sam crossed her arms and shook her white-blond hair out of her face. "I can hold on a while longer. I might have to get a loan and expand, offer something besides books. Furniture? Maybe antiques. I don't know." She dropped her arms, resignation in the movement.

"I don't mean to hog your time," Maisie said. Sam didn't seem glad to see her; maybe coming here had been too pushy, asking too much. "I'll leave if you're busy." Maisie counted to five, trying not to let her disappointment show. She didn't want to leave. Her New York and Beach Cove feelings about going to the village were two different things entirely.

"It's okay. Stay." Sam pinched the bridge of her nose. When she looked back at Maisie, the blue of her eyes had brightened. "Now that you've finally found your way back."

"Sam, I didn't want to hurt anyone's feelings. I hope you know that."

"I know that you didn't *want* to, Maise." Sam leaned forward. "But that doesn't mean you *didn't*. But I get it." She sighed.

Maisie nodded. "I know. I'm—"

"Don't say you're sorry again. Sorry has nothing to do with it. Hey, don't worry, Maisie. It's all right."

But it wasn't. There was a distance between them that had Maisie knead her fingers and Sam look at the floor. What could Maisie do to scrape away the icy wall she'd put between them?

"Can I buy you a cappuccino, Sam? Pretty please?"

Sam shook her head, but the left corner of her mouth pulled up in appreciation of Maisie's effort. "Sounds nice, but I can't. Larry said he'd meet me for lunch."

Maisie nodded, unable to never mind the rejection even though she deserved it. "How's Larry? Still busy?"

In The-Time-Before, Larry had rarely been present. As a professor at Bay University's history department, he'd been too busy with teaching and research. And very, *very* busy working his way up the ladder. Once Sam's husband sunk his teeth into something, he didn't let go, be it project or career.

Sam lifted an eyebrow. "Oh, yes. To catch you up quick, we had a... I don't know, a falling-out. Happened a few years ago."

Maisie frowned. "I'm sorry." Not so much for the falling-out, but for not being there when Sam needed a shoulder.

Sam shrugged. "We found our way in the end."

"Is he working less?" He'd always promised and never cut back then.

"No." Sam chuckled, but there was no mirth in the sound. "I'm working more, so I don't notice that he's never around so much anymore. I've given up fighting for his attention, but I still like him enough to stay married. It's just what it is."

"That sounds...good?" Maisie tried to stay neutral. Larry had never been Maisie's favorite. In her opinion, Sam deserved better. She deserved someone who was there for her. At least sometimes. But Maisie wasn't in the relationship, and so she knew only the bits Sam chose to share. Like the rest of them, she grudgingly acknowledged that Sam, smart and intuitive, knew best. She had the right to stick it out with Larry if that's what her heart wanted.

Sam shrugged. "Doesn't sound great, does it? But it works for us. He's got a room in Bay Port, so he stays there when he has to work late. I'm not constantly unsettled because I'm waiting for him to come home. It helps."

"It's a long drive," Maisie agreed. Bay Port was an hour commute each way, and Sam was stuck in Beach Cove since she couldn't pick up her store and move it. Larry could've snagged a position at Merewif Community College and cut his commute in half, but he'd wanted to be at a research university.

"His research is going great," Sam volunteered. Maybe she felt the urge to defend Larry. "He just got a grant to go to Syria for some ancient manuscripts that have recently been discovered."

"Oh, whoa." Maisie tried to be impressed, but she could only view Larry's research travels through the lens of Sam's loneliness.

Sam chuckled again. "It really is okay, Maise. I've taken up yoga, and I found that I'm much more balanced when he's not home all the time. I think he's making me nervous. Not like bad-nervous, just like...well..."

"I think I know what you mean." In their later years, Maisie's life had been most peaceful when Robert hadn't been home. She'd liked having him at home; even after the first glow of newlywed love had subsided, he'd been great company. But Maisie had been most at peace when she'd been on her own, at least while Robert had been alive. After she'd lost him, all that solitary peace had shattered into a myriad of spiny splinters. Now, burrs of loneliness hooked themselves into her skin when she was alone. "It's not the same when they're dead," Maisie blurted out.

"Oof." Sam glanced at her. "Yeah. I shouldn't have —"

"Of course you should've." Maisie held up her hands in apology. "That just came out, sorry. *I* shouldn't have. What I meant is, with Robert, it was most peaceful when I knew he was at work and I was alone, or with all of you. I knew where he was. I knew he'd be back. When he was home, something in me constantly followed him as if I had feelers on him, tasting the air between us, making sure I had him... I don't know. *Encompassed.* I always knew what his moods were, and what he needed and wanted and all that."

Sam smiled, and some of the old warmth crept back in the air between them. "I have no idea what you're talking about. I just like the quiet when Larry's gone."

"Oh, very funny." Maisie smiled back. Even if Sam's experiences weren't the same as hers, she saw the light of recognition in Sam's eyes. "Tell me about yourself. You know—" Maisie cleared her throat, embarrassed. "It occurred to me that I don't even know if you have a kid."

"If I have a what?" Sam raised a single eyebrow.

"You could have a baby at home, for all I know. I mean...it's possible, right? There was enough time. All of you could have had more kids. Two or three, even."

"Um, no. I don't have a child, let alone three." Sam shook her head enough to set her hair swaying. "What I did have was a hysterectomy. My hormones were going haywire, and in essence they said it'd be easier to take the whole skedaddle out instead of figuring out what's wrong."

"I'm... I don't know what I am. Is sorry the correct sentiment?"

"I'm not sure, either."

"How long ago was that?"

"A year or so after you went to New York. Right about the time I stopped texting. Maybe..." Sam grimaced. "Maybe exactly that time."

Maisie gritted her teeth. "Oh, Sam. You should've said."

Sam sighed. "Should I have? Didn't seem like you had any energy left for my uterus. Which, you know, one more time. I totally understand."

Maisie hesitated. "I wish...so many things. I didn't text because I didn't love you. I did. I do."

"You love me?" Sam grinned. "How much? A lot?"

"Golly." Maisie grinned back. "To the beach and back."

"Good. More than that and I wouldn't believe you. But since the beach is right around the corner: sounds legit."

"So come have coffee with me. It's not even eleven, how early can Larry want his lunch?"

Sam thought for a moment, then she pulled her cell out. "Not as late as I do," she murmured, her fingers tapping. "There. Lunch is canceled. I think maybe he said my butt looks big in these jeans anyway. If he didn't, he probably thought it."

"Your butt is perfect," Maisie said, not having had a single glimpse of it since Sam was wearing an oversized knitted sweater. "And I *love* your sweater."

"I do too. It's the best. Guess what, I made it myself. I can knit now." Sam went back into her cubby and reappeared, purse slung over her shoulder. "Café Dharma closed last year, and Tom knows too much already. But there's a new little coffee shop on Main. You'll like it."

They walked through the town, diving in and out of tiny side streets so Maisie could have a look at this front yard or that shop window.

"I don't even see these things anymore," Sam said, waiting for Maisie to finish wistfully fingering the April Cornell tablecloths outside Maison de Sand, the village's tiny home goods store.

"I haven't bought a tablecloth in ages," Maisie said glumly. "I used to have so many. Wonder what happened to them?"

"Check *him* out, not the linen." Sam's elbow dug into Maisie's ribs.

"Who?" Maisie looked up. A few hundred yards ahead, a man had stepped out of the Beach Cove Pharmacy. His pepper hair put him in his fifties or sixties, and his shoulders slouched in the way of tall people trying not to loom.

Sam lowered her voice. "That's Vincent Grey, your new neighbor. He moved here from London a few years ago and bought Carriage House. The agent said Grey wanted the orchard out back."

Maisie glanced at her friend. "Interested?" she asked casually.

"In the orchard or Grey?" Sam whispered. "He's my best customer but just a tad strange if you ask me. As far as I can tell, he hasn't made many friends. Keeps to himself, even though he's very polite when you talk to him."

"'kay."

"Also I'm married."

"True. I forgot. You couldn't be interested in handsome tall men if you tried."

Sam chuckled, taking it in stride. "Sure you forgot, I don't—Oh, he's coming this way, stop talking."

Maisie shook her head. "Aren't we too old for that sort of thing, especially since we're not inter—"

"You started it," Sam muttered, cutting Maisie off.

"Mrs. Bowers." Vincent Grey stopped and smiled. It was a peaceful smile from behind heavily lidded eyes, in a face marked by time, and weather, and something Maisie couldn't put her finger on. "What excellent luck to meet you here. Did you get new books since I last came to your store? I was about to stop by the store and ask."

"I did get a few boxes at a barn auction," Sam admitted. "They've been sitting in an attic for the last fifty years, maybe longer. I haven't opened them yet, though. Could be there are only old textbooks and moldy primers inside."

"I don't know about mold, but old textbooks can be fascinating," Vincent Grey replied thoughtfully, his voice as calm as his eyes. "Depending on the subject." He smiled at Maisie.

Maisie smiled back.

"This is my friend Maisie Jameson," Sam said. "She's only visiting now, but she owns Beach House and used to live there."

"I do know Beach House." Vincent offered his hand with a slight inclination of his head. "I live down the road and walk past it most days. It is nice to finally meet you, Mrs. Jameson."

Maisie put her hand into his. It was large and dry and calloused as if he was a laborer, but his fingers were long and elegant, and his fingernails immaculate. "Nice to meet you, too. Please call me Maisie."

She felt Sam's eyes flit to her.

"Thank you, Maisie. My name is Vincent. Vince, if you'd be so kind."

Maisie nodded and let go. "Sure, Vince."

His eyes were the greyish blue of a stormy sky. As if she'd found him out, Vince dropped his gaze and inclined his head in another hinted-at bow. "Mrs. Bowers, Maisie. Good day."

"Bye," Sam and Maisie said in unison.

Vince stepped off the sidewalk and passed them, continuing on his way.

"So," Sam said after he'd disappeared from view. "What do you think?"

"He's very polite, just as you said. A little strange?"

Sam looked pleased at Maisie's acumen. "Nail on the head, sister."

Maisie hesitated. She could tell Sam wanted more. "Old-fashioned?"

"Another good one."

They continued walking. "Not in a bad way, though, am I right?" Maisie wondered who she was asking. Sam or herself?

"Uh, no. Just unbelievably formal. I've never had a bad feeling about him, but he's always—I don't know. Extra. I definitely can tell when I've had an interaction with him. It affects me. But not in a bad way."

Sam had always been sensitive to what she laxly called a person's vibe. But Maisie had felt it, too. It was as if Vince Grey gave the air a taste. She wanted to know more about him, what he did, and what his story was. But it was only passing curiosity, and since Sam's man-sensors were up, Maisie didn't ask.

"If I were a horse, I'd calm right down if he talked to me," Sam mused.

Maisie had to laugh. "What? A horse?" But again, she knew what Sam meant. There'd been something calming to Vince, to the way he took time for each word he said. She smiled. "Since you aren't a horse, how does he make you feel as a human?"

"Not sure." Sam narrowed her eyes. "Calm, but suspicious."

"All men are suspicious," Maisie muttered.

"So they are."

The bubbly mood that had floated Maisie a moment ago fizzled away. All men were suspicious, and all women, too. Teens were suspicious. Everybody was suspicious. That's what happened when your child disappeared. Trust ceased to be an option.

The new coffee place was cute and predictable, exactly what a tourist would expect to find in a seaside town like Beach Cove. The wood was stained Dark Espresso, the food included crêpes with Nutella or strawberries, and the college-age kids who prepared them thought the café might be a chain but weren't sure.

In a back corner, side by side, steaming paper cups before them and heads bent over phones, sat Jim and Ashley. Jim murmured something and his wife, glued to her screen, nodded.

Maisie sat with her back to the door so she could watch them. Sam, after an uncertain look at Maisie, chose the chair opposite. A pretty young woman with a discreet nose piercing and heavy dreadlocks in a ponytail brought coffee and menus. Maisie didn't recognize her.

"Don't you want to go say hi?" Sam murmured, picking up a laminated card and pointing it like a thumb over her shoulder.

Maisie shook her head. "Let's give them some space. They went to check out the beach where Brandie left him. They can't have learned anything I don't already know. Maybe they're planning what to do next."

"Okay," Sam said and began to pry the lid off her paper cup.

Maisie watched Ashley frown, then say something to Jim. Now he frowned as well and took her phone, using two fingers to magnify the screen.

Maisie wanted to run over, yank the phone from his hands, and see what was so interesting. Was it to do with Alex? Was it a clue they'd uncovered, something she'd missed? A Sherlock Holmesian insight that would tell them something? Anything at all?

Maisie would pay gold simply to know whether Alex went left or right after he'd thrown his empty bag in the trash. Any detail was worth all she owned.

"Hey," Sam said.

Maisie looked at her.

"Are you crying?" Sam pushed her cup aside.

"No, of course not." Maisie hadn't cried in years. She had no tears left in her. Only an acrid fear that she was missing something, that there was something she should do for Alex, that she'd failed following a lead. Maisie rubbed a fingertip under her eye and showed it to Sam for proof: dry.

"Okay. Hey... I was just thinking I'd better get back to the store after all." Sam reached for the purse dangling from the back of her chair. "I think Mr. Grey might still stop by if I'm open. He actually buys books when he does. I better go."

"I didn't frighten you away, did I?" Maisie frowned. "I swear I wasn't crying, Sam. Come sit.

You had an entire lunch date penciled into your day."

"Still." Sam stood, smiling apologetically. She reached for the lid and pressed it back on her cup. "I'm sorry I said that; I know you weren't crying. I'm an idiot. But I honestly can't afford to lose a sale. Taxes and all that. I've got to hustle. Okay? Are you going to be okay?"

"Sure." Maisie squelched her insecurities as best she could. It wasn't for her to question Sam's motives for running off. "Can I buy everyone dinner tonight, you think?"

"Oh! I don't—I mean, it's a nice thought, but I don't know what everyone's schedule's like. I'd have to check with Larry, too. Send a text?" Sam took a couple of steps toward the door, looking back over her shoulder.

Clearly Maisie was expected to stay. Not walk her friend back. "Sure." Maisie gave a perfunctory wave and turned back to her coffee.

Sam was running away. Maisie wished she wouldn't. But Maisie was the grandmaster of running away, and she hadn't said bye either, not even over her shoulder. She'd just gotten up and walked out the door. Not a single look spared for her friends.

Sam had all the right in the world to run away and not explain herself.

Maisie sipped her coffee, slow and methodical. At least here she wasn't alone, and she could keep an eye on the podcasters. See if their faces gave something away. Wait if they spotted her. Wonder if they had questions. Or news.

News. That dreaded, hoped-for word.

Maisie couldn't stand it, couldn't *stand* waiting for news. It made her skin crawl, made her want to run and scream and huddle in a corner all at the same time. But she had to wait for news. Just as a long time ago, she'd had to get up at night whenever baby Alex needed milk, or soothing, or a clean diaper. She was his mother. She did what she had to, no matter how she felt about it. Doing her duty didn't make her special, either, even if not every mother got called on to step up the same. Some got lucky and were spared. Maisie wondered whether the lucky ones thanked fate every night for being granted peace even though they had kids.

Kid. One.

One was enough.

No wonder she'd made Sam uncomfortable. Maisie didn't want to be in her own obsessive, suffering, hurting company either. She'd run from herself too if she could.

But for her there was nowhere to go, and so she sat, her eyes on the podcasters.

Chapter 11

Cate checked the slim gold watch on her wrist. Time to leave for school. She glanced at the table. Emily had made breakfast, and she and Claire were scrolling on their phones as they ate eggs and waffles. Cate could smell the maple syrup across the kitchen. It made her swallow, and she cleared her throat. Gross. Like some Pavlovian dog. Cate took a sip of her frozen mango-and-collards shake. It wasn't that bad.

"Do you have to go to work today, Mom?" Emily looked up.

"I only have one class in the afternoon…" Cate checked her watch again, already having forgotten the time again. "Oh. I better leave though, I've got a meeting. Are you ready, Claire?"

"Yep." Claire stood, eyes never leaving her phone. She grabbed the backpack hanging on her chair and slung it over her shoulder. The girl looked like she was in a commercial, all blond hair and long legs.

"Put the phone away," Cate said mechanically.

"Okay." Claire stuffed the phone into a side pocket on her backpack.

Cate sighed. "Come on, baby." Claire was a smart kid, but unlike her older sister Emily, Claire was passive. Not rebellious but also not engaged. At her age, Em had raised hell and high water over the smallest things.

She'd calmed down after Alex had vanished. All the local teens had. There'd been a couple of exceptions, kids that fought their fears by acting up for a time. Emily's friend Lily, who now was working at the new coffee place, had had a rough few years of it.

"I'll clean up." Emily stood and stacked Claire's plate on her own. "And then I have to memorize some lines."

Point proved. "Thank you, sweetheart."

Emily had always meant to be a doctor. But in the middle of her residency at Bay Port Hospital, she'd suddenly discovered that she *wanted* to be an actor.

Cate sighed. She suspected that the hospital had reminded Em too forcefully of all the things that could've happened to Alex. Cate hadn't weighed in on Emily's decisions. She wanted her oldest to find her path herself, even if there were bends in her road. Expensive bends.

Allen had raged. He'd refused to let Emily move back in with them, threatening that he wasn't going to support her any longer. But that was one time Cate had put her foot down; something she seldom did. Cate's mother had been a cold, narcissistic woman who'd never offered safety; on the contrary. When she held Em in her arms for the first time, Cate had sworn to herself that no matter what, she'd have her children's back. If they should fall, she'd catch them. Always. Her daughters would always be welcome to live with her.

So, Cate had offered Allen an alternative. If he didn't want to live in the same house as Emily, *he* could move out.

Allen had stayed. But Cate knew he'd considered the offer. In the end, she knew he wouldn't leave—he'd built his life and house and reputation in Beach Cove, and he wasn't about to give that up for the price of one wasted education.

"Let's go." She picked up the hobo bag that held the essays she'd graded the night before, put an arm around Claire's waist, and steered toward the door.

Her stomach lurched. "Oh." Cate swayed.

"Mom. Are you okay?"

"Yeah. I'm fi—" Her stomach lurched again.

"Mom." Emily came over and took hold of her arm. "You don't look so good."

"I'm... I better go to the bathroom." Cate's toes prickled, and cold sweat started to bead on her forehead; she wiped it away.

"I'll drive Claire to school." Emily plucked the key to her old Honda from the hook by the front door.

Claire hitched her backpack higher. "People, I can walk. It's like two minutes down the road."

"It's fifteen minutes. And your sister is going to drive you." Cate took a breath. The times of kids walking everywhere by themselves were over. At least for her teen.

"How about we walk together?" Emily offered.

"It's fine, you can drive me."

"Thank you, milady," Emily smirked. "Mom, go lay down. I'll be back in five."

"Stay until she's in the school building," Cate muttered, but then she had to turn on her heel and rush to the bathroom.

She locked the door and leaned over the sink, her nausea rising and ebbing in waves. Was it the coffee? She hadn't had breakfast before going to Beach House, and Tommy's coffee had been extra-strong. Normally, Cate had a nice breakfast and a cup of milky Earl Grey.

After a while of waiting for the retching that never came, the nausea lessened. Cate washed her face with cold water, went into the bedroom, and called the school to ask for a substitute to stand in. She only had one class. The substitute could easily go through the assigned reading with the kids.

By the time she'd ended the call and sent the substitute an email with instructions, Cate had heard the front door open and close again.

"I'm in the bedroom, Emily!" Cate called, closing her laptop.

Allen appeared at the door. "Cate?"

She sat up. "Allen! I didn't expect you home."

"I came back a day early. *I* didn't expect *you* home."

Carefully, Cate set the laptop on her nightstand. "Don't you have one more day of workshopping?"

Allen came into the bedroom. He looked like someone running a relaxation retreat for apoplectic managers might be expected to look. Nice khakis, button-up shirt with sleeves rolled up, no tie. His hair was moussed the way he liked it. Casual, yet clean-cut. "Marlene took over," he said.

Cate dug in her memory for the name until she remembered that Marlene was Allen's newest mentee. "Already? Is she that capable?"

Allen shrugged. "I had to get out. It was one workshop too many. Remind me to never again put them back-to-back like that." He slumped onto the bed; a tired, hard-working man come home to rest.

Cate saw his eyes flick to her feet.

The ugly slippers.

She swung her feet off the bed and kicked the slippers under the bed. Then she picked up her laptop and carried it to the desk. "You rest, Allen. Do you want me to make you a green smoothie? I have frozen mango."

Allen closed his eyes, one hand on his flat stomach, one hand on his forehead. "No," he murmured. "I just need to relax."

He'd seen the slippers and was shutting down on her.

Another wave of dizziness rolled over Cate, just enough to make her touch the wall to steady herself.

"I've canceled my class," Cate said quietly, regretting the email to the principal already. It was only one class. Barely worth the trouble of bringing in a substitute.

"Hmm." Allen's chest was rising and sinking with regular breaths.

Cate knew he wasn't falling asleep. Not yet, not Allen. No, this was his cue for her to leave him alone.

She slipped out of the room and pulled the door shut behind her. Luckily, she was still dressed. She hadn't even gotten as far as taking her pantyhose off. Cate stepped into her flats, grabbed her purse off the counter, and left the house.

"Mom?" Emily was unfolding herself from the driver's seat as Cate walked down the driveway.

"Did you watch Claire go in?" Cate couldn't help it. Whoever had kidnapped Alex was still out there. Every day that Cate had spent searching for Alex, fear had grown in her mind until it felt like a cage around her brain.

"Mom, yes. I did." Emily came over to her. "She's fine."

Emily understood because she'd been frightened out of her wits as well back then. Even though Emily wasn't overly protective of her sister herself, she sweetly acknowledged Cate's need to guard her daughters. "Thank you, sweetheart."

"Why aren't you in bed? You look like you have to throw up."

"Oh, I just had too much coffee. I'm fine." Following Em's gaze to her white knuckles, Cate loosened her grip on the purse. "I thought I'd take a walk down to the store. Get something for my headache."

"Nausea and headache, huh? Do you have a migraine?"

Cate shrugged. "Listen, sweetheart, Dad just came home. He's resting in the bedroom. Better not disturb him, he's exhausted."

"Ah." The look her daughter gave her was far too knowing for Cate's taste. "Do you want me to walk with you?" Em offered.

"No, but thanks." Cate felt a sudden rush of love for her older daughter. What a beautiful person she was. She reached for Emily's hand. "You learn your lines. Meet your friends. Have fun. Do you need money?"

Emily smiled. She had a job in the hospital. Not as a doctor, but at the check-in desk. It seemed enough to cover her personal expenses and pay for her second career as an actor. "I'm fine, Mom. Call me if you feel sick again, I'll pick you up. You don't have a fever, do you?"

Cate put a hand to her forehead, but it was cool and dry now. "I think it was the excitement of the morning. Seeing Maisie again, you know? And that coffee. I'm not used to coffee, and I haven't had breakfast."

Emily nodded; her medical instincts were satisfied. "Get a treat at the bakery; you should eat something. I'll see you later?"

"Of course." Cate let go of Em's hand and turned toward the sidewalk with a smile. The brief exchange had warmed her heart; she so loved her daughter. Both of them. They were wonderful kids. Smart, strong, and independent. They were all she needed to be happy.

Chapter 12

"Mrs. J?"

Maisie stopped typing and looked up from her phone. "Hi, Ashley."

Ashley exchanged a look with her husband. "We didn't see you before. Have you been here long?"

Maisie nodded. "I came with a friend, but she had to leave. I didn't want to bother you."

"You should've." Jim smiled and shrugged into his bright yellow anorak. The sort of high-tech anorak someone in a rescue team would wear.

"Did you find the beach?" Maisie set her phone on the table.

"Sure." Ashley nodded eagerly, and Maisie wondered what pleased the young woman so. Finding the beach or the beach itself? "We drove to a couple of other spots, too. There are so many beautiful beaches in Beach Cove! I always figured the coastline in Maine was all rugged cliffs and rocks."

"No." How could anyone not know about the beaches in Maine? "There are plenty of sand beaches, especially near Beach Cove. That's how the town got its name. Though I read that in the olden days, it was called Liban's Cove."

"Liban? Where does that name come from?"

Maisie shrugged. "It didn't say." The name was a tidbit she'd learned from leafing through an old guide Sam had found at one of her barn auctions. "Maybe an early settler? Well, people started to call it Beach Cove for obvious reasons, and the name stuck. There are very few places where the water is this warm. It's great for swimming."

"Not warm enough for me, I'm sure. I'm more of a hot tub girl."

An image of her old white-and-blue swimsuit suddenly popped into Maisie's mind. Was it still waiting in some drawer in Beach House? "Alex was an excellent swimmer," she said absentmindedly.

"Why...are you saying that?" Jim threw her a watchful look.

It took Maisie a moment to realize that he thought she was commenting on Alex's disappearance. Probably because one of the most obvious answers to the mystery was that the sea had swallowed him. Only if it had, it should've given something back, too, and they'd never found proof that Alex had drowned. Maisie shook her head. "I was thinking about the beaches. I didn't mean anything."

"I think you did. What made you?" Jim insisted. "Don't you think Alex could've drowned? Maybe it was an accident."

"Oof. Okay. Well, there are no currents, riptides, or sharks in the cove. Nothing was found, not his body, not the backpack, nothing. As for drowning himself on purpose, I already told you he'd never have considered it. I'm sure you've found out about his father. But Robert killed himself because Alex had gone missing, not because he had some genetic defect Alex might've inherited. There's not a shred of doubt in my mind."

Maisie glanced at the college kid at the coffee machine and lowered her voice. The more complete a picture she'd paint for the podcasters, the faster they'd put aside theories that didn't pan out. "Alex was a fantastic swimmer. He grew up in the water, you know. I figure that even *if* he'd try to drown himself, he couldn't just march into the water. His survival instinct wouldn't have let him drown, and there was no evidence that he picked up rocks to weigh himself down. His book bag wasn't heavy, either. He kept his books in the school locker, and they were all accounted for. So was anything else."

"I get what you're saying," Ashley said thoughtfully. "Like, his muscle memory would've kicked in. Hmm. Maybe. Were there no other people on the beach?"

Maisie sat back. "Not that we know. Of course, there's again only Brandie's word for it. But nobody has come forward. The local people were desperate to help; they'd have come forward. And nobody saw any strangers sticking around Beach Cove that week. I mean, it doesn't mean people didn't drive through it, but no one remembered seeing a new face in the village or at the beaches that day."

Jim pointed at the chair Sam had abandoned.

"Can we sit? Just for a moment."

"Yes." Maisie's heartbeat quickened as if this was the preamble to an important conversation. A whisper that they'd found something, a murmur that they knew what had happened.

It was silly to feel like that. They were only making a podcast, and there was nothing new for them to discover. Every stone on that beach had been turned over twice; Maisie herself had made sure of that. Barring somebody coming forward, she had all the information Beach Cove could provide.

The couple pulled out chairs and sat.

"Are you at all suspicious of Brandie?" Ashley asked softly, leaning forward. "She was the last one to be with your son. It would be natural."

Automatically, Maisie leaned back as if her body wanted to restore the distance between them. "No."

"When you say that there is *again* only Brandie's word for it," Jim added, stressing the words Maisie had used. "Do you have any—"

"No." Maisie held up a hand to stop him. "There is nothing to implicate Brandie. Everything in her story checked out. As far as we know."

"Why do you feel like you should say it like that?"

"Like what?"

"You know, saying 'as far as we know.' That seems to imply that you think there's more to the story. Things she hasn't told you."

Maisie took a breath. "There *is* more, whether or not Brandie knows it. There's the entire question of *where is Alex?*" She could see they didn't follow her.

"Okay."

The couple scooted their chairs closer; now they were the ones hoping there'd be a reveal, a hidden clue coming up. Maisie's stomach ached. There wasn't. But—

"Between us only, okay? I do wish I could sit Brandie down and ask her what I want to know." She exhaled. It wasn't something she wanted to get out to the public, let alone broadcast on a popular podcast.

Maisie had enough experience with the media to know that every sentence, every word could be spun to suit the narrator's purpose. Usually, what suited the narrator was the version he thought entertained his audience the most. And in the eternal battle for ratings, only the most shocking spins and most open-ended implications would do.

"You didn't get a chance to do that?" Ashley asked. "Talk with her?"

"By the time the real questions came up, talking with Brandie had become a job for the police. Especially since she'd already lied to me. They knew what my questions were because I'd told them. And they got answers." Maisie exhaled. "I'd still love to talk with her, but it's not a good idea."

"No?" Jim asked.

"No," Maisie said firmly. "I'd keep asking her the same question over and over. There's no sense doing that. I'd be like a hamster on a wheel, going over the same thing again and again and again. It's good I don't have access to Brandie. I mean it." Her voice was steady and convincing because Maisie didn't want them to go down the rabbit hole of what-did-Brandie-know. It was unproductive.

Ashley tilted her head. "What question would that be, though?"

"What question would what be?"

"The one you'd ask over and over."

Maisie looked at her. "Well, what happened to my son. What happened, of course."

"Of course." Ashley's face fell with disappointment. "I thought you might've had one more specific."

"One way or the other that's what it all boils down to."

Ashley checked her phone and pointed at Jim. "We have to go, pick up Amanda and JJ. They're still at the beach."

Maisie blinked. "Why? Anything to do with the search?"

There was pity in Ashley's brown eyes. "No, no. It's just, they love hanging out at the beach. Jim was cold, so he and I came here to warm up with a cup of coffee."

"Oh. Right." That was it then. No news, no nothing. Maisie felt herself deflate as if her lungs had been punctured. Air out of an old balloon. Flat tire.

Once again, she'd let hope clutch her in its golden grip. It seemed that losing hope wasn't something she was able to learn. She didn't have that particular talent. She was the kind that crashed and crashed again, knowing better yet never learning the lesson.

"I'm tired, I'm going…" She petered out.

"Home?" Jim suggested, twisting out of his chair already.

"Yeah," Maisie muttered. "Home. I guess."

"We'll see you later."

"Are you done for the day?"

"I think we'll try and get a few more soundbites for the podcast. The ocean, the wind. Listeners like to get the atmosphere, you know?"

Maisie sighed. Atmosphere wasn't going to solve the mystery. "Sure. Have fun."

"We'll see you back at the house, Mrs. J." The podcasters shuffled out the door.

Who knew if they'd even been talking about Alex all this time? But she had to keep positive, couldn't let herself feel like this; they'd still get Alex lots of publicity. She should've—

"Ma'am?"

Maisie looked up. The young barista with the piercing stood in front of her, a large plate of steaming crêpes in her hand. The folded pancakes were drizzled with caramel and generously topped with sliced strawberries and whipped cream.

"Did you order this, ma'am?"

Maisie looked at the plate. It was lunchtime, and she'd only had half a bagel for breakfast. "No, I didn't." She took her purse and stood. "I'm sorry, wrong table."

The barista hesitated, glancing back at the counter. Now that Jim and Ashley had left, Maisie was the only customer left. "I must've made a mistake. Do you want it?"

"Um…" The sweet scent rose into Maisie's nostrils, and her stomach gurgled enthusiastically in response. Embarrassed, she pressed a hand against it.

The barista smiled. "Have it on the house, please. The strawberries are super fresh, I got them in this morning." Without waiting for an answer, she set the plate on the table and added a napkin-wrapped bundle of silverware from her apron pocket.

Maisie sat again, trying to keep it together. Sam, the podcasters—they'd been the only other people in here all morning. Nobody had ordered food; there was no mistake.

Always look for the helpers, she heard that gentle voice from her childhood.

"Thanks," she murmured and swallowed the urge to cry. "Thank you."

"Enjoy." The barista gave a casual nod—no big deal—and turned. When she reached her counter, she busied herself polishing the coffee machine, studiously keeping her back to Maisie.

Slowly, Maisie peeled the fork from the napkin and cut a corner off. It was good. Sweet and warm, soft and creamy. Maisie hadn't had crêpes in… She couldn't remember when she'd last had something sweet, let alone the delicate French pancakes. She picked up her knife to cut off a bigger bite, dipped it into the warm caramel puddling on the plate, and then scooped strawberry on it.

She'd forgotten how sweet food could be… A little sigh escaped her.

The barista definitely was one of the helpers.

"Look. We can fix this." Ellie put her hands on her hips.

"Yeah?" Maisie shaded her eyes against the afternoon sun and bravely surveyed the damage.

She'd walked past the Fish Market just when Ellie had stepped out to close the shop for lunch. Ellie had waved and called her over, hooked her arm under Maisie's, and declared they'd have lunch together at Beach House. Maisie's heart, already warmed by the kind barista, warmed even more—despite being stuffed full of strawberries and cream, she'd dreaded returning to her big, empty house.

Unfortunately, Ellie had found out on the short drive that Maisie hadn't yet checked on her beloved garden and ordered her to get it over with.

Well, here they were, standing on the patio. The garden, or what was left of it anyway, spread out in front of them.

Maisie cleared her throat. "I don't think this can be fixed, Ells. It's a mess."

When she'd left, the garden had been a riot of color and composition, a hard-earned mirage of petals, buds, and butterflies. Now, not so much. Maisie went down the steps and touched a brown umbel hanging off a woody stalk. She frowned at the cluster of desiccated flowers before letting it droop again; her inner gardener itched to pull out the dead plant, but why even start? She looked around. The ornamental grasses nearby looked like fistfuls of straw. And it got worse... Maisie braced herself and let her gaze wander over deadhead roses, rotted foxgloves, broken peonies, drowned hydrangeas.

She raised an eyebrow, amazed by the damage. Of course, she'd been aware of fighting a losing battle against nature every time she'd yanked a weed, but this was *too much*. Strawberries and cream or no.

"Ugh. Let's go back inside. There's no way. It was so much work just *maintaining* it, there's no way I can get it back from"—Maisie gesticulated with both hands at the ruin—"*that*. It's too much. It's too late. I should've hired a landscaper."

"Why didn't you?" Ellie threw her a sidelong look. "You had Liz check on the house."

"I didn't think I could afford a gardener," Maisie hedged. She could've splurged, but she hadn't had any intention of ever again living in Beach House. She wasn't even going to stay long.

"All right, then don't tell me." Ellie turned. "Let's go in. I think I heard the delicious sound of the pizza delivery car. The exhaust pipe is wonky."

Ellie had called her son from the car, asking him to send a large arugula pizza to Maisie's house. Ellie had done this without consulting Maisie first, and Maisie didn't have the heart to tell her friend that she'd already gobbled up one hearty lunch.

Now, Ellie cleared her throat. "Are you going to say hi to Tommy before you leave, Maise?"

Maisie kept her voice even. "Of course. I'd love to see him again."

"Don't lie," Ellie muttered. "I can hear it in your voice; you're trying too hard. You don't want to, do you?"

Maisie stopped, her hand on the door to the sunroom. "I want to see Tommy so bad it hurts. He's the closest I can get to seeing Alex."

Ellie's voice softened. "And how much does that hurt?"

"So much." Maisie could hear her voice turn brittle. "But that doesn't mean I won't do it. Come on in."

Ellie followed her into the sunroom. Robert had claimed it was a conservatory, but Maisie had said that was taking it too far and it wasn't that big. Whatever its proper title, it was still plenty spacious and had a domed ceiling made of a little cast iron and a lot of glass.

"Maisie, it's a crime to let that garden rot away." Ellie plopped into a wicker chair and crossed her legs, then slanted them sideways and studied them fondly. "Every time I'm in here, I feel like I'm on the set for the Great Gatsby or something."

"Ha, the Great Gatsby. I wish." Maisie sat on the wicker couch. "The fan doesn't work." She pointed at the large Havana fan that hung from the center of the dome.

"Never did. You love it anyway."

"Always have." The sunroom had been Maisie's happy place, back when she'd still had happy places. The garden had been another one. And the beach, of course. The cliffs with their gulls and sun-dappled blueberry forests, too. In fact, all of Beach Cove had been Maisie's happy place. Alex too had loved living here.

"Maisie, I wish you'd come back for good."

Maisie looked up. "Do you want to go to the beach? I haven't been down there yet."

Ellie stood. "Let's not forget the pizza. I was about to ask whether we should have a beach picnic." She smiled. "Remember? Eating sand makes dreams come true."

Maisie stood as well. They'd used to say that to the kids when they'd complained about sand in their food—someone had always been sure to drop their treat. *Eating sand makes dreams come true.* She smiled. She'd forgotten about that.

"Think Liz threw away the old picnic blanket?" Maisie asked.

"I hope she washed it and put it away; I have very fond memories of the picnic blanket. And your old picnic plates. The aqua ones with the little fishes on them?"

Maisie remembered. All the watermelons, peach and pecan pies, hot dogs, burgers, and salads that had danced over those plates... "Liz saved them; I saw the stack in the kitchen cabinet. Those things are indestructible."

She hadn't meant to go to the beach. Yet again, the words had simply risen from her soul and slipped by her brain. Though her heart knew that sand and sea hadn't claimed him, Maisie had imagined so many ways her child could have met foul play on the beach, she thought she'd given herself a sand allergy.

But with Ellie at her side and a peppery arugula pizza to keep them both grounded, it suddenly seemed as if Maisie could risk the beach after all.

Chapter 13

Sam closed her laptop and took off her reading glasses, setting them on the desk that filled the minuscule office in her store. Farsightedness had hit her early, and she'd had to start using glasses in her late thirties. Lots of people didn't need them even in their fifties. She rubbed her face. *Don't let the crummy sales numbers from the last two years get to you.*

Sam let her head fall back and sighed at the ceiling. Nice try...but she'd never been any good at lying to herself. It wasn't the numbers; the numbers hadn't been good for the last two *hundred* years. The store always somehow managed to scrape by.

But Maisie had finally found her way back to it, and Sam had immediately behaved like a resentful jerk. She'd walked out on her best friend, abandoning her in the café at a vulnerable moment. Why'd she done that, for crying out loud? She *wanted* to be with Maisie and talk. She wanted Maisie to let down her guard and be vulnerable so Sam could help share the burden. Sam shook her head as exasperation tipped into annoyance. Why not run off like a scared penguin instead? That was going to get her closer to Maisie for sure.

Vincent Grey had not stopped by. And now it was past lunch and she was hungry. She'd texted Larry, telling him she'd be available for lunch after all. He hadn't answered, of course. Larry wasn't good about checking his phone; half the time he left it in the car when he was in his office and vice versa. Another hurdle in communicating with her husband was the fact that he didn't like to reply to texts. It was probably some weird flex of his, but Sam had been married long enough to know that worrying about Larry's idiosyncrasies was not a good use of her energy.

Mechanically, she checked her own phone. Past one... If he'd meant to have lunch with her, he would've picked her up already.

Fine.

The feeling of exasperation in her chest grew until her legs fairly twitched with the need to move. Sam stood and left her office. The bell hadn't tinkled all morning, but sometimes she didn't catch the bell. Maybe her hearing was getting as bad as her eyesight?

Sam went on an idle tour of the store, patrolling the empty aisles. She rearranged a couple of discontented books, then restlessly returned to the counter. Like a bored bartender, she polished the surface with a kitchen towel. *Not enough*. The unsettled feeling drove her to do more; she went to open the door, moving it back and forth a few times. The bell worked just fine. Sam inhaled, tasting the salty air. The sun was almost at its zenith, the mist of the morning long burned away.

Shading her eyes, Sam stepped onto the sidewalk. The bookstore had plenty of windows, but wood and paper swallowed the light inside and created a mellow, timeless twilight. Maybe that's why she'd needed glasses so early?

Sam held her face into the sun, trying to ignore her rumbling stomach. She checked her phone again when something moved in the corner of her eye. Looking up, Sam caught a flash of red hair and army-green sweater disappear down Marina Alley.

Bonnie?

The alley was only a few steps away, and Sam, still driven to move, walked down Main Street to the mouth of Marina Alley. The narrow street led straight down to the town's small marina. From her elevated position, Sam could see a motorboat taking off, streaking the water white. Sam squinted; she had trouble reading a book without glasses, but at least her far vision was excellent. That was Bonnie steering the boat, her hair fluttering in the wind. And she wasn't alone; beside her sat someone else. There was a navy sweater next to Bonnie's green one.

Sam rubbed her chin. A man. Must be a man, judging from the breadth of the blue shoulders and the short hair.

The dinghy reached Bonnie's beat-up fishing vessel, an old Down-East lobster boat with a small tumblehome at the stern. They climbed aboard, splashes of color against the white hull. A few moments later, the vessel puttered off toward the open sea.

Sam watched the boat until it rounded the cliffs and she lost sight of it. Late morning was a weird time to go fishing, wasn't it? Lost in thought, Sam let her gaze wander up the rugged cliffs that rose from the water until her eyes came to rest on the forest above.

She should take a walk before the underbrush grew too dense. There were some places only the locals knew because, by the time the tourists arrived, lots of nice spots and paths were overgrown. The forest swallowed them back, unwilling to share its best berry patches and most tranquil ponds with people that didn't stick it out year-round.

The sudden desire to go to the forest, to find spring flowers and sit on mossy rocks almost startled Sam. Should she rush home, swap her flats for her boots? Just *go*, the way Bonnie just did?

Sam huffed impatiently. She couldn't simply leave the store. Just because her business was down in the dumps didn't mean she could skip out. On the contrary, it meant she had to double-down. Not go sit on mossy rocks. Keep the door open for customers. Generations had managed before her, and she would manage as well.

Slowly, Sam turned back.

Bonnie might not have much money—everyone knew she lived off the land and was barely ever even seen buying groceries at the market. Let alone keep a car. But she seemed to make it work. She'd inherited her family's waterfront plot, a trailer, a fishing boat, and a nice lobster territory. And good genes. No doubt Bonnie found company whenever she wanted it.

Few people were as free as Bonnie. Sam was aware of a jealous twinge in her heart. That sort of freedom was something she could only yearn for, as unreal and unlikely as a dream. Sam was too enslaved to the comforts of her life to trade them in. Sitting at a bonfire in a field by the ocean sounded better than watching re-runs of The Golden Girls, but it didn't mean Sam was going to give up her TV and sofa and cozy living room. And yet, it seemed that the yearning to do exactly that and finally be free was a big motivator. It drove Sam. All of them.

She cast a last glance at the water and the trees. Sapphire and emerald, calling her.

She'd get out there as soon as she could. And she'd make sure to take the girls. Maisie, especially; she could use a hike.

They all could use more of what was out there.

Slowly, Sam made her way back to the store. She reached for the door, then realized that it wasn't shut closed. It gaped open only an inch or so, but she'd pulled it all the way closed before she left, hadn't she? Yes. She always did. Sam inhaled. Bad idea to leave her store unlocked... There were some precious books on the shelves. And while there wasn't much cash in the register, Sam couldn't afford to lose a dime.

"Hello?" Gripping the cool, smooth brass knob, Sam pulled the door open farther and peeked inside. Carefully, since in the end, she'd still rather lose her possessions than her life. "Hello?"

"Oh hello. There you are, Mrs. Bowers."

"Yes." Relieved, Sam let out the breath she'd been holding. She knew that voice.

Vincent Grey stepped out of an aisle, an open book in his hand. He looked surprised when he saw her standing at the door. "I hope I didn't intrude? I assumed you were in your office."

Sam shook her head. "It's fine, I just stepped outside to—" She stopped, at a loss for an explanation. To snoop on Bonnie? "I wanted to see the water and the sky." Sam smiled, feeling self-conscious. But there it was. A middle-aged businesswoman, running off to smell the flowers...not exactly professional.

"It is a beautiful day," Mr. Grey confirmed kindly, and Sam thought she saw a twinkle in his hooded eyes.

Smiling back, she went to stand behind the counter like a good storekeeper. "Would you just like to browse, or can I help you with something? I could get the boxes I mentioned earlier if you like."

Mr. Grey carefully closed the book in his hands and placed it on the counter. "This is a second edition of The Orchardist. It is a fairly rare find. I've been looking for it for a while."

Sam picked up the slim, inconspicuous volume and studied the green quarter calf binding. She didn't remember it. "Was it in the tall pile by the window?"

"It was in a rather short pile at the bottom of the stairs." Mr. Grey pointed at a couple of stacks of newly harvested books.

"Ah. I haven't gotten to those yet." Sam held the book up and nodded at her office. "Would you mind if I..."

"Absolutely." Mr. Grey turned to the nearest shelf. "Take your time. There's plenty to occupy me."

"Thanks." Sam waited until her customer disappeared down an aisle in search of more treasure. Then she went into the cubby and opened her laptop to research the price for a second edition of The Orchardist. Fair condition.

When she found a suggestion, she blinked. More than ten bucks, then.

Her heart started to beat a little faster. Okay. Bracing herself, she grabbed the book and went back out.

"Are you all right?" Mr. Grey's voice came from the side, startling her.

"Oh yes. Well, I priced this one at—" She couldn't help but take a quick breath. "Four hundred and thirty-two dollars."

Mr. Grey's eyes crinkled, making him look like a British spy from the heyday. "Four hundred and thirty," he said earnestly.

The muscles in Sam's throat clenched. "Done," she croaked. Four hundred and thirty would cover overhead *and* the boxes of attic books she'd bought.

"I'll take these two as well if you care to let them go." Mr. Grey put two more books, already priced in pencil at fifteen dollars each, on the counter.

"I don't mind at all," Sam said with feeling and rang the books up.

Mr. Grey pulled a leather wallet from his coat and counted the bills on the counter.

Sam handed him his change and then rifled through the mess under the counter for a bag. She'd stopped stocking her own branded bags, but at this price point... "Here we go." A sturdy, clean tote bag from the farmer's market honey stand. Good enough.

"Thank you very much." Mr. Grey took the bag from her. "I'm looking forward to a cozy fire and The Orchardist tonight."

"That does sound nice." Maybe if Larry would stay at the university, she'd make a fire herself... Pour a glass of pinot and leisurely rummage through one of those new book boxes.

"Do you happen to enjoy fruit trees?" Mr. Grey's eyes were half-closed as he regarded her.

Sam leaned against the counter and smiled. Some lonely people went to the doctor for a chat. Others went to their local book dealer. She liked that—bookstore loners had the best stories.

"Sure." Who didn't like a pear tree? Plum trees,

apple trees... "They're nice."

Grey chuckled. "Thomas Bucknall did as well. He's the fellow who wrote The Orchardist."

"I don't know that I've heard his name before," Sam confessed. She knew a ton of authors; it came with the job. Nevertheless, Mr. Grey always knew more yet. Sam used to take it as a challenge. But sometime last fall, when the maple trees had turned orange and the scent of pumpkin spice lattes wafted up and down Main Street, she'd conceded. She'd stopped trying to out-author Vincent Grey. The man was freakishly well-read.

"Mr. Bucknall was known for taking a rather random yet strong interest in fruit trees."

"Is that right?"

His lips drifted into a private smile. "He was a member of parliament."

"Oh."

"Even so he kept his family seat in St. Albans, where he experimented with grafts. I believe one of his daughters married into the Shakespeare family, though I'm afraid that sums up my knowledge about Mr. Bucknall."

"I'm guessing that's St. Albans, England, then?" Sam lifted an eyebrow. She'd only heard of St. Albans in Queens, in connection with a burglary in which valuable books were stolen. She'd made a point to remember in case she'd come across booty peddled from the theft.

"That's my understanding as well." Mr. Grey inclined his head. "Well, I mustn't keep you any longer.

Thank you and good day to you, my dear Mrs. Bowers." He left, the doorbell tinkling goodbye.

"Such a strange day," Sam said to her empty store. "I mean, St. Albans? Who just *knows* stuff like that?"

She drummed her fingers on the counter until the last echo of the bell had ceased, then pulled out her phone. "Listen, Cate? I'm going to close the store for the rest of the day. Do you have time for a walk at the beach? I need to—I don't know, I just need to take a walk on the beach with you. Air my brain out. Meet you in a half hour?"

Chapter 14

The sun had soaked up the morning mist over the sea and was beaming triumphantly in the sky as Maisie stepped off the last wooden stair and onto the beach. Her shoes sunk deep into the fine white sand as if her feet had finally come home and meant to stay.

With every new step she took, more warm sand trickled into Maisie's moccasins. She stopped. The picnic blanket and melamine plates she'd tucked under her arm were slipping, and her hands were full, holding two long-stemmed wine glasses, a heavy bottle of cold chardonnay, and a stack of paper napkins with little red poinsettias on them. She readjusted her grip.

"Have you been to the beach a lot since you left Beach Cove?" Ellie asked behind her.

"I haven't been at all."

"Wait, what? You haven't been to the beach in *ten years*?"

Maisie let her left moccasin slip off her heel and shook her foot to get the sand out. "I haven't even really *seen* the sea since I left. Other than driving by once in a blue moon, the way you do when you live in New York."

Ellie huffed, loud enough for Maisie to grin. "That's just weird, Maisie. I couldn't stay away. I know it sounds dumb, but I get homesick when I don't go to the beach for too long. And I *live* here."

"I know." Compared to losing a child, not going to the beach wasn't exactly a biggie, but… A lump rose in Maisie's throat as she gazed at the waves. The sea was forever rushing toward the beach, eager to write messages in seaweed and driftwood on the sand. The vigilant gulls stood guard as they had for thousands of years, watching and waiting to see who could decipher the script.

There was no hurt or lingering resentment in the murmur of the waves. The sea welcomed her back without bitterness.

"Are you crying, Maisie?" Ellie asked. "You're all hunched over."

Maisie straightened and wiped the sleeve of her shirt over her eyes, letting the bottle of chardonnay cool her cheek for a moment. "No, I'm not." But when she looked, there were tear stains on the sleeve. Maisie stared at them. "Oh." The lump in her throat rose like the cork on a warm bottle of champagne. "I guess I am? I guess—" She sniveled a sob away, tried to blink the haze from her eyes. "Ellie?"

"Hang on, sister. I got ya."

Maisie, her vision blurred by tears that kept puddling in her eyes, felt bottle and glasses tucked from her hands. She lost napkins, plates, the blanket, until her hands were free to wipe her cheeks.

"Sit," Ellie ordered. "I'd cry too if I hadn't been to the beach in ten years."

"It's silly." Small sobs cobbled her words into a breaking staccato as if she was five, not fifty. "I could've gone, but I didn't *feel* like it." Maisie sniffled, kicked off her moccasins, and sat cross-legged on the blanket.

"Maybe you wanted to, but you didn't have time?" Ellie pressed one of the old Christmas napkins into her hand.

Maisie blew her nose. "Course I had time. I was busy but…*ten years*. There was time." She glanced at her friend, who cheerfully poured chardonnay into the glasses.

"You had enough to deal with, and you just didn't realize you wanted to go," Ellie decided. "We're salty old women with seawater in our veins, not blood. You need the beach as much as the rest of us. Go ahead and fuss a little. Here." Ellie held out a glass, filled to the brim with white wine.

"That's full." A few drops spilled onto her hand, mingling with the tears she'd rubbed off her cheeks. Maisie smiled, even though her eyes burned. "Better wine than tears, I guess."

"I know. Enjoy." Ellie lifted her own glass, looking pleased. "It's so good to have you back."

"Thanks, Ellie." The wine was cool and crisp, and Maisie drank deeply. "I'm sorry I cried."

A gull screamed, diving low to check on them.

"You know, I think you should stop saying you're

sorry," Ellie said suddenly.

"But I am," Maisie said. "I don't want to be so... I failed Alex, and then Robert, and then you."

Ellie stared at the ocean, her large eyes unseeing. "I don't think what we have *can* be failed. Despite your taking off and all that."

"I didn't care when I left," Maisie admitted, letting the wine wash up her shame. "I can't stand myself for it."

"We love you, Maisie." Ellie sighed. "I admit we *tried* not to miss you somewhere around year five. But it didn't work. Not for me and not for Sam or Cate, either. You're stuck with us."

Maisie moistened her lips. "That's—"

"And seems you're stuck with the beach, too," Ellie pointed out. "What with having to cry because you're back and all that."

"Ugh." Maisie emptied her glass and held it out, waggling it from side to side. The sun and the wine and the feelings started to swim like minnows in her head. No, her *head* was starting to swim. *She* was the minnow. Wait—was she? Maisie blinked. "I don't drink much anymore, but this is good."

"Isn't it, though?" Ellie refilled both their glasses, but this time stopped a couple of inches short of the rim. "Tom only just found out about this vineyard. I'm telling you, that boy has a way with—"

"Are we supposed to cup our hands, or did you bring more glasses, or what?"

Maisie looked up. "Sam? Cate? Where did you two come from?"

"Sand covers all tracks and swallows all sounds," Cate declared mysteriously. She took the last few steps and sank onto the blanket. Sam stood for a moment, looking unsure, but then she sat too, squeezing in between Ellie and Cate.

Maisie threw a glance at Ellie, who was back at studying the wine label, unperturbed. "I'd have brought more glasses if I'd known you'd be here."

"That's okay." Without further ado, Cate lifted the glass from Maisie's hand and took a sip. "Mm, that's good. Sam, try it. Tommy's been holding out on us."

Sam took the glass and drank, then gave a long, satisfied sigh. "Tell Tom to get more of that, Ells." She handed the glass back to Maisie.

Maisie would never share a glass with anyone in the city, but here, with her girls, it felt right. She took a sip. When she looked up, she found three pairs of sea blue eyes on her.

Maisie swallowed. "What?"

"She's making progress," Ellie murmured to Cate and Sam. "The beach helps."

"What do you mean?" Maisie protested. "What progress?"

Cate slung an arm across Maisie's shoulders. "Progress getting back, is what Ellie means. You're finding your way back to yourself."

"Back *where*?" Maisie blinked and handed the glass to Sam. "I think I've had enough."

"Is that *pizza* in the pizza box there?" Sam emptied the glass, and Cate topped her off.

"Tommy made it," Maisie explained. Now, the words came sluggishly. Very un-minnow-like.

Her friends glanced at each other, and Cate smiled. "We know, Maisie. Tommy's been making the pizza for a while."

"Ha. Yeah." Maisie didn't have to explain anything to *them.* They were way ahead of her. She leaned unceremoniously across Ellie's lap and flipped the lid open; the aroma of bacon, caramelized onions, and melted Gruyère rose into the air. She swallowed. "It smells ah-mazing."

"Hang on, tiger." Ellie started to shovel large, gooey slices on plates and handed them out.

Maisie closed her eyes as the savory taste flooded her tongue.

"Yummy, isn't it? Stay in Beach Cove and you can eat Tom's pizza every day!" Cate wiggled her eyebrows, chewing. "It's good to see you eat again, woman."

Maisie nodded, her mouth too full to speak. Her eyes drifted along the waterline. The beach was empty but for a single person walking alone. If she were to squint and pinch the person's length between thumb and forefinger, he'd measure only an inch. But it was only because of the distance; in fact, he must be quite tall. His shoulders stooped as if he was searching the dried kelp for something.

"Is that Vincent Grey from the Carriage House?" Cate asked casually, not sounding like she expected an answer.

Maisie took another slice from the box and

looked again. Vincent. Vince, actually. Now and then Vince bent down, maybe to check for a rock or a piece of sea glass glistening in the surf.

Beach treasures.

Maisie used to collect them too. Everyone did. Smooth chips of glass, shimmering shells, robin-egg stones rounded to perfection by centuries of waves, the intricately turned houses of sea creatures. Each find was unique, as random and irresistible as a picture drawn by a small child.

"I need to go and see if there's sea glass." Maisie set her half-eaten slice on a napkin. "Right now."

Sam crammed the last of her pizza into her mouth and wiped her hands. "Coming," she mumbled.

"I'm having another piece." Cate pulled two slices apart and offered one to Ellie, who took it.

"Hey, are those your podcasters?" Brushing sand off her jeans, Sam squinted.

Maisie turned and shaded her eyes. "Yes, that's them." There they were, a small crew ambling along the waterline as if they didn't have a care in the world.

"Are you coming?" Sam started down the beach.

Duty shackled Maisie to the spot and sobered her as effectively as a bucket of ice water. "Maybe they're looking for me."

Sam stopped and looked at her. "Should we go meet them?"

"Um…" Maisie hesitated. They hadn't noticed her yet. Jim was chasing Ashley into the surf, and she screamed as the waves splashed her. Amanda and JJ took off their shoes, and then they all stood at the edge of the sea, laughing and watching the waves wash over their toes.

"Did they come to work, or did they come to play?" Sam muttered and returned to the blanket.

Cate raised an eyebrow, chewing. "I don't see any equipment. I figured they'd bring a camera or something?"

Ellie looked up, too. "Have they started doing anything constructive yet?"

Maisie shrugged helplessly. Had they? They'd asked her some questions so far. "I mean, they'll still reach a lot of people putting it on the podcast, right?"

"Yeah. Yes, they will," Ellie murmured. "You can't lose with this one, Maise."

The women watched as the podcasters kneeled and started to scoop sand.

"Are they building a sandcastle?" Sam muttered. "How are they—Oh no, Maisie. Hey."

Maisie suddenly became aware of Sam holding her arm. She straightened her shoulders. "I'm okay. I'm fine."

"Okay." Sam took her hands away, and Maisie managed to lift the corners of her mouth.

"Points for effort, Maise, though that's a wane smile if there ever was one. Girls—" Sam turned to Cate and Ellie. "Maybe we should take a little walk? Get her mind off the sand-castling over there?"

"Sounds good. Maisie?" Ellie put an arm around

Maisie's waist.

"Yes. Let's walk."

All of them rose, kicked off their shoes if they hadn't already, and went down to the water. The cove was never very cold, but the sea's touch brought Maisie back into her body. She felt exhausted, and not because of the alcohol or the sun.

"Talk to me, Maisie," Cate muttered. "How do you feel? You practically drooped when you saw them."

Maisie tried to pull together a string of thoughts to explain, a logical rope leading out of her head and to her friends. "I hoped they'd do something new. Find the missing puzzle piece. Or at least try. I know I have to stop hoping for a miracle, but it's…so hard."

"But it's not likely that they *can* find a new clue, right?" Ellie said softly. A wave rolled in and she sidestepped it. "I mean, we know the facts inside out. Way better than they ever will. We were there when it happened."

"And yet we don't know where Alex is," Sam pointed out. "There's very much a piece we're missing. Maybe it's a case of not seeing the forest for the trees? I think anything's worth a shot, even letting a bunch of podcasters play in the sand. They're young. It doesn't mean they're not good at what they're supposed to be doing. Who knows, maybe they're discussing their next move right now."

Maisie rolled up her jeans that were already soggy from the splashing water. Then she straightened and looked at her friends, who were standing around her as if guarding her. Slowly, Maisie drew a breath, pulling the salty air all the way down to the pit of her fears. "Do you think he's dead?" she asked.

She'd never asked them before. She'd never asked anyone.

He needed to be alive.

"Aw." Ellie leaned her head against Maisie's shoulder, her hair soft and sad on Maisie's arm. "Yes, Maisie. I think so."

"If he were alive, he'd have found a way to let you know." Cate put a hand on Maisie's other shoulder, a gentle anchor to keep Maisie from washing into the sea. "I think he's been dead for a long time."

Maisie felt a tearless shudder go through her. It was a seismic shift of her soul, a fault line breaking in her mind. She looked at Sam. Sam knew. Sam always knew. "Sam? Do you think Alex is dead, too?"

Sam closed her eyes. Then she opened them again, her gaze wide and deep like the sea herself. "Yes, Maisie. I think so." Her voice was gentle, but there was no room for doubt. "I'm sorry."

Maisie exhaled softly, the wind carrying her breath over the water and to the sea. The sea, this ancient keeper of sighs and souls, answered with a small wave that engulfed Maisie's ankles in foam.

"But that's only my feeling, Maisie. Don't let us tell you to let go," Sam said. "None of us can do that. Nobody can."

"Your face is going all white," Ellie said. "Hang in there, Maise."

Maisie didn't move.

Cate tightened her grip on Maisie's shoulder.

"You don't have to make a call on whether or not he's alive. I sure wouldn't if it was one of my daughters. Whatever we feel, we simply don't know what happened."

Maisie nodded. Cate was right. And so was Sam. But it was too late; the seed of knowledge in Maisie's stomach, buried so laboriously under fear and hope, was finally unfurling and claiming its space.

Of course he was dead. They were right. She'd known. She hadn't given in the way Robert had, but holding out against her gut feeling had slowly been killing her, too.

"Did you ever have some sort of... I don't know, service? I don't mean like a funeral." Ellie cleared her throat. "I mean like a—a celebration of him. To remember the good. He was such a good kid. He really was."

Maisie shook her head. Celebration? She didn't understand Ellie's words.

"That sounds nice." Cate nodded. "Alex was a sweetheart. I would love to celebrate him. You know, think about all the good things about him."

"Maisie?" Sam asked. "You can cry, by the way. I wasn't mad at your crying in the coffee place. I was just struggling with my stupidity."

"I'm not crying," Maisie said automatically. She felt sick, nauseated with grief for her child.

Then, "We love Alex, too," Ellie said into the silence. "I know it's different, but... I mean, Tommy—" Ellie's voice broke and she cleared her throat. "We've got you, Maisie. We promise."

"Beach sisters, remember?" Cate said. "It doesn't just stop because you've been away for a bit."

"Okay," was all Maisie trusted herself to say.

"You're a good mother," Ellie said. "You deserve to hold on to that part of you. You deserve to remember the good parts."

"No," Maisie stammered. "Guys, too much." All the guilt she felt for failing her son... She suddenly couldn't stay upright under the weight.

"Let it come up, Maisie. Get it out here. That's the only way we can help you carry it," Sam murmured.

"It'll tear me up," she whispered. She'd suppressed so much for so long, letting it out would rip her in half.

"We'll glue you back together." Sam smiled and wiped the hair out of Maisie's face.

"It doesn't have to be like some big event," Cate said. "Let's have a picnic. We'll make some food he liked, have it in a place he liked to hang out, and tell stories about him."

Reeling, Maisie tried to lean on the support and understanding her friends offered. She'd tried to do it alone, and it hadn't worked. She'd tried for ten years, and she'd done Alex not a bit of good. "He likes blueberry pie," she whispered.

Ellie caught the words before the breeze carried them off. "Blueberry pie. Got that, girls?"

"I'll bake one," Cate promised. "We'll have a blueberry-pie celebration. I think that's lovely, yes? Where should we go?"

Sam pointed at the forest rising on the cliffs in

the northeast. "To the blueberry patches, probably. We already got the pie, and the kids loved picking the berries."

Maisie remembered the straggly berry bushes. "Alex did," she confirmed, her voice growing stronger. "I haven't thought about picking berries with him in forever." Her friends were right. Alex deserved to be celebrated with love. At least she'd been able to give him a whole sunny childhood full of beach, and blueberries, and friends.

"If it'd been you who'd disappeared instead— You'd want Alex to remember the good bits," Ellie said. "You wouldn't want him to be in constant pain."

"That's how I feel," Cate said. "If I die, I want the girls to remember the good stuff. If I knew they'd be upset for years…that'd be the worst."

"Of course they'd be upset for years," Sam said sternly. "You're their *mom*. But if I die, you can be upset for six months. No longer. And once a month you have to meet and have pie in my honor. I'm serious."

"All right already." Ellie sounded exasperated, waving them down. "One celebration at a time." She held her hand, palm down, into the center of their circle. "Do it."

Sam crossed her arms. "Ells, we're in our *fifties*."

Ellie grinned. "Go on, Grumpy, you're not too old for me."

"You're not fifty yet, Sam," Cate pointed out.

Sam scoffed but put her hand on top of Ellie's.

"Ugh. Don't leave me hanging," she muttered at Maisie.

Cate added her hand to the stack. "You too, Maise."

Maisie, too raw to talk, laid her hand on top. Because they were her friends. Blueberry pies, insensitivity, and everything else included.

Ellie cleared her throat. "One, two...uh, or is this too silly? Are we still doing the counting, or—?"

"Three!" Cate called.

Maybe their minds had forgotten, but their muscles hadn't.

"Beach sisters!" The call erupted from their mouths as their hands flew in the air.

For a moment, Maisie was too shocked to do anything but stare at her friends. They stared right back. None of them seemed to have expected the yelling.

Then, "Hey, no!" Cate shouted and pointed at the blanket they'd left behind. "The gulls are stealing our food!"

Maisie turned in time to see a herring gull flap its strong gray wings, carrying off the leftover pie in her beak. The gull barely made it into the sky before her buddies dive-bombed her, trying to steal her prey.

"Okay, so that happened," Sam said.

"The gull?" Ellie wanted to know.

"Or the yelling." Sam ran a hand through her short hair, looking embarrassed. "I mean, the gull, too. Though I'm not one for congealed Gruyère anyway. The birds are welcome to it."

"We better clean up anyway. The napkins are blowing all over." Ellie started toward their blanket, unceremoniously pulling Maisie along by her hand. "It's going to be all right, Maise," she muttered as she plodded through the sand. "You'll see."

Maisie glanced over her shoulder, at Sam and Cate, and the sea.

They'd brought back a part of her she'd locked away for a good reason. Now that it was summoned, would she be able to live with it?

Chapter 15

Ellie stepped out of the shower and wrapped a towel around her body, then slung a second one around her hair and tucked the ends into a turban. She checked the mirror. Without her long, wavy hair to balance them out, her eyebrows looked too dark and strong. Wild.

With a few impatient strokes, she applied foundation because Dale would appreciate it. Usually, she didn't bother much about makeup anymore. Some sunscreen was all she used. But it was a good idea to make an effort... Dale hadn't paid much attention to her for the last couple of years. Not in the bedroom, not out of the bedroom. To be fair, she hadn't given him much attention, either. They were so busy with their jobs and whatnot. Ellie didn't miss anything, but that wasn't a good attitude. She should at least try.

After a while, she leaned back to assess her handiwork in the mirror. The brown eyeshadow made the blue of her irises pop, and the lipstick was pretty but...well. She grabbed a wipe and rubbed it off again. It'd just smear her teeth, or flake, or stain her glass.

Ellie slipped into a blue dress that showed off her curves and twiddled her almost-dry hair into an updo, pulling out a couple of curls to frame her face. Was that look still with the times? She hadn't looked at a high-gloss magazine for ages; maybe she should ask Cate for some. Ellie turned once or twice in front of the mirror and gave up.

Good enough, anyway. No need to overthink things.

The front door creaked, letting her know that Dale had come home.

Ellie checked her phone. Almost seven-thirty. Outside, the sun had set, but the afterglow still held the dark at bay. Ellie stepped into a pair of kitten heels, wiped off the dust that had collected on the patent-leather toe caps, and hurried downstairs. Her husband stood in the door to the kitchen, his back to her.

"Dale?"

"Yes." He cleared his throat before he turned. The skin under his eyes looked like wrinkled paper, and his brow was creased. But when he saw her, Dale smiled. "You look nice, Ellie."

"Thank you." She smiled back, unsure how to return the compliment. Dale was handsome enough with his moussed-up hair, blue eyes, and the seductive half-smile that naturally curled his lips. But it felt wrong to talk about his hair when her husband seemed so tired. He was exhausted. Weary.

Dale dropped his gaze. "I know. It's been a long

day and a longer week." The smile dissolved like a shadow in the night.

"Did anything bad happen?" Ellie tucked the loose strands behind her ears.

"No, no, just the usual mess. Never mind, it's not important." The smile returned. "Erm—look, Ells, I'm sorry I'm late. Did you make dinner already? I brought this." Dale pulled a bottle of wine from a paper bag on the kitchen chair.

Ellie eyed the wine bottle. Red, supermarket.

Her stomach dropped with disappointment. "Dale, we were supposed to go out tonight. Thai food, remember?" So much for her husband's effort at turning up the romance. She tugged on her dress. It was uncomfortably tight across her chest and hips. Worse, she felt embarrassed for having made an effort.

Dale ran a hand through his hair, then leaned forward and peeked into the kitchen. "I thought we said we'd make lobster. Didn't we? Yeah, sure. We did."

Ellie tucked her chin down, giving Dale an upside-down look. "No, we didn't say that. We said Thai and to have lobster some other time. Remember?"

Dale rocked back, set the bottle of red on the sofa table, and half-closed his eyes. He looked like a cat sneaking up to a bowl of forbidden milk. He reached over and pulled Ellie into a hug.

She felt herself stiffen but then gave in and rested her forehead on his shoulder. "Fine," she mumbled into his shirt and inhaled. Dale smelt of aftershave and...cigarette smoke?

She lifted her head to look at his face. "Did you smoke? You smell like cigarettes."

His blue eyes twinkled down at her. "I don't smoke. Never have, never will. But—" He lifted his arm off Ellie and smelled his shirt sleeve. "I had a bunch of meetings with crazy people that do. Ugh. Hey." He stepped back, holding Ellie at arm's length. "I'm going to go grab a shower, okay? Why don't you go get the lobsters from the Fish Market?"

Ellie frowned. The Fish Market was only ten minutes away and she could take the car, but she was all dressed up and ready to go out. "Really? You want me to go fish in the tank for lobsters? And then cook?"

"Sure. Why not? We could have a cozy evening at home. Huh?" He put his finger under her chin, tipping her face up. His hand, too, smelled of stale nicotine.

Ellie stepped back. "Dale, honestly, I'm not feeling it. I'm not going to hobble over in my tight skirt and high heels to fish lobsters I already said I didn't want to have from the tank, hobble back, and cook them while you take a shower, just so we can have them with a cheap bottle of the wrong color wine."

"Well, if you put it like *that*..."

How else would she put it? Ellie turned away. "Why don't we not do this tonight? You look exhausted anyway."

Dale sighed. "I'm sorry, Ellie. I am. I must've forgotten about going out. I really understood you were going to make—you're right. I'm bone-tired."

"Okay." The truth was just that. Truth. It didn't hurt her feelings. Everybody made mistakes, and at least she could get out of the dress. Ellie nodded, suppressing a twinge of guilt at her eagerness to let the date night go. "Let's forget about it. I'll just make some pasta, how about that?"

"That's great, Ellie." His blue eyes softened, and the tension lines of his smile disappeared. "Listen, it's been a mess at work, all day. I had these zoning problems pop up, and it could mean... Of course it should all work out in the end, but it's a lot of schmoozing and phone calls and meetings. You know how I hate that."

"Uh-huh." If she knew anything about her husband, it was that Dale was exceptionally good at talking people into things. He *liked* doing it. "Go ahead and have your shower. Toss your shirt in the basket; I have to do laundry anyway."

"Thanks, Ellie. Hey—I love you."

Surprised, Ellie looked back. "I love you too, Dale."

His smile looked genuine. Sweet and a little crooked, not as toothy as before. "I'll be quick."

"No hurry. I'm fine." Ellie smiled back to prove that there were no hard feelings about the forgotten date and went into the kitchen, where she waited until she heard his footsteps on the stairs. Relief washed over her. She leaned into the feeling, letting it soothe her so she could feel kinder toward her husband. Everybody had hard days at the job, even Dale. She'd had plenty of them. So it was okay. Everything was okay. It was just a little glitch.

Humming a tuneless melody, Ellie opened the cabinet and grabbed a pack of pasta. Then another one. She weighed them in her hands, unsure. One or two?

Before she knew what she was doing, she'd texted Tommy, asking whether he could come home for dinner. He texted back that yes, he could be there in a few.

Ellie ran water into a pot and lit the burner.

It was strange though that after all that effort, after going to the trouble of finding her in the store to set up their date instead of simply calling, Dale had forgotten about the date. Maybe those zoning problems were worse than he let on. Maybe the deal wasn't going to happen. Bummer. But they were fine financially. And if Dale's project came to a standstill over paperwork, the cute little town of Seaside Bay would be safe from being developed a little longer.

While the water was heating, Ellie went into her bedroom. She could hear the shower running in the bathroom, but Dale wasn't singing as usual. Maybe he was shaving? Ellie pulled open her dresser drawer and got out fuzzy socks that felt like heaven after the narrow kitten heels.

She tossed the dress on the chair in the corner; she'd put it into the donation pile later since it seriously didn't fit anymore. Then she swapped her lacy bra for a soft cotton tank and pulled on a navy sweatshirt and brushed flannel sweats. Last but not least, she let down her hair and pulled it into a ponytail, then took a tissue from the box and rubbed the worst of the eyeshadow off.

The mirror reflected cozy, warm, cuddly, and Ellie smiled at herself. Way better than Thai food. And way, *way* better than driving an hour to Bay Port with Dale.

Chapter 16

For once, there was none of that briny mist that usually hugged the cove in the mornings. Maisie carried her cup of Earl Grey out on the patio, frowning over her teacup at the tumbledown garden. Even blue skies and rays of golden sun couldn't make it look better. A clump of grass pointed its long, brown stalks at her like accusing fingers.

Maisie set her cup down. The bushes growing along the stone wall to the road had managed a handful of pale roses. That was better than nothing; at least they were alive and kicking. Though at this time of year, they'd used to droop with fragrant yellow roses. No matter how many vases she'd filled with them, there'd been plenty more to pick. Alex hadn't been a natural gardener and never learned to tell one plant from the other, but even he had liked the stone wall roses. Maisie knew because when the bouquets started to wilt, he'd let her know. *Mom, look. You need to change the flowers.*

Maisie pulled Robert's robe tighter around herself. A suitable attire to visit a dying garden, wasn't it?

She took the patio steps one by one, lifting the hem of the robe like a ballgown so she wouldn't stumble. A few of the stones had cracked, and weeds crawled out of cracks and clefts.

She'd have to get on that. If Maisie was going to sell Beach House, she'd have to get at least the patio back in shape.

She reached the rose bushes, plucked a twig of brown leaves, and studied them. There were still a few green spots, small and localized as if the plant was experimenting with investments in chlorophyll. See if it was worth it. Whether it made enough sugar to cover production cost.

Maisie's fingertip expertly trailed the serrated edge of a leaf. She could try hosing the bushes off to wash off some of the salt the ocean breeze had put there. And she could cut dead parts back so that the new growth got more light. She nodded; yes. She could do it while she waited for the podcasters to finish writing the scripts they were working on. Maisie turned to the sea beyond the lawn.

Well, lawn.

More like dandelion and crabgrass, purslane and lambsquarter, chickweed and shepherd's purse. Mother Nature had eagerly reclaimed what was hers. The wild glory that used to be the lawn stirred Maisie's jealousy. Unlike herself, Mother Nature had nursed her picks with skill and enthusiasm in the last decade. Dandelions dotted the field like little suns, and wild carrot blossoms played clouds. Sturdy purple thistles waved at the red-winged blackbirds and flycatchers that were darting after bugs, inviting them to sit.

Only Maisie's white woodruff had managed to join the fun on the field. It'd escaped her garden, content to hug weeds into wild bouquets.

Maisie tilted her head, assessing, and decided that while the rolling lawn had been grand and very much to Robert's orderly taste, a field of wildflowers was charming and very much to her taste. Plus, it was maintenance-free.

Maisie returned to the patio, touching a brave bud here, plucking a dead leaf there, and letting her thoughts wander as she listened to the waves lapping at the beach.

The night before, the podcasters had eaten at Tom's café. Maisie hadn't joined them. In fact, she'd skipped dinner altogether. Even now she didn't feel hungry. But if she was going to go on this celebratory blueberry hike with the girls, she had to eat something so she wouldn't run out of energy.

She pressed a hand against her stomach. Visiting Alex's favorite places to remember him had sounded a lot better when she'd been surrounded by friends. Now that she was alone, doubts crept in. It was a lot to face. It was a lot to let come up. It was very much against her rules.

Her tea had turned cold, and when she took a sip, the bitter tannins shriveled her taste buds. She grimaced.

"Mrs. Jameson?" Jim, hair messy and eyes squinting sleepily into the sun, stood barefoot in the door to the sunroom. Conservatory. Sunroom.

"Yes?"

"Everything all right?"

Maisie lifted her cup as evidence. "The tea's bitter. Did you sleep well?"

"I did." He blinked, pleased. "Must be the air or something. I was out like a light last night. Usually, I have to take something to sleep at all."

"You do? How old are you?" Maisie had given up on sleeping pills since they left her fuzzy-brained the next day. But what could possibly be in young Jim's closet that didn't let him sleep?

"There's always something to worry about, isn't there?" He scratched his arm.

Maisie lowered her chin. There wasn't always something to worry about, was there? Not really. "Um, I was talking myself into going to the bakery. I'm guessing you and your team wouldn't mind bagels for breakfast again?"

Jim patted down his hair. "That'd be great. Maybe after breakfast, we can talk about the case."

Maisie glanced at her feet in old flip-flops she'd found in the garage, toes wet with dew. She wasn't dressed. What was she doing, strutting around the garden like this? She needed to dress. Get ready. Be prepared. "Yes. That's what we're here for. I want to know what you think."

Jim nodded and glanced at the sea. "The view is spectacular."

Ready to get inside and get going, Maisie glanced over her shoulder. "Sure is." The water, forever in motion, glittered in the sun.

"You don't live here all year? I totally would."

As if she was going to stand there in a robe, explaining her innermost motivations. Maisie made a shooing gesture with her hands. The kid was blocking her way. "Let's get going. If you don't mind…"

Jim held up his open palms and disappeared into the house.

"Good morning."

Startled, Maisie turned.

"Good morning." At the corner gate stood a man. Vincent Grey. Vince.

Maisie clutched the robe closed at her throat. The one time she was not dressed and ready to take on the world! "Good morning."

"I hope I don't interrupt. I was wondering…" Vincent Grey inclined his head. His silver hair managed to be both short and windswept, and he wore a loose black sweater with a wide neckline that made him look like a free-spirited French painter from the sixties. In his hands, he held a potted plant and a parcel wrapped in paper. "If it is too early…" He tilted his head at the road, letting her know he could leave.

"A little bit, but it's fine," Maisie said, embarrassed. Should she walk over? The distance was all the protection from scrutiny she had. "Can I help you with something?" she called out, hoping it'd be enough.

"No, no. I was only going to…" Vince set both parcel and plant onto the stone pillar.

"Oh." Maisie hesitated. Vincent had brought gifts

—it was rude not to go thank him. But she stood rooted to her spot, welded there by the robe, the bad hair, the grass clinging to her wet feet.

Vince smiled. "I thought I'd be neighborly and bring a welcome-back gift. But I'm afraid I'm out of practice with neighbors; my timing is off. I hope you don't mind if I leave these for you instead of carrying them back?"

"Oh – uh... Sure! Thank you!" Warmth rose in her cheeks. "How kind of you, Vince."

Tall, shoulders slightly stooped, Vince waved and walked on towards the village.

Maisie followed him with her eyes until he was out of sight. Then, flip-flops smacking on the stones, Maisie went to gather Vincent's presents. It was a sweet gesture, and it was true that they were neighbors now. In a sense. She didn't really live here.

Planted in the small, aged terracotta pot was a tiny apple tree, its trunk only as long as her forearm and as slim as her pointer finger. White tape wrapped neatly around the midsection. Surprised, Maisie touched the tape. It looked like Vince had grafted the tree himself by taping a scion from a good fruit tree onto new rootstock. It was a thoughtful present, especially for welcoming a neighbor. A plate of brownies or a potted kalanchoe from the gift store would've been plenty for the occasion.

Maisie blinked at her tiny tree. She wasn't going to be able to care for it... It wouldn't survive in her city apartment. There wasn't enough sunlight from the windows to let it grow, even if it could stay in the pot. Which it couldn't.

Swaying between a neighbor's appreciation and a gardener's apprehension, Maisie set the tree down by her feet, picked up the second gift, and pulled the printed tissue paper off.

A book, an old one. She turned it over. It looked like something Sam would sell in her store. Whatever the book was about, this was nice... A young tree and an old book. Curious, Maisie lifted the green cover. She smiled. When was the last time she'd been simply curious? She couldn't remember.

Drawings of trees and grafts, paragraphs on nursing trees to coax out the best fruit.

Carefully leafing through the pages, Maisie spotted sentences that had been underlined with a fountain pen and ruler. The ink, once black, had faded with age.

She closed the book, touched by the sweet peculiarity of the gift. It complemented the self-made tree. It complemented Vincent Grey and his French-artist shirt.

Terracotta in hands, book tucked under her arm, Maisie flip-flopped her way back to the house. So this made it official; she had a new neighbor. She and Robert had always thought themselves lucky that nobody lived in the small carriage house down the street. A long time ago, it'd belonged to the Beach House estate. But even though both estate and lands had been broken up long ago, Robert had felt possessive about it.

Maisie climbed the stairs to the patio and set

down the pot. The tree was better off outside, even though it was so small. Maybe if she planted it by the gate, it'd get enough water to root after she left? But there wasn't enough sunlight for a fruit tree over there... Maybe she'd put it by the patio, then. The soil dried out faster, but at least the tree would have light and a view. Still better than a stunted life in a glum city apartment.

Maisie let herself into the sunroom and sat in one of the wicker chairs for another look at her book. It was charming—a little like Vince himself. She let the book fall open where it liked and started reading, soon sinking into the secret lives of apple trees.

"Mrs. Jameson? Do you want me to go get bagels?" Ashley appeared in front of Maisie, dressed in jeans and a sweater.

"Your sweater is the color of a Red Delicious." Maisie closed the book and swiped the hair out of her eyes. "No, I'll go myself, I need the exercise. I hope the bakery is still there."

"Okay." Ashley tugged the sleeves of her Red Delicious sweater over her hands. "It's my college color," she explained. "I thought I'd wear it since we're going hiking today. You know, explore the area." Her smile was a little embarrassed. "I got lost once when I was six. Just for a couple of hours, no harm done. But ever since, I like to wear bright colors. In case I get... I get..." She frowned.

"Lost again?" Maisie rose from her chair. It sounded as if at least some harm had been done. Ashley couldn't even say she'd been lost. "Good idea."

"Thanks," Ashley looked over her shoulder into the kitchen, and Maisie suddenly noted the smell of coffee and the sound of chatter from the other podcasters. "Um, Mrs. Jameson?"

"Yes?"

"Do you think Alex could've gotten lost in the forest? I had a look at the map yesterday. It's such a large area. Unbroken forest, once you get away from the sea."

"It is." Maisie nodded. She and Alex—sometimes even Robert, if he'd had time—had often gone walking in the forest. For years, they'd brought sandwiches so they could spend the long summer days, picking blueberries and huckleberries, mushrooms and wildflowers. When Alex finally outgrew his berry basket, Maisie had gone with Sam, Cate, and Ellie, though they usually ended up eating what they picked on the spot. Alex too had still gone to the forest with his friends, visiting the cliffs that looked out on the sea and the old berry patches. Not to pick berries, but to make forbidden campfires and toast marshmallows.

"Alex wouldn't have gotten lost in the forest." Maisie shook her head. "He knew his way around like all kids in town. He even had a compass in his backpack, and he knew how to use it." She held up a finger, anticipating the next question that was sure to come. "Even if he'd been desperate over the breakup with Brandie. Which I doubt he was. He wasn't the sort to get desperate."

"Did the police search out there?" Ashley's eyes were wide open, her own traumatic experience shining through.

Maisie smiled, feeling pity. She wished she could help Ashley, but Maisie didn't even know what exactly had happened to the girl. "They sent a helicopter out, and some of us checked all the places the teens usually went. But most of the search parties focused on the beach and the village. Like the streets leading in and out of town, too. You know in case…"

"In case he was kidnapped?" Ashley finished pensively. "That makes sense."

"The police thought so. Oh, and they had boats go along the coastline." She pointed at Ashley's sandals. "By the way, you might put on shoes for the forest. Sneakers are good."

Ashley looked at her feet. "You're right; I better change them. Well, I'm going to get a cup of coffee first. Sure you don't want me to get the bagels? You looked so absorbed by your book. I didn't mean to interrupt you."

"No, I got it. There's cereal in the pantry to tide you over until I'm back." Clutching her book, Maisie went upstairs to get dressed.

All that talk about the forest made her recall little images of the past. Like the little Longaberger basket Alex had loved so much. He'd used to hug it to his belly with his chubby little arms. And when, at four years old, he'd gone through an Emily Shortcake phase, he'd named the basket Poppy and told everyone it was his berry best friend.

Maisie had forgotten all about Poppy Longaberger and the way Baby Alex had giggled himself silly over his little berry joke.

The girls were right. Alex deserved to have all the good things remembered. Not only the horror. The searches, the constant mulling as to exactly what terrible thing had happened. Alex was much, much more than that. Smiles and sandwiches, pilfered smores, all the love a sweet boy could give—Maisie needed to find those memories again.

If it'd been her that had disappeared, she'd have wanted Alex to do the same. Remember the good things. Remember the fun and the warmth. Remember how much she loved him.

Chapter 17

Cate hurried along Main Street, frowning at each empty parking space she passed. She'd left the car far away from the market, figuring that on a beautiful Saturday like this, all the spots by the harbor would be taken. But even though it was going on noon, she seemed to be the only one hustling around town to get the weekend shopping done.

When her favorite parking spot of all—a single slot right in front of the jewelry store—was empty as well, Cate snorted in disbelief. Her feet hurt from all the walking just to get there. She was exhausted. And that spot was *always* taken.

Cate took a wheezing breath. She was out of shape. Lumps and sweat everywhere. It was disgusting. She needed to find a diet she could stick to. And start an exercise program, something structured. She had to put some research in, too, because her back and knees were aching just thinking about sports.

Cate sighed at the futility of it all. Maybe after all these years of trying and failing, it was time to rethink her approach? Maybe what she needed was to relax. Meditate. Twenty minutes each morning and afternoon were supposed to do wonders. Though how people found an extra forty minutes in their day was beyond Cate. Maybe start with positivity; that didn't cost time. It was a beautiful Saturday morning, wasn't it? Yes. The town was fresh and empty, and she looked forward to a picnic with her friends. It'd be so great.

Trying to catch her breath, Cate slowed down. Didn't she read that kettlebells were best for building the core? She could get a magazine when she got the ingredients for blueberry pie and chicken sandwiches. Though it'd been a while since she last made the sandwiches, and maybe she should bring something more involved? But what?

Cate passed the fountain and automatically scanned the notes tacked to the community board. Somebody needed a sweater.

She had one that she could put into the wishing box below the board. It was from that cute shop in Seaside Bay... Cate had splurged on it because it'd been a Christmas present for Allen. Allen had never worn it once. It didn't fit or scratched his neck; she forgot. Maybe he'd never tried it on. After picking it up from the closet floor one time too many, Cate had tossed it in the donation bin in the basement. He hadn't missed it.

She stopped to make a note about the sweater on her phone and went on.

It *was* a good sweater. Better quality than what Cate bought for herself. But still, she should've known better. She knew Allen was particular about his clothes, much more sensitive to feel and fit than she.

Maybe because she was wearing whatever fitted around her these days. She didn't get to be picky.

She'd finally reached her goal. The sliding doors to the food market opened, and with a sigh of relief, Cate stepped into the store. Soothing music hummed in the background, and the rich scents of vegetables, baked bread, and hand-poured soaps twined into a welcoming aroma. Cate wrested a red basket from the stack by the door and started browsing the narrow aisles.

Intrigued by the colorful array of vitamin bottles, she picked one and read the label. Melatonin, a sleep-aid.

Allen was still in bed. He'd had a hard time falling asleep last night. At some point, he'd given up and moved to the couch in his study. He could use a sleep-aid. But Cate had tried melatonin before, and it had given her nightmares. Allen wouldn't thank her for *that*.

She put the bottle back. If anything, she needed something to help her lose weight. But the thing to do was to eat less, not hope for a solution in pill form. Cate moved on to the produce section, where she selected celery and plum tomatoes for her basket, passing on the little plastic bags. Save the oceans.

It was funny though how someone so successful

at teaching relaxation techniques could be such a ball of stress himself. Allen claimed it was the traveling. Maybe. Cate hadn't asked how his techniques then helped business managers who traveled a lot. But Allen didn't deserve to be questioned. His workshops filled and earned money.

Cate herself preferred a hot bath and a nice glass of chilled chardonnay. It put her to sleep faster and tasted a lot better.

Browsing the selection, she picked a bottle. It was a brand she liked. Sam liked it too. So did Ellie, and Maisie... Cate stopped. Did she know whether Maisie liked this one? She smiled, putting the bottle into her basket. If not, Maisie would be a sport about it. Chardonnay never ended up in the donation bin, did it?

Maybe she should get some grapes. A classy touch. Maisie was classy, so she'd enjoy that.

Cate returned to the produce section and started browsing. The cilantro didn't look super fresh.

Suddenly something clattered, followed by a stifled curse. A handful of limes rolled across the floor toward her. Cate looked up.

A man in his fifties held on to the citrus basket, preventing more limes from falling out. His eyebrows rose in apology as he met her glance.

Cate smiled. She'd been there. The aisles really were too narrow.

One of the limes bumped against her shoe, and she picked it up. The man put the basket back on the stand and, picking up limes as he passed them, came over to her.

"Can happen to anyone," Cate assured him as she handed him the lime. He wasn't handsome with his widow's peak and round face, but the laugh-lines crinkling the corners of his eyes made it look like he had a sense of humor. She liked that.

"You're very kind," the man said earnestly. "I'm afraid I've never been any good at pick-up limes."

"No worries," Cate replied. Then his words trickled through; an involuntary snort of laughter broke from her. Surprised, she clapped a hand over her mouth.

The man winked and then retraced his steps to the basket, picking up more limes on his way.

Cate fled into the bread aisle, where she hid behind a display of sesame burgers.

Had the man just *flirted* with her? She rubbed a hand over her cheek, finding it warm to the touch. How silly of her. She was as embarrassed as a schoolgirl and for no reason. He'd only been joking. With that unruly curly hair and the less-than-chiseled jaw, he probably relied on his humor a lot; no big deal. Squaring her shoulders, Cate stepped out from her spot to continue shopping.

Just then, the man passed the open end of the aisle. Their eyes met, and they both smiled.

Then he was gone again.

Cate's heart beat faster. Staring at the toast, she tried to focus. What bread for chicken sandwiches? She'd forgotten.

She was married with grown kids. And a husband.

But also...how sweet, a moment like that. Like back in the day, before she'd met Allen and still sometimes felt like she had it.

Cate felt lighter as she moved around, choosing her meat and cheese and mayonnaise. She had another glimpse of the lime-man as he left the market, carrying two grocery bags, but he didn't notice her. Half of her was relieved; more smiles would've been too much.

And the other half of her was curious. Would he have smiled again? What if she'd stopped and talked?

Cate pondered that while she set her things on the belt and re-packed them into her bag.

Here was the thing. If she *would* have talked to the stranger, he'd have turned out to be perfectly uninteresting. Whatever it was that made her smile would've left.

She pulled out her wallet to pay.

It was good they hadn't introduced themselves. This way, the stranger had simply given Cate a little gift. A small compliment of attention. She hadn't gotten one in—well, that was depressing... But then, it wasn't *like* that in marriage, was it? Getting compliments and all that.

When Cate left the supermarket, the sun shone a little brighter than before. Maybe she'd do something more than just sandwiches after all. Something nice.

Cate stopped. She could get pretty napkins. She

was passing by Maison de Sand anyway, and there was enough time. Why had she felt so hassled before? She had plenty of time to enjoy her shopping.

At the next opportunity, Cate swerved left. Of course, a few grapes and pretty napkins couldn't make Maisie stay in Beach Cove. It wasn't for Cate to meddle with Maisie's grieving process.

Though, to be honest, Maisie *should* stay. They needed her in Beach Cove. Things hadn't been the same without Maisie. It wasn't that they didn't have pretty napkins without Maisie. It was that they didn't have *picnics* without her. They barely ever met anymore.

And Cate needed her friends more than she liked to admit. Sometimes, the hole Maisie had left in Beach Cove was too big for Cate to handle.

Chapter 18

Maisie pulled an old roll of kitchen paper from the backpack. "Was I bringing entire rolls of kitchen paper on our hikes?"

"Dunno." Ellie, elbows propped up on the kitchen island, face in hands, was watching her. "Where are your podcasters? On the hunt for clues?"

"More like lunch at the Corner Café. Though they took their laptops to brainstorm." Maisie studied the contents of a cloudy plastic bag. A first-aid kit, Band-Aid-papers peeling with age. Nothing in there was sterile anymore. She tossed the bag into the trash, then went to the fridge. "I'm afraid the most celebratory thing I have is diet coke. And I have crackers I can bring to the picnic." She should've remembered to pick up a blueberry pie at the bakery when she was getting the breakfast bagels. Vince had thrown her off course with his gifts.

"Don't worry about it," Ellie said. "I made fish cakes and shrimp quiche to share."

"Shrimp quiche?" Maisie cast her mind back to some of Ellie's baked creations when she'd been in her experimental phase. "Sounds nice. Does it taste good?"

"You know, I'm not sure. I haven't made one before." Ellie tapped a finger thoughtfully on the counter. "It *smelled* good what with the shrimps and eggs and cheese."

Maisie took a bottle of water, closed the fridge, and joined Ellie at the kitchen island. "What cheese did you use?"

Ellie arched an eyebrow. "The recipe had a lot of stars. People liked it."

Maisie smiled. "I'm sure. It's nice of you to have gone to the trouble, Ells." Unlike herself, Ellie had put effort into her picnic dish.

"So what's that brainstorming session about?" Ellie asked. "What are they going to do next?"

Maisie put the water bottle into the backpack and cinched it shut. "I suppose that's what they have to figure out. But someone said they should interview the cops." Which was fine, though the cops knew nothing Maisie hadn't already told Jim and Ashley.

"It's good they're doing it, Maisie. It shows they're serious about the episode. You don't interview cops and then not air it. It's bad for their reputation. Or something."

Maisie sighed. "After their day of playing at the beach, I'm scared they'll ditch the story. There's nothing much to talk about and nothing new to report. I've been burned before by the media, Ellie. And I can't afford to waste time."

"Aww." Ellie's voice was soft. "They're good at what they do. And they care."

"But who knows how much material disappears in their drawers, right? Media always cater to ratings first. They have to."

Ellie shook her head. "Maybe. But remember how good it'd be to reach their audience." She was silent for a moment. "Also, you don't know what they have. It's possible they're not telling you everything. You know. Out of consideration."

Maisie looked up, but her friend's eyes were clear and innocent. "Consideration for my feelings? Do you know something I don't? Did they say anything to you?"

"Maise, I'd tell you. I haven't even seen them. But you know...they might be looking into some lead but not let us know. If it doesn't pan out, we won't be disappointed."

Maisie raised her eyebrows. "I wish they'd had a lead, false or not. But they better tell me." The doorbell rang, electrifying Maisie. "Hang on, Ellie."

Outside stood Sam and Cate.

"Hey!" and "Hi, Maise," they said and casually passed her to enter the house.

"Come in." Maisie closed the door just as Ellie, her pack slung over the shoulder, joined them in the hall.

And suddenly, Maisie's anxiety surged. Her job was to *find* Alex. Not celebrate him. Celebrating wasn't going to help. She was just eager to go snack on quiche and give herself a good ol' time with her friends. She had no right. Alex wasn't having a good time. Maybe he was shackled, maybe he was—

Maisie pressed a hand to her heart as if she could loosen the panic's grip.

How had she gotten here, how had she managed to lose focus like this? She'd meant to stay clear, not waste time. Maisie tried to draw a breath and couldn't. "Listen, girls," she croaked. "I've got to…"

Six sea blue eyes turned to her in alarm. "Hey!" Cate stopped telling a story about limes and rushed to Maisie's side. "It's all right. Here. Sit." She took Maisie's arm and helped her sit on the floor, back propped against the door, knees drawn to the chest. "Take a breath. Deep as you can."

Maisie tried, her mouth opening and closing.

"Breathe, girl," Sam ordered, her voice rising.

Cate kneeled and took Maisie's hand, rubbing it with her own. "You're calm. You can take a breath," she whispered.

Again, Maisie opened her mouth and this time, she managed to draw oxygen. "I can't go," she whispered. There was pressure on her chest, and it wasn't coming from her lungs. Her heart *hurt*. Panic, wearing the guise of a heart attack. "I need to stay here. The podcast—I need to stay here in case they come back. I should be here. I have to help."

"Okay. That's okay." Ellie exchanged a glance with Cate. "You stay here if you want to. It's not a problem. We can all stay."

"I have to." Each breath was a little easier, and for a while, it was all Maisie focused on. Then her panic changed, taking its real shape. It was—sadness? Maisie propped her elbows on her knees, covered her eyes with her palms, and buried her fingers in her hair. She should never have come back to Beach Cove. Too much. It was too much. Grief enveloped her like a dark shroud.

"Hey." Sam sat beside her, laying her head on Maisie's shoulder. When Sam spoke, her voice was quiet and firm. "I hate to break it to you, Maise. But they don't *need* you. The podcasters, you know. You don't have to worry about them."

Cate cleared her throat. "Sam, are you sure?"

"Maisie, you *can* leave the house," Sam continued. "You're not trapped the way you were when Alex first went missing. That's the past, and it's over. Now is different."

Cate and Ellie murmured agreement.

Maisie let her hands drop. "I haven't had this much anxiety for years. It's what I get for coming back here."

"But don't you agree?" Sam probed gently. She lifted her head to look into Maisie's eyes. "Do you think you can leave the house?"

"What if they need something from me? What if I could help and I'm not available? If it means a delay in something that can't be delayed? I know it's unlikely. But so is a car accident, and we still strap kids into car seats every single time we drive to the store. Because it doesn't matter how unlikely it is. You simply don't take the risk."

Sam nodded. "But we're not driving around with kids. You have a phone. They can reach you whenever they want."

"Not if I'm up in the forest."

Ellie sat in front of her and put a hand on Maisie's knee. "Maise, you told Jim and Ashley everything you know, and there hasn't been any news for ten years. You don't need to worry about taking a walk."

"I can't stay here." They had to understand this.

"What?" Cate shifted her weight with a huff. Her friends now formed a small fort around Maisie. "What's this now?" Cate asked.

"You're right, Ellie." Maisie nodded slowly, the last of the panic still fluttering in her chest. "I don't need to be so worried. But..." She blew out a long, slow breath through pursed lips. "I just had a panic attack, and I haven't had one in a long while. I can't be in Beach Cove. I can't be in this house. I thought it'd be okay, but it's not. I'm only going to stay until I know the podcasters are set, and then I'll go back to New York."

It was so quiet Maisie heard the sea whooshing behind the house. Sam looked frozen, Ellie shocked, Cate resigned.

Maisie couldn't blame them. "I wish I didn't have to. But I do. Like Sam said, back then is over. Now is different. Everything is different."

"But it seemed like—I don't know. We were going to do this for Alex. You thought it was a good idea," Ellie murmured.

"I never said it was a good idea." Defensiveness rose in her as if she'd been accused of wrongdoing. "I said I'd go." Maisie pressed her lips together, feeling like a liar. Because even if she hadn't said it in so many words, she'd thought it. She'd thought her friends had it right, that she should remember the good times and re-visit the old places Alex used to like. She'd almost let them talk her into feeling that it was safe doing this like that. But for her, feeling safe meant forgetting her duty as a mother.

Yet another wave of feelings hit Maisie as if the lid she'd kept so tight all these years had finally been lifted, shoved aside by her friends, her old home, her memories. This time, it wasn't fear or grief. It was remorse.

She had no right to judge the podcasters for lollygagging instead of solving her problems; she'd been the first to run and check out the beach and the garden and the coffee place to eat fancy pancakes. Instead of hanging out with her friends and gabbing with the neighbor, she should've dipped in and out of Beach Cove the way she'd planned.

"You're all over the place, Maisie." Sam got to her feet, uncurling like a cat. "You can do whatever you want. But I mean—what do you want?"

"I want to go back to the city and my work," Maisie replied automatically. Get away from this lifted-lid chaos, these false hopes and unproductive feelings. Get back to helping others, holding down the fort, scour the internet for John Does, every night, all night.

"Maisie, I think we should go on this hike," Cate said suddenly. "I think it would be good for you if you came with us."

"If I came with you?" Maisie repeated the words

like a confused toddler. She'd just declared she didn't want to go. How was it every time she made a decision, one of her friends threw a stick into the spokes?

Nobody replied. Maisie leaned her head back against the wall, exhausted. The doorbell. The bell had triggered it all. She'd come back just to be the captive of the doorbell again.

"I think Cate's right. Alex wouldn't want you to miss out on a walk with your friends," Ellie said, her voice as soothing as a trickling brook. "Maisie, it's been ten years. He'd want you to go out and have a picnic with us and remember the good times. Honest."

"You don't know that, Ellie." Maisie smiled, exhausted by the winds of her emotions. Alex wouldn't want her to let go for even one second. He'd want her to do whatever she could to find him and bring him back.

"I do know because I've got Tommy." Ellie smiled an apology. "He keeps telling me."

"Tommy…" Tommy had been so like Alex. Until he wasn't because he was home, and he was safe.

Ellie nodded. "I told him about the picnic. That we were going to go to Alex's favorite blueberry field from when he was little."

Maisie looked at her friend. "Which blueberry field?"

"The one we took the boys to when they were just able to pick by themselves? Remember how Alex told us it was one of his earliest memories? Or wait

—maybe that was at our house, and he was telling Tommy about it? I can't remember exactly, but I know he said that. It's a good place; nice and dry. It was the only place that never had any mosquitoes because there was never any standing water."

The last of the cold feeling in her chest started to ebb away as Maisie remembered. She knew which field in the woods Ellie was talking about. A large clearing really, a warm, sunny spot that somehow never had bugs. Ellie was right. Alex had loved their trips there.

Maisie squeezed her eyes shut, surprised by her wish to see the field again. "You think it's okay if I leave? I won't mess up if I do?" She'd been on the job without fail for ten years, and it hadn't brought Alex back. Yes, she could go for a couple of hours, and nothing would happen. She wouldn't be missed. She hadn't been missed in ten years.

Cate stood laboriously, reaching for Maisie's hand and pulling her up as well. "I think it'd be lovely. I think you would enjoy it. I think it'd make you stronger. I think it'll help. Don't be scared."

Maisie wanted to trust her. But none of her friends was bringing up the fact that in their opinion, Alex had passed on. He was gone as far as they were concerned, and to them, Maisie was fighting a fight that was over.

Maisie swallowed, trying to move the lid back where it belonged. "I'm not scared." She pulled her hand out of Cate's. "Sorry for…for being all over the place."

Sam stepped forward and pulled her into a hug that almost toppled Maisie off her feet. "For the last time, stop apologizing," Sam growled. "You have nothing to apologize for. You're allowed to fall apart."

Maisie bit her lip to keep tears back. She'd failed everyone. She'd failed Alex and Robert. And Maisie had failed her friends by putting up walls and thinking thoughts that didn't do them justice. "Okay," Maisie mumbled into Sam's neck.

"So can you come? I agree with Cate; I think you should." Sam let Maisie go.

Maisie forced herself to nod. She'd come full circle. Somehow, the girls did that to her.

So she'd go to this picnic because her friends wanted to go, and they wanted her to go. She'd go not to celebrate anything but to not let the girls down yet again. And then she would hand the key to her house to Jim and his crew, telling them to lock up Beach House when they'd had enough.

Maisie was going to go back to the city.

At least that way, she could help other parents find their kids.

Chapter 19

The toe of her hiking boot caught under a root. Sam stumbled but managed to avoid a tumble onto the forest path.

"You okay?" Cate called over her shoulder.

"Yeah." Sam disentangled her foot from the wily bit of spruce and bent to rub her ankle. It hurt—she'd pulled something. Her head ached, too. She'd wanted to come here so badly, had so looked forward to the trees, the air, the views…but the moment they'd entered the forest, she'd been on high alert. The unrelenting flow of adrenaline was starting to wear her down. Was this how Maisie felt all the time?

Sam waved to Cate, who'd stopped. "You go on; I have to fix my shoe. I'll catch up in a sec."

"I can wait." Cate huffed as she talked. She was heavier than the rest of them, and the steep path had left her breathless.

"It just makes it harder to get going again," Sam warned. "Go on, or we'll lose them entirely. I'll catch up no problem." Ellie and Maisie were out of sight already. Sam had been trying to keep Cate from falling behind too far, even though she'd felt like rushing ahead to burn off the stress she felt.

"Oh, okay fine. I guess you've got a point," Cate mumbled and staggered on, clearly too exhausted to make a case for the buddy system.

Sam lowered herself onto the forest floor. The pine needles from last year's shedding were sun-warm, soft, and smelled like the summer that was yet to come.

Sam threaded her laces through the uppermost eyelets and pulled them tight to support the ankle. Then she pulled her water bottle from her pack and took a swig.

The forest was quiet.

It'd been at least a year since Sam last came here. Maybe longer. But some things didn't change, at least not that much. There had always been wood thrushes singing somewhere and flickers dancing up and down branches like nervous hall monitors. There'd been warblers and veeries and yellow-bellied sapsuckers. Sam used to observe them with Larry's field binoculars.

Now, nothing.

Not even a chipmunk squeaking alarm. No wood mouse rustling under the leaf litter.

Maybe all the critters were holding their breath because they weren't used to hikers anymore? In the off-season, the animals certainly had the place to themselves. Could be they didn't appreciate the intrusion of four loud, middle-aged women, huffing and puffing like steam trains in the quiet forest.

Could be.

But it *was* eerie.

Sam stowed the water bottle and stood, suddenly unnerved. She was alone now. It used to feel so peaceful up here, but not anymore. The forest was watching. Maybe sasquatches were real after all... She shouldn't have laughed at Larry, just because her otherwise so professorial husband had a weakness for the mythical creatures. Was it because he felt like she did now when he came up here?

Sam frowned, swung her pack onto her sweaty back, and started walking uphill. *Long stride and crooked knee: try it out and you will see.* They'd sung that to the kids when they climbed up here to pick. The blueberries Sam glimpsed were far from ripe. And bears didn't come for green berries.

Blueberries, blueberry, blueberry pie...

Chanting in her head didn't help either. Sam peeked over her shoulder.

But there was nothing following, nothing disappearing behind the trunks of spruces and white pines. Just trees, happy trees. And sunbeams, dappling the ground. And *quiet*.

Sam rubbed the gooseflesh off her arms and walked faster, relieved when she spotted the rest of their little caravan. Good. They had to stick together, keep Maisie's anxiety at bay. Sam hurried until she could hear Ellie talking; it seemed the conversation had turned to the mating behavior of sturgeons. Good old Ellie with her fish.

Sam fell in with her friends; Cate was just ahead.

With every step Cate took, the red backpack danced. Almost like Bonnie's red hair had danced in the wind when she'd rowed the dinghy to her fishing boat.

Who'd been the man beside her?

Sam narrowed her eyes as if she could see his face among the tree trunks if she squinted hard enough. There'd been something so familiar about the width of the shoulder, the color of the sweater. One of Larry's? Was that what it was? He was having an affair with Bonnie?

Sam allowed herself a little grin. No.

Of course not. Larry would never.

Larry was solid, but even if he weren't, Larry wouldn't be able to talk Bonnie into an affair. Larry was certainly handsome enough with his silvery hair, tan skin, and intense eyes. But seducing women wasn't his forte; he'd try and get his paramour to sign a non-disclosure contract before sleeping with her. Bonnie didn't seem like the type that would sign anything, and Larry was big about keeping his affairs in order. No pun intended, ha.

"You okay, Sam?" Cate was looking over her shoulder, her face shiny with perspiration.

"Fixed up and caught up." Sam nodded. "Go on, you're doing good."

"I hope we'll get there soon." Cate sighed and resumed her slog up the hill.

"Hmm-mm."

But then, who knew what Bonnie would do. Sam had never talked more than a few words with the woman, and it was obvious that Bonnie didn't play by rules. Any rules, including ones Sam dreamed up.

A beautiful fisherwoman. With a wide-shouldered man beside her.

Sam bit the inside of her cheeks, chewing on it.

Nah.

Though Larry had been a little weird lately. More than usual, even. She simply had to trust that he was strange because he was being his own strange self, not because he had an affair.

And the sweater of the man in the boat—Larry never wore bulky sweaters like that. He didn't go in for rugged. Larry wore woven lambswool turtlenecks, corduroy sports coats, whatever he figured made him look intellectual. Sam had pointed that out once. The conversation hadn't ended well.

She grinned. Maybe a lunch date with her weirdo husband *would* be nice. It truly had been a while. Once she got out of this forest, she'd give him a call. See whether he wanted to cook dinner together.

"Oof." With a twist of her shoulders, Cate threw her backpack on the ground. Sam, not having paid attention, stopped sharply to avoid stumbling over it. "I can't take another step."

Maisie turned, her hands on her hips. Her face was serene; unlike Sam, she seemed to enjoy being here. "I'm out of breath myself."

Ellie sat down and pulled a bottle of water from her pack. "I'm surprised how overgrown the path is. Like, does nobody come up here anymore?"

Sam wanted to keep going, but since everyone was taking a break, she sat as well. Maisie glanced at the phone in her hand.

"We do, I guess," Sam said, just to fill the silence. She narrowed her eyes at the pines that surrounded them. They stood thick, shoulder to shoulder, and gave away nothing. "Maise, it's okay," she said louder than she'd intended. "You talked with them just before you left."

"And you keep checking over your shoulder, Sam," Ellie remarked, peeking over Sam's head down the path they'd just climbed. "What's going on?"

Sam could lie, say it was a mosquito bugging her. She sighed. "I feel weird," she admitted instead, simply to share the burden. Maisie kept swiping on her phone, but her shoulders stiffened.

"Yeah?" Ellie's eyebrows rose, but Cate shook her head and pointed at Maisie. Mistake. Maisie was dealing with enough; she didn't need to know that Sam felt off.

"So I had a really good day at the store yesterday," Sam continued casually. "Guess who came in and bought a pricey book, cash down and no questions asked." She nodded at Ellie. *Come on, girl. Get us out of the conversational quagmire I steered us into.*

Ellie nodded back. "Mr. Grey."

Sam opened her hands in fake-surprise. "How'd you know that?"

Ellie winked at Maisie, who'd resurfaced from her phone at the mention of the store and was pulling a snack from her bag. "Easy. He's the only one that buys expensive books off-season. Wished I'd had wealthy customers like that."

Maisie pensively weighed her granola bar in her palm. "How expensive are we talking, Sam?"

Sam raised an eyebrow. "Well, *Vince*..." She grinned. Grey had never offered his first name to anyone else she knew, let alone a nick—

"All right." Maisie waved her hand, motioning for Sam to get over herself.

"Hehe. Well, it was almost half of a blue one."

"Of what?"

"Of a blue one," Sam said. "Isn't that what they call a thousand-dollar-bill? A blue one?"

Cate tilted her head. "A blue one? I've never heard that."

"I don't think there *are* thousand-dollar bills," Ellie said. "Like, they don't exist. Blue or otherwise. I mean, if anything, they're probably green, no?"

Sam shrugged. "Anyway. He paid four hundred and then some for the book."

Maisie's hand holding the cereal bar dropped into her lap. "How much?"

"I know. And it's not the first time he's spent money on books, either. He's almost single-handedly been keeping my store in the blue."

"Green," Ellie threw in. "Pretty sure it's green for doing good and red for doing poorly."

"Are you impressed, Maise?" Cate chuckled. "I hear you met him."

"I'm...surprised. What book did he buy, Sam?"

"The Orchardist."

"Oh." Maisie suddenly looked at the trees as if leaves were the most interesting thing in the world.

"Maise?" Cate asked, fanning herself. "Do you know something about the book, Maisie? Do tell."

"Well." Maisie's smile was uncertain. "I think he gave the book to me. He also gave me an apple tree in a pot."

"He *what*?" Sam sat up. Cate stopped fanning herself, and Ellie's eyes were bright with interest. "Why would he do that?" Nothing like a rhetorical question—it was pretty clear why Grey had given the book to Maisie. Delicate and skinny, soft silver hair fluttering in the breeze and eyes as bright as ever... she was a middle-aged stunner.

"It was a welcoming gift. We're neighbors." Maisie raised an eyebrow. "He's bought the carriage house, right?"

"He sure has," Ellie confirmed gleefully.

Sam smiled. "He's nice, Maisie. Always polite. Filthy rich, too. Either that, or he knows how to splurge on the right things."

Maisie's eyes widened as if she wanted to roll them. "I'm sure he's nice. I don't care if he's rich."

"It doesn't hurt." Cate laughed quietly.

"Stop it." Maisie's voice was cold. And dead-serious.

Sam felt her smile slip away, same as Ellie's and Cate's.

"Maise," Cate said. "We're just kidding around."

"I know. I'm sorry. I'm not...I just can't do that again. I don't want to go there."

Sam leaned forward. "Do what? Be in love?"

Maisie straightened her shoulders. "Yes."

Sam felt the other two women quiet. "Can't or won't?"

Maisie took a deep breath. "Won't. I won't go through it again."

Sam leaned back. It wasn't for her to judge, and this was not the time to freak Maisie out. "Okay." Sam stood, patting pine needles off her jeans. "Swearing off men is never a bad idea. Am I right? Are we ready to go on?"

Without a word, the other women rose and shouldered their backpacks.

Some things, love and fear among them, couldn't be reasoned. They just were. Everyone had to deal with them on their own when the time came.

Chapter 20

Maisie stopped, hitching her thumbs under the backpack straps to relieve the weight. She barely recognized the path. The trees had changed, their canopies denser than she remembered. Below the woody cliff they were scaling, the ocean still sang its song. But the new leaves blocked the sea breeze, and without relief, the stagnant heat was becoming oppressive.

Maisie peeked at the spots of sky visible between the branches above. The forecast hadn't predicted rain or even one of Beach Cove's rare thunderstorms, but clouds had appeared nevertheless. Not puffy white ones... Clouds that looked like they'd come out of an old diesel exhaust pipe.

Ellie caught up with Maisie; Cate and Sam followed.

"Was it here the path went off to the left?" Ellie rubbed her shoulder where the strap of her pack had left a red impression on the skin. Tiny beads of sweat covered her forehead, and her long hair frizzed with humidity. "Wasn't there a boulder?"

"There was," Cate said, breathlessly leaning

against the trunk of a spruce. "We must've gone too far. I haven't been here in ages. It looks different, doesn't it?"

Sam took off her backpack, dropped it on the ground, and pressed her hands into her lower back, arching her spine. "It really does look different." She unhooked her bottle and took a drink. "I'm trying to figure out why it's so quiet. Can you guys hear that?"

"Can we hear the quiet?" Cate smiled faintly.

"Is it more quiet than usual?" Maisie frowned and listened. Was it quiet? Yes—there was nothing, no humming in the air, no buzzing. Even the mosquitoes seemed to have let off. She hadn't noticed before... Her thoughts had whispered all the time. Maybe she should have noticed *that.* The quieter it was, the more thoughts and memories crowded in on her. But she hadn't. She hadn't been paying attention at all. Anxiety rose in her chest like a wave ready to break. She took a breath. Tree. Backpack. Friend. She took another breath, managing to make it deeper than the last.

"Take the birds, for example." Sam pointed at the tree branches.

"What birds?" Ellie craned her neck and squinted.

"That's the thing. There aren't any. I wonder why. Maybe I've never been up here this early in the year? I can't remember. Funny, isn't it? After living in Beach Cove all my life."

"I've only been once or twice," Cate said. "But never alone. I'm always talking with someone, so I never notice anything. Unusual or otherwise."

Ellie murmured in agreement.

Maisie took a last, deep breath. Her anxiety had ebbed away as fast as it'd come. That oak over there... "Isn't this the tree where Emily threw the big tantrum?"

They all looked at the oak, trying to match their memories to the roots and rocks and bark of the present. Toddler Emily had thrown a tantrum because she'd had fewer berries in her basket than Tommy. Allegedly, since they'd made sure all kids got similar amounts of blueberries and huckleberries.

"She threw her basket against that rock there." Ellie pointed at a boulder, hidden in the brush.

"Oh right." Cate chuckled. "She was such a handful."

"And you loved every minute of it," Sam remarked. "It appealed to your hidden wild side."

"Please. I'm a middle-aged married mother-teacher. I don't have a wild side." Cate sighed.

Even Maisie had to smile now. Yes, Cate did have a bit of a wild side. Cate hadn't let Emily get away with too much, but they'd all known she admired her girl's free spirit. There'd been less of it after Alex had disappeared, and Cate had claimed she was glad about it. But it'd been only a claim. The light in her eyes when she'd told them about Emily's adventures had been the real thing.

"You're just good at hiding it, Cate. But anyway, the lighting should be in there." Ellie pointed a finger into the thicket.

"Oh dear." Cate squinted at the brush. "Nobody's gone in there for years."

"I thought they maintained the trails." Sam checked over her shoulder as if she could catch the lazy culprits sneaking off.

"Who are they?" Ellie asked, distracted.

"You know. *They*. Whoever maintained the trails." Sam rubbed her neck. The sun had given it a red glow. Maisie should've packed sunscreen for her fair friend. "I bet trail maintenance went the way of the budget cuts."

"And there's the rub. Hamlet, Shakespeare," Cate said. "Though scratch is more like it. Look at those thorns."

Maisie too studied the former opening to the blueberry patch. "Let's see—lots of brambles. Raspberry...and the thick ones are blackberry. Um. I don't think I want to break a path through blackberry brambles."

"And that little lovely down there?" Ellie pointed. "That's poison ivy. Leaves of three, let me be."

"Oh. Oh no. I'm not doing poison ivy. Been there, done that." Sam shook her head. "I like having skin."

They all looked at Cate. She was the only one of them—the only *person* Maisie knew at all—that didn't react to poison ivy.

Helplessly, Cate lifted her hands. "What do you want me to do? Even if I rip out the poison ivy, I can't break through blackberry bushes. We need gardening shears or clippers."

"Or a machete," Ellie threw in. "I'd quite like to

see you hacking your way through the forest with a machete."

Cate waved her off, but Maisie had to grin. Sweet Cate, chopping her way through the deciduous jungle with large knives...

Cate slipped her pack off and dropped it. "Oof. I'll be waiting in the shade here. Did anyone bring bug repellent? I don't trust the peace."

When nobody spoke, Maisie shrugged. "I have some, but it's old." She took off her backpack and pulled the small spray bottle from a pouch. "I found it in the mudroom. Don't know if it still works, but I used it myself and so far, so good." She handed the spray to Cate.

"Let's have the picnic right here," Elie suggested.

"Here? In the middle of the path?" Sam looked around, frowning critically. "That's not very celebratory."

"It's not like anyone will interrupt us." Cate squatted down on a large, smooth root jutting from the forest floor. "Fine by me."

"Fine by me, too." Maisie sat on the soft ground. The entire celebration thing was freaking her out anyway, her anxiety rolling in and out like ocean waves. The blueberry patch could wait. Everything could wait until she knew where Alex was. She didn't have a reason to celebrate until she had him back.

"This is not what we meant to do!" Sam threw a hand up in frustration.

Maisie glanced at her, surprised.

"But Sa-am," Ellie whined. "What do you want us to *do*?" She walked to the bushes and took one of the thorny vines between forefinger and thumb and bent it. As soon as she let go, it whipped back, almost hitting her arm. "See? We can't get in there. We'll have to come back."

"This is not good," Sam muttered under her breath, and Maisie didn't miss Sam's gaze flicker to her.

Maisie lowered her head. Of all her friends, Sam was the only one who didn't have kids. Tommy and Alex had forever hung out at Beach house and Ellie's place, and even Cate's because they'd been friends with Emily. But Sam had seen a lot less of the kids. Yet she seemed most intent on getting to the spot Alex had liked. To celebrate the good memories.

Anxiety fingered Maisie's trachea. "Sam, it's okay," she said. Or croaked. Maisie rubbed a hand over her throat. "I don't want to sit on the path either. Let's go have the picnic on the cliff. We can look out at the sea. Alex loved the cliff more than blueberries anyway. I know the kids had bonfires there."

Cate lit up. "Oh, lovely! There's going to be a breeze over there. Yes, let's do that instead." She handed the bug spray back to Maisie and stood. "Okay, Sam?"

"Come on, Sam," Ellie coaxed. "Let's get to the wine and grapes part!"

"I have grapes, too." Cate laughed. "Grapes for everyone."

Sam rolled her head as if her neck was aching.

"Oh, fine. But it's not what we meant to do. For the record, I wanted to stick to the plan."

"Recorded." Maisie stood and slung her pack over one shoulder. The cliff was no more than fifteen minutes walking downhill. Grapes sounded good. Cool wine sounded good. Even the crackers she'd brought didn't sound so bad anymore. "Let's go. I'm hungry. Are you?"

Sam threw a dark look at the brambles barring their way. Despite her blond hair, pale skin, and sea-glass eyes, Sam excelled at throwing dark looks. "I really need a drink," she muttered.

Maisie took another sip of the cold chardonnay. The cooler bag stuffed with ice had done its job, and the wine rolled sweet and fresh and clear over her tongue. She looked around. They'd picked a beautiful spot. Good thing they'd come here instead of squatting among weeds and berry bushes.

The sea below was calm, and the sun kissed the lazy waves green and turquoise before they rolled against the cliff. Gulls and cormorants sat on rocks, preening and drying. The aroma of the sugar kelp and bladderwrack, dulse and sea lettuce that were drying in the shallow tide pools hugged Maisie like an old friend. "How peaceful," she murmured, more to herself than anyone else.

Ellie heard her anyway. She'd been lying flat on

her back, seemingly asleep, but now she turned her head and blinked at Maisie. "I don't know how you stand living away from the sea."

Maisie let her glass sink. "I live. That's all. Where and when and how doesn't matter anymore. All that matters is that I do whatever I can to get him back."

Ellie inhaled as if she wanted to say something, but then she simply closed her mouth and nodded.

"Maisie, is there any of your quiche left?" Cate called from the right. "It's so good."

It was. It was really good. Maisie lifted her glass at Ellie, who put on an exaggerated I-told-you-so look.

"There is, but I didn't make it. Ellie did."

"Truth." Ellie propped herself up on her elbows and checked the container she'd brought. "There's one slice left, and it's got your name on it, Cate darling."

Cate got up from where she'd been leaning against a rock in the shade and brought her plate over. Ellie scooped the rest of the quiche on it. "More wine?"

Cate nodded. "Don't mind if I do, though I'm starting to enjoy this a little bit too much. You don't want to carry me back down the mountain."

"Never mind carrying!" Sam called. "We'll use you as a sled."

"Well, I'm fat enough," Cate retorted dryly. "At least y'all fit."

Ellie and Sam started assuring her that she looked almost perfect and didn't they all have a little extra padding just for sitting on rocks by the sea.

Maisie didn't join but soaked up the sun, banter, and companionship when suddenly, new voices reached her ears. She sat up, scanning the forest line. There it was again – another group of hikers was coming their way.

Maisie squinted at the newcomers who were coming straight toward them, but they were still too far to see their faces.

There was no avoiding the group. Maisie looked away; she didn't want to meet anyone. She let her thoughts drift, wishing she'd be at the beach, walking in the water. She should make sure to get a proper beach walk in before she left home again. No—what was she doing? Maisie's breath almost hitched as she caught up with her thoughts.

She couldn't take leisurely beach walks while her son lived in who-knew-what conditions. She couldn't sit with her friends, laughing and sipping wine. The times were long gone when all she had to worry about were her drooping dahlias or matching the pillows in the sunroom to the green of the sea. Watching full moons over the ocean, fishing for crabs in tide pools with her son, small restaurants —her life had been enchanted. She'd had her turn. Now it was time to step up, not let Beach Cove seduce her into—

"Maisie?" Ellie said.

"What?" She looked up.

Ellie was shielding her eyes against the spring sun. "Aren't those your podcasters? They're coming over here."

Maisie stood and swayed for a moment, blood rushing in her ears. She shook her head. "I knew it. I knew they'd need me."

Ellie stood too, waving at the young people climbing across the rocks toward them. "I don't think they need anything," she muttered softly. "Look at them; they're happy. They're just taking a walk."

Sam stood, brushing sand and shell-crumble off her pants.

"Hi!" Ashley waved. Like the rest of them, she wore shorts and a long-sleeved t-shirt, baseball cap and sneakers. Her red sweater was knotted around her waist.

Maisie took some small steps toward them, tense like a coil. What were they doing up here? "Do you need me?" she called out, the words brittle in her throat.

Ashley shook her head but also exchanged a glance with Jim.

Maisie forced herself to inhale. Too many people had exchanged glances and then told her not to worry. Maisie worried. She'd worried all along.

Finally, the podcasters reached them.

"It's so hot today!" Jim said, wiping his forehead. "I thought there'd still be snow on the ground in Maine!"

"Beach Cove is always a little ahead of schedule," Sam said. "What brings you up here? Do you need Maisie for something? What's going on?"

"No, nothing like that. We had no idea you were up here!" Ashley said, hiking her thumbs under the straps of her pack. "A woman in town mentioned that people like it up here. We figured there was a reason, and I gotta give it to Beach Cove—wow." She beamed at the view.

Maisie tilted her head, not trusting the cheerful tone of Ashley's voice. "Okay. Well, nice to see you. Any new insights?"

"Did the woman have red hair?" Sam interrupted.

Jim nodded while Ashley returned her eyes to Maisie. "We talked with the cops, but they said the same things you already told us."

"Hmm." Of course they did. Officer Clayton would always make sure Maisie was the first to hear when there was a development. Not that there had been any.

"This is beautiful." Jim pointed at the sea. "You're so lucky to live...here..." He glanced at Maisie.

The kid was just trying to be nice. "It's pretty," Maisie confirmed weakly.

"And are you up here for the view?" Ashley asked suddenly.

"There's a blueberry field Alex liked." Cate had joined them. "We meant to have a picnic there."

"Really? Where?" Again, she glanced at her husband.

"The path is grown over," Maisie said. This glance, she could decipher. "The cops went over the forest with a helicopter. We even had some search parties up here."

"Okay." Ashley narrowed her eyes; the wheels in her head were whirring so loudly, Maisie could almost hear them.

"Did they use dogs?" Jim asked after a short pause.

"Dogs?" Maisie frowned as the image of the search dogs, nose on the ground and eyes glazed over with concentration, came back to her. "Only on the beach and in town. That's how they traced him walking to the water. But then they lost his scent."

"Oh. Well... Not *those* kind of dogs; we know about them. No, the, um...the other dogs," Ashley murmured.

From the corner of her eyes, Maisie noticed Sam crossing her arms.

"Cadaver dogs," Jim said quietly.

"We don't call them that anymore! He means human-remains detection dogs," Ashley corrected her husband.

Maisie shook her head. "No?"

"The cops didn't use any back then as far as we know." Ellie put an arm around Maisie. "Um. I mean, you could bring one in, couldn't you? Everyone loves a dog. It'd be good for the podcast."

Maisie blinked, bewildered. "If the dogs didn't find his scent, how are they going to...going to find..."

Ellie hugged Maisie tighter. "An engaging episode gets more buzz, Maise. And then more people listen to it. It's our best chance to reach that one person that knows something."

Jim nodded, looking relieved. "Exactly. We know someone who's got the right dogs. Would you mind if we check a few places? Like up here? Your friend's spot on; dogs make for good ratings."

"Fine." Maisie's legs were tired. She was cold. Empty. There was still the entire hike back down. All she wanted was to be back in her house. Lock the doors and go to bed.

She extracted herself from Ellie's arm and went to stuff her things back into her backpack. "I have to get home," she explained when her friends gathered around her. "I can't do this. I shouldn't have come here. You stay. I don't want to spoil your—"

"Fiddlesticks we stay," Cate said warmly. "Of course we're coming with you, Maisie."

She didn't want them. She didn't want anyone. "No, you should—"

"Don't even start," Cate said, her voice a warning.

Maisie closed her mouth and nodded meekly. She knew that tone. Cate could make an entire high school hush down and do as she told with that tone.

"We didn't mean to chase you away," Ashley said. Regret tinged her words, enough to make Maisie look up.

"You do what you came here to do," she said shortly.

Ashley nodded. "I'll make the call for the dogs right now," she promised, pulling out her cell phone and tapping at the screen.

Maisie snapped her backpack closed and slung it over her shoulder, then started walking. "Cell phones don't work up here."

"Wait, we're coming," Ellie said, hurrying to her spot. She started stuffing things back into her pack, then caught up with Maisie. "Don't twist your ankle running over the rocks like that."

Cate huffed after them. "Maisie, it's not going to change a thing if they bring dogs. If he's not here, the dogs aren't going to put him there either. Wait, where's Sam?"

They turned. Sam, backpack in hand, was talking to Jim. They waited until she joined them.

"What was that about?" Ellie asked.

Sam shrugged. "I told them I'd show the dog handlers the blueberry patch. Someone should."

"Why?"

"You know." Sam's voice quieted. "No reason. But just—in case. To be thorough. I'll show them the other hangouts too."

"Oh." Ellie was silent for a few beats while Maisie sped up, propelled by nerves. "You know what, Sam? I'll ask Tommy to join you. He knows best where they hung out."

"We should've looked more up here," Maisie said suddenly. Anxiety wrung the words from her, crowding them out of her chest. "Why did we never come up here with dogs before?"

"Because nobody thought it was worth the trouble. The dogs lost his scent on the beach," Cate said calmly. "The volunteers searched the woods. Don't let this freak you out, Maise."

"Alex loved coming up here," Maisie insisted.

She'd always been satisfied that the forest had been checked, had searched here herself when the volunteers had left to return to their own lives. Why did everyone suddenly think cadaver dogs were a good idea? Was this what she'd missed? What if she hadn't been thorough enough? What if she'd focused on the wrong things? "We should've gotten the dogs up here a long time ago," she repeated breathlessly.

"No, we shouldn't have," Ellie said calmly, marching at her side. "There was no reason. I'm sorry this is happening, Maisie. They're just trying to make an interesting podcast."

Maisie nodded, mute.

"We had a plan, a plan that was developed with the cops and made sense. Alex was at the beach; the dogs tracked him to the waterline. We checked all the road points and the areas around Beach Cove. The dogs couldn't check the entire county."

Cate hummed in agreement behind them.

"Sam?" Maisie looked over her shoulder at her intuitive friend. The one whose opinion she trusted. The one who had never before insisted they go to the forest.

Sam blinked a few times as if she wanted to say something. Then she pressed her lips into a tight line. "Let them go ahead with the dogs. It can't hurt."

Maisie turned back, trying not to slide in the loose gravel on the path.

It can't hurt.

Yet there was a pain in her heart that hurt

enough to scare the living daylights out of her.

Chapter 21

"What we need is a nice, relaxing evening at home." Ellie fell onto the sofa in Maisie's living room and patted the seat beside her.

"Don't you have to go home?" Maisie sounded slightly desperate. "It's almost seven."

"Nope," Ellie said contentedly. They'd decided that Maisie needed some real food after the disturbing images conjured up by the podcasters' dog-talk. Maisie, stick figure that she was, naturally hadn't wanted food, but they'd told her that there was no way they'd leave her hungry and alone in that vast house of hers, that she was welcome, and to stop it already. Then they'd frog-marched her into a little brewery that served a mean barbeque. Without asking, Sam had ordered lobster rolls for everyone, fries and clams and beer, BBQ sample platters to share, and extra double-creamy coleslaw.

It'd been glorious.

Ellie sighed happily. Even Maisie, who'd been on an emotional rollercoaster ever since she'd set foot into Beach Cove, had eventually eaten half her lobster roll and gnawed, ladylike, on a couple of ribs.

"You look very satisfied." Maisie sat beside Ellie.

"I love that brewery. Do you want to watch something?"

Maisie gazed at the French doors. "You know what *I* love? Gardening."

"Fair enough." Back in the day, Maisie had forever been rooting around between her flowers, weeding and pruning. "You should get back to it."

"I can't get anything done in the two days I'm staying here." Maisie leaned back and picked up the remote. "Not even worth getting started."

Ellie swallowed. Two days? Was that all Maisie gave herself—and her friends? She cleared her throat. "Not sure you have an argument there. If I could go to Italy for two days, I'd still make sure to eat all I could. Not sit in my hotel room and think there wasn't a point to it because there wasn't enough time."

"The two things have different timelines, Ellie. Eating gives immediate satisfaction," Maisie remarked. "Gardening gives delayed satisfaction. You have to put in the work now, but you won't see the fruits of your labor until later. Sometimes years later."

"But then, can you say you love gardening? Or do you just love looking at a pretty garden?"

Maisie studied the remote in her hand. Then she smiled. "You're right. I love gardening. Obviously, I enjoy looking at the fruits of my labor, but I love getting my hands dirty too."

"So then..." Ellie circled her hand in the air.

Sometimes, people needed to draw the conclusions themselves.

"So then—" Maisie set the remote control back onto the glass coffee table. "Gardening is Italy. We'll go and garden. Right now."

"Wait, what?" Ellie sat up. "Like, *right* now? I thought we'd relax, watch a little TV... I think there's a rerun of Golden Girls tonight. I've never watched it, and I desperately want to." Ellie was the first to admit she wasn't a natural-born gardener. Her back still kind of ached from the backpack.

"You don't have to come with me." Maisie stood and left the living room.

She'd had a suspicious twinkle in her eye. Probably knew that they meant to watch her and looking for clever ways of getting rid of them.

Ellie moaned and made a weak attempt to get off the sofa, but it was very soft and very comfy. "Oh, Maisie, I take that back! It's totally not worth it!" she called, falling back into the warm, snuggly leather. "Gardening isn't Italy at all, yeah?"

Maisie reappeared at the door in red rubber boots and a waxed barn jacket. In her hand, she held another pair of boots, and over her arm hung a second jacket.

Okay. She wasn't here for her amusement. Ellie hauled herself on her legs, even though they still ached from the steep trail, and her belly was super full of—

"Since you're on babysitting duty," Maisie said

heartlessly, "you'll need these. Here." She unloaded her outerwear onto the sofa. "I'll see you in the garden." Without another look, she marched off.

"Oof." Ellie picked up the jacket. It'd clearly been Robert's, since it was fourteen sizes too large and ten years too dusty. She sighed. Last-ditch effort. "Let's stop this after-dinner manual-labor nonsense," she called weakly after Maisie. "And anyway, it's too dark."

Instead of a response, light flooded the garden.

Ellie rolled her eyes. Dale made good money, but Robert had been properly rich. Of *course* there were lights in the garden. "Okay," she muttered, trying to sound dark.

But she couldn't make it stick. The lobster rolls had been too melt-in-the-mouth, and the grilled pork too moist for her to truly be annoyed. She just sounded...*buttery*. Maybe it wouldn't hurt to burn off some calories pulling weeds. Ellie stepped into the rubber boots and pulled on the jacket, feeling like it was large enough to drag on the floor behind her like some weird waxed train.

"There you are." Maisie reappeared, walking to the French doors and opening them into the night garden.

"I can hear thunder." Ellie looked up. The lights were too bright to see the sky. "I think a storm's coming."

"Welcome to my life," Maisie murmured. "Listen, Ellie, I'm just kidding. You go back in and watch TV if you like—but you did accidentally convince me about going myself. I really do want to do some gardening, even if it's for nothing."

"Oh. Um... No, now I want to come." It was nice to have rung a chord. If Maisie wanted to do something she loved, that was great, actually. "Just let me warn you; I know fish, but I can't tell a flower from a weed."

Maisie nodded and walked out. Ellie followed even though the thunder grumbled louder.

"So that depends on context," Maisie said softly. "It's only a weed if it's in the wrong place at the wrong time. Otherwise, weeds can be beautiful—just as beautiful as something grown in a nursery."

"What? Nah." Ellie had a lot of weeds at home. Some of them were okay. But they didn't look *beautiful*.

Maisie chuckled. "See this bed over there?" She waved Ellie deeper into the garden.

"It's too dark back here." But Ellie followed. Her friend hadn't set foot in this garden in years—but of course she remembered every single plant she'd planted.

"I guess it's a little dark." Maisie looked up as if she'd only now noticed that the lights didn't reach this far, then inspected the raised bed. "Hmm. Doesn't matter; it's all rotted away anyway. But I used to let milk thistles grow here." She pointed. "They bloom late in summer, but they're gorgeous. And earlier in the year, there was healall and meadowsweet. Not as showy, but pretty enough, and honeybees and butterflies like them. I always had some lavender and hydrangeas in the background."

Ellie smiled. "I know thistles but not healall or meadowsweet. I'll have to look them up. Pretty names though."

"Aren't they?"

"So you grew weeds here? I never noticed it. It all looked so pretty and colorful."

"Calling them weeds is like... It's like saying that not all the fish in the sea are real fish, only tuna and salmon."

"Thanks for the fish analogy, my dear." Ellie chuckled and wrapped the jacket tighter around herself. A cool breeze blew from the sea, playing with her hair. "See, this I don't understand, Maisie. How are you holed up in New York City of all places in the world, when you have this garden waiting for you? I mean, I do understand. Painful memories. But there's also so much beauty here, isn't there?" She took a breath. "And us. We're here too."

In the dim light, Maisie frowned. "I know. But it... doesn't matter."

"Mm-hmm." Ellie waited to see whether Maisie would say more. Because what Maisie meant was that she, Maisie herself, didn't matter. Her life for the life of her son. It hurt Ellie.

But Maisie had had time to reconnect with her home a little. The house and the garden, the beach, the little bakery around the corner, the walks. Her friends and her friends' lives. Ellie had seen the light they'd brought to Maisie's eyes. She'd heard how Maisie's last sentence had petered out. As if Maisie was becoming less sure that her own joy in life was really so unimportant in the face of her son's disappearance.

Maybe it was. Ellie couldn't imagine losing Tommy; she couldn't picture how she would react. She'd thought about it many, many times, only to draw back with a shudder and put in a quick phone call to check on him. She tucked her long hair behind her ear and looked over her shoulder. Down at the beach, the breaking waves had gotten louder. "Since we're not weeding—what should we do? What does one do in a garden at night?"

"Smooch, usually." Maisie laughed quietly as if she'd made an inside joke. It wasn't hard to deduce her thoughts had gone to her husband and happier times. "I didn't say there wasn't weeding to do. This is all rotted. And we still have to clean up the flower beds where I *don't* let the weeds grow."

"Oh, okay." Ellie shivered. After brewing all day, the weather was going to break. The grumbling in the sky had reached threatening levels and a raindrop landed on her shoulder, splattering off the wax and onto her cheek. She wiped it off. "Let's better hurry. I'm a tiny little bit scared of thunderstorms."

"I forgot that." Maisie looked up, her pale face a shimmering oval in the twilight. "Seriously Ellie, why don't you go and watch your movie? You can still see me out here. If I get lonely, I promise I'll come in to sit with you."

Ellie hesitated. She should stay with Maisie, keep

up the chatter to distract her from brooding over the podcasters' cadaver-dog escapades.

The sky growled again.

Um... For as long as she could remember, storms turned her heart into jelly and her knees into pudding. Maybe because of her long ancestral line of fishermen, many of whom the sea had claimed for herself.

"Trust me, I'm okay," Maisie said. She wiped a strand of hair from Ellie's face. "Don't be brave. I'm sorry I forgot about the storm. Go on inside. I promise I won't panic."

Lightning split the sky over the cove with a deafening roar, and for a second, Ellie saw the roiling waves. Any fishers trapped out there would be praying for mercy.

"You're crazy, staying out here." Stress raised her voice. The house was a quick jog from where she stood.

"What you gonna do about it," Maisie said in a New York accent that made her sound like a *famiglia* boss.

A nervous laugh escaped Ellie. "Okay. Okay. I'm going back in. I'll make sure to drag you inside when you get struck by a lightning bolt."

Maisie nodded. "Good. That sounds good. I'll only stay for a bit."

Raindrops, fat and warm like worms, started to splash off Ellie's waxed jacket. "Ugh." She yanked the collar higher. Maisie was fine. The garden was her thing, not Ellie's. Ellie turned and ran the short distance to the house, her hands shaking with relief as she pulled the door shut behind her.

Through the glass, she could see Maisie shrug off her jacket and drop it on the ground, then walk further back into the garden. What was she doing? She was only wearing a thin blouse. She'd get soaked.

Ellie squinted. The light from the house barely reached back to where Maisie stood. A flash made Ellie flinch in fright, but she kept her eyes on her friend. When the thunder boomed barely one count after the lightning, Maisie stood in the back of her garden, her face lifted to the sky, rain splashing on her, her palms raised and open to the sky.

Ellie shook her head. The image had something pagan to it, something wild. Maisie wasn't wild. She was posh and perfect. Put together.

Ellie took off her own jacket and tossed it on a side chair. Should she be worried? Was Maisie losing it? Or was this what she needed—a cleansing?

Ellie chewed on her cheek, keeping her eyes on Maisie. Then she pulled out her phone. "Cate?"

"Yes. What's going on?"

"Maisie's out in the rain. She took off her jacket and is—just standing there, looking up at the sky. Think it's normal?"

"Hmm." Cate took a moment to consider. "Uh, probably it's normal? Could be she's letting off steam after all that dog talk. Where is she? On the beach?"

"In her garden."

"Oh, garden's good." Cate sounded relieved. "But keep an eye on her."

"Okay. Thank you. Bye." Ellie hung up. Another boom and another lightning, this one showing Maisie bent at the waist, pulling weeds in the streaming rain.

Pulling weeds was good. A little craziness in the rain was probably good, too.

It was almost time for the Golden Girls rerun. And there'd been some walnut ice cream in Maisie's freezer earlier. It must belong to one of the podcasters, but a bowl of reassuring sweetness and a few jokes sounded just about right. But first... Ellie lifted her phone again and dialed Dale's number.

Dale liked to have dinner late. Ellie had made sure to stock the fridge with the ingredients for his specialty frittata. Her thoughts flashed to the gorgeous lobsters Bonnie had brought her. Dale had better not have gone and gotten one of them.

He didn't answer.

Ellie let her phone sink. Maybe he was listening to music and couldn't hear his phone?

Or he'd muted his phone for a meeting and forgot to put the volume back on.

Or he'd fallen asleep on the sofa.

She swallowed her unease. Her husband was unavailable for two minutes, and she was uneasy? That's not who she was.

She was the kind of woman that took care of her friends and had a huge bowl of ice cream while watching a favorite sitcom.

Ellie brought Robert's old coat back into the mudroom and hung it on a hook. She stepped out of her boots and returned those to their tray as well.

Then she helped herself to ice cream and went back into the living room. A glance told her that Maisie was still weeding, working her way closer to the house.

Ellie switched on the TV and sank into the comfort of the sofa.

Things were all right. Things would turn out all right.

And Dale wasn't only a good husband.

Dale was a great husband.

Chapter 22

Maisie poured herself a cup of coffee. The morning mist blanketed the kitchen window; it was always there after a night of rain. Something scraped over the wooden floor above, and she titled her head. So the podcasters had come home the night before after all.

Jim had texted her they'd go out for food… But nothing was open late in Beach Cove this time of year. In summer, when the tourists came, sure. But in May? Unless restaurant hours had changed while she'd been in New York, Jimmy hadn't been quite forthright with her. Why not? She wasn't his mom to give him a curfew…

She took a sip of her steaming brew, letting it roll over her tongue. Almost as good as back then. Robert had known how to make good coffee—another thing she hadn't even realized she'd missed. Coffee. Such a tiny spot in the big picture, barely there. And yet, it made for a moment.

Maisie swirled her mug.

Ellie hadn't left until about ten the night before. It had taken that long to reassure her that Maisie wasn't going off the deep end. And it was probably good Ellie didn't know that Maisie had weeded until well after midnight. The thrumming rain and crashing thunder had distracted her from her worries. It'd been the most restful thing Maisie had experienced in a long time. It'd set something free—something more than her pent-up desire to garden, even though she couldn't put her finger on it.

But pulling dead stems and rotten roots from the soil had felt like a drug; she hadn't been able to stop. Her hands had reached out, again and again, to give the plants that were still clinging on a fighting chance in the battle for sunlight, water, soil.

Maisie took another sip.

The podcasters were coming down the staircase now; the old wood creaked its familiar melody.

"Good morning, Mrs. Jameson." Jim appeared in the door. He wore jeans and a T-shirt though his hair was unbrushed and unruly, and he was barefoot.

"Good morning." Maisie busied herself with the coffee machine. Alex had come down barefoot in the mornings too, even in winter.

"Coffee?" She nodded at the mugs she'd pulled from the cabinet.

"That'd be great." Jim padded over to her and took a mug.

Maisie poured.

"I hope we didn't wake you last night. We came in pretty late. Sorry."

"You don't have to apologize; I didn't hear a thing." She glanced at him. He was blowing into his coffee, steaming up his glasses. Irritated, he shook his head to get the fog off the lenses, and Maisie smiled. They were just kids, after all. They were trying to do good.

"We made a driftwood bonfire on the beach and forgot the time," Jim said, still sounding contrite.

Maisie tilted her head. That must've been some driftwood. "It rained. There was a storm," she pointed out mildly.

He took an exaggerated sip, letting the mug hide his face. Then he raked his fingers through his hair. "Okay, actually, we went to meet a friend near Boston."

"You went all the way to Boston last night? And back?"

"Well, yeah." He looked at the mug in his hands.

"Cream?"

"Oh. Yes please."

Maisie got the carton of half-and-half from the fridge and handed it to Jim.

He poured. "Yes, so—this friend owns the sort of dogs we'd need."

She'd known it before he'd said it. But the panic she'd felt the day before wasn't there anymore. Mostly. "How did it go?"

"Well, he's got two he can bring up here. Freddy and Pamela."

"Pamela?" Maisie was more of a cat person. But if she'd had a dog, she'd definitely call her Pamela too. Pam.

"I know, right?" Jim grinned. "They are cute."

"What sort of dogs are they?"

"They're cada—"

Maisie held up her hand. She didn't need to hear that word again. Ever. "What breed, I mean."

Jim's pale cheeks flushed a light pink. "Freddy's a golden retriever. He's young. Pam's a basset."

Maisie couldn't help but smile again. Basset hounds were the short-legged wrinkly ones with floppy ears, weren't they? She'd never even thought of owning a dog. Robert had been allergic, and they'd traveled too much. But a hound called Pam? She sounded like good gardening company... And Freddy sounded like he'd enjoy a nice long walk at the beach.

Maybe in a different life, she'd have adopted herself a couple of dogs. And cats. Both.

She cleared her throat, suddenly becoming aware that Jim was watching her. "What did your friend have to say?" she asked.

"Yeah, he's bringing them." Jim checked his watch. "They're on the way right now. We'll be heading out to meet him in an hour or so. He'll call when he gets close."

That soon? Mechanically, Maisie nodded. She'd gotten what she wanted, hadn't she? The podcasters were doing something to find Alex. One way or the other, they'd found a way to bring new facts to the table.

Unlikely as it was—what if they found something? People said that knowing was better than not knowing.

Maisie wasn't so sure that was true. Sometimes, not knowing was the better alternative.

"Do you have any plans for today?" Jim asked.

She exhaled. "No, I don't." She hadn't even noticed—but none of her friends had said they wanted to meet today.

No one was on babysitting duty today.

The stairs creaked again, and Ashley walked into the kitchen. She too was barefoot despite the cold floors. "Good morning, Mrs. Jameson. How are you today?" she asked.

Instead of answering, Maisie filled another mug with coffee and handed it to Ashley. She pointed at the creamer, but Ashley smiled and shook her head. "I'm trying to quit dairy." She snuggled into Jim's side, smiling sleepily at him.

Maisie recognized the look. A long eternity ago, she'd looked at Robert like that. It was a good look for a wife to have. Love, adoration, good sex—all that was wrapped up in it.

"It might be good to have some company today, Mrs. Jameson," Jim said. "Are your friends around?" He gave his wife the slightest nudge, clearly trying to be inconspicuous. Ashley instantly straightened.

"I'll be all right," Maisie said. Sam and Ellie had businesses to run, and Cate had not only her job but kids to take care of.

She wished she could call Robert. She wished he'd be with her, a shoulder to lean on. But he'd made his choice. Supporting her hadn't been it.

Never wish. Never wish. The weight of her

wishes could pull her under quicker than an anchor tied to the neck.

Maisie took a deep breath. As always, she needed to get over herself, do what needed to be done instead of wallowing. "Call me the moment you have any news." She looked first in Jim's, then in Ashley's eyes.

The rest of the little crew came padding into the kitchen, looking for caffeine, and Maisie was glad to have something to do with her hands. She poured and handed mugs to Amanda and JJ, who nodded their thanks.

"We will," Ashley promised.

"Whatever it is. If you don't find anything—I want to know. I have a right to know."

"Of course. I'll text you even if nothing's happening."

Let me know if you do find anything. Let me know the moment you find him.

Maisie wanted to say it but couldn't get the words out. Her throat felt tight. After a moment, she gave up trying.

Chapter 23

Cate's phone vibrated, and she stepped into a doorway to find it in her purse. Thankfully, it wasn't as hot as it'd been on that unfortunate hike the day before. There were some clouds in the sky which helped; she wasn't sweating so much. Though still enough. And her knee hurt from that long march down the cliff.

A text from Allen, asking her to get him gas pills.

Cate frowned and bent to rub her knee. She'd just *been* to the market, picking up the milk she'd forgotten. If she went back now, she wouldn't be able to drive Claire to her soccer meet at two, and Cate had been looking forward to catching up with her youngest. But going back to the market meant that Emily had to drive Claire instead.

Another text. Allen wanted them for his trip tomorrow and could she please not forget. He hadn't slept well and was trying to get things off his list so he could rest.

Cate sighed. If only he'd get a grip on his sleep problems. Maybe he should stop watching so much TV at night; that blue light from the screen was no good for sleeping. Though she'd never had a problem reading on her screen herself; her eyes often fell shut before she could finish the chapter. Anyway, she should text Emily...

As she scrolled through numbers, Cate remembered seeing an advert for the Cove Pharmacy in the Starfish Report. The pharmacy had closed after old Mrs. Terry died of pneumonia, but someone from Merewif had bought it not too long ago.

It was really close to where she'd parked the car. She could easily stop by for the pills and make it back in time to drive Claire.

Cate texted Allen to take it easy and started walking again, already almost at the pharmacy's door.

When she reached it, the pretty brass detail on the green door was polished, and the window display had changed. In the center stood a driftwood table with an old-fashioned double-pan scale. On the upper plate was an apple. On the lower plate were a few orange pharmacy bottles, some toppled over to dramatically spill pills.

Well, what about that. Pharmacists made their living selling medicine, yet this lady was promoting eating fruits instead. How nice.

Cate pushed open the green door and stepped into the cool interior. The scents of anise and lavender made her inhale deeply and contentedly; she looked around. Sunlight poured over the old wooden shelves, lighting colorful containers and pretty packets.

Towelettes and bandages, sun cream and poison

ivy lotion, soaps, breath mints, and shaving brushes.

Cate walked around, looking at all the interesting little offerings. Maybe she should get one of those delicious-looking Peach Perfect face masks, do a little relaxing herself when Allen was gone? Maisie, Sam, and Ellie—they'd all been blessed with perfect skin, while she seemed to forever battle old pimples and new wrinkles.

"I won't be able to sell you one of those."

Startled, Cate whirled around.

Behind the marble counter stood the man. The lime-man from the market. His hazel eyes were fixed on her, his face expressionless, his hands pushed into the pockets of an immaculate lab coat.

"Oh, I'm sorry!" Cate dropped the mask back, feeling her cheeks flush warm. Was the store not yet open after all? But no, she was sure she'd seen the announcement in the newspaper. And the door *had* been open. She glanced at the shelf, but there was no sign explaining why she couldn't get a mask. "Um, why not?"

"It'd be unethical to let you buy it," he said calmly.

Again, Cate squinted at the facemasks. Was it one of the ingredients? Animal Experiments? "Why unethical?" she finally asked.

"You're perfect already."

"Oh. *Oh!* Um. Thank you. I guess." Cate tried to squash her embarrassed smile, but she could feel it tug hard on her lips.

He'd gotten her again.

"How can I help you, ma'am?" The pharmacist smiled back and again, deep laugh lines crinkled his eyes.

"I, uh..." There was no way Cate could ask him for gas pills now. She'd just have to go back to the market. "I just wanted to stop by, have a look at the new pharmacy. It's very pretty. Much brighter than before."

For a moment, the pharmacist looked thoughtfully out of the window. Then he lifted the hinged door and came out from behind the counter.

Cate's heart started to flutter, and she cleared her throat.

Silly. She was an overweight, middle-aged, married schoolteacher with kids and a retirement fund. Her heart shouldn't beat faster for anything other than climbing stairs.

The pharmacist came over to where she stood rooted to the spot and offered his hand. "My name is Calvin. I'm so pleased to meet you."

Again, Cate felt her smile widen on its own. "I'm Cate. Nice to meet you, Calvin. I hope you're enjoying your limes?"

His eyes sparkled, but his voice stayed as serious as his face. "I do very much, thank you." He let go of her hand. "May I show you around?"

Cate looked over her shoulder. Was there more to it than this? Back when it'd been Mrs. Terry's pharmacy, there'd only been the one room. "Sure. Please."

Calvin nodded, waving for her to follow. Cate did, feeling a bit uneasy. But instead of waving her to follow him behind the counter and out of the familiar room, Calvin only led her to the shelf on the far wall. "You will like this," he said and pointed with a conspiratorial nod.

Cate leaned closer. She was supposed to like... what?

Calvin drew an important breath. "That's right. Sunscreen. There's some pink tubes here, and over there they are blue, and this one is *white*."

Cate straightened back up. With any other stranger, she might've been weirded out. But looking at Calvin's intelligent eyes and deadpan face, she only felt amused. "I see. Very nice."

He nodded. "There's more. On the stand over here—" Again he waved her to follow and Cate did, "—are key fobs. All sorts, see? Tassled. Some are... *without* a tassel. It's very creative." He raised an eyebrow. "And there are some adorable pocket-sized tissue packs stacked to your left. We could count them, make sure none are missing. Do you have time?"

What a strange man. Cate smiled but shook her head. "I don't have time, fascinating as your tour is."

"I'm afraid I'm limited by my surroundings. I'm afraid—" He hesitated.

"Yes?"

"That my store *bores* you?" Again, his face gave nothing away. Only the twinkle in his eyes told her that he was having her on.

Cate giggled. "No, it's been interesting. But I do have to go."

"If you're sure." Again, Calvin held out his hand,

and Cate shook.

She'd never shook hello and goodbye with a pharmacist before, but she was glad to do it. Definitely gladder than she should be. "Bye."

"Bye."

Cate turned and headed for the door, aware that Calvin was watching her.

Once outside, she hurried around the corner. Then she stopped, rearranged her purse strap, and took a breath. And another one. She couldn't have this...*this* with a stranger. She was so parched for compliments that a silly line got her all confused. She was seeing things just because he was a little funny and a little sweet. Pathetic.

She'd never set foot into Calvin's pharmacy again.

Maybe if she'd been single, lonely, and looking.

But she wasn't. She couldn't. She wasn't. Of course she wasn't.

Cate pulled her cell phone from her purse and texted Emily, asking her to drive her sister to the soccer meet. Then she started back toward the market.

Her knee hurt. She'd pulled a ligament on the hike or something.

It was too bad. There were pills *right around the corner*, to be had for the asking. But there was no way she could ask Calvin for Allen's *gas pills*.

Cate stopped. What? Why couldn't she, for crying out loud? What was so precious about her that she couldn't admit to the existence of a stomach? He was a pharmacist. He knew about stomachs. And he wasn't *that* charming. A few funny remarks and flatteries couldn't throw her *that* much.

Cate gritted her teeth. It was the exact medicine she needed to take herself. Go right back in, ask for gas pills, explain they were for her husband. Put her feet on the ground where they belonged, let Calvin know he was wasting his charm on her.

She texted Emily again, saying she'd drive Claire herself after all.

Then Cate took a deep breath of the clean, salty air coming from the harbor, smoothed her skirt over her fat hips, and marched herself back into the pharmacy.

Chapter 24

"Hello?"

"Yes?" Maisie gave the pepperweed a last yank, finally pulling the massive root. She straightened, clutching her trowel.

Where *was* the speaker? She shaded her eyes against the bright morning sun. "Oh! Good morning." Vincent Grey stood by the gate. She waved him to come into the garden. "The latch is rusty; you have to press hard."

Hours of heavy-duty gardening with spade and pitchfork under the sun—she was drenched in sweat and streaked with soil, but it hardly mattered. Maisie tossed the pepperweed onto the pile in the wheelbarrow. Pepperweed was invasive; she'd have to make sure to bag it later, not just throw it on the compost. Maisie slipped off her gardening gloves and blotted her forehead with the sleeve of her blouse as she watched Vince come toward her.

Her visitor looked…nice. Though not what she used to think of as attractive, that clean-cut business-style Robert had personified. Impeccably groomed, suit, tie. She used to like a man that wore a tie.

Vince didn't wear one. Instead, he was in a short-sleeved patterned shirt and rather old-fashioned black pants held by suspenders. Again, his short gray hair managed to look windswept. And again, he looked as if he belonged to a time and place where tree-lined alleys led to vineyards and wooden easels. "I don't want to bother you," he said, smiling an apology.

Maisie smiled back. "I'm glad you stopped by. I always forget to take breaks, but I think I do need one."

The apology dissolved as his smile spread to his eyes. "I see you are gardening."

She nodded. "Thank you very much for the book and the apple tree. They are beautiful gifts."

"I'm glad you liked them."

"I do. Though I'm worried the tree might not survive here when I'm gone. My apartment in New York City doesn't get much sunlight, and it won't like being inside in a pot much longer." She paused, letting her words hang in the air. She wanted him to know she wasn't going to stay, not be a neighbor for long. The tree-matter was secondary, but maybe he'd take it back to give it a better chance.

Vince didn't speak right away, but it didn't feel like he was pondering her words. On the contrary, it felt like he was giving her time to think. Finally, he said, "I remember your friend mentioning that you were only visiting Beach Cove, so I made the tree as hardy as I could. I'm afraid we never can be sure how they turn out. But if you feel like giving it a chance, I would suggest planting it here, where it belongs and can thrive. If it manages to take root, it will care for itself." His eyes didn't leave hers. "Beginnings are important. Don't you think, Maisie?"

"Yes, I agree," Maisie replied. Her name in his mouth made her feel odd—as if he'd been a cherished friend in a former life that she'd forgotten. Maisie shifted her weight, simply to reassure herself that she still stood in her garden and on her own two feet, not those of someone who'd lived well before her. "I'll make sure to put the tree into the ground today. Maybe I can get a bag of mulch at the hardware store. That should help." How much longer was she going to stay? One day? Two?

Vince folded his hands behind his back. "You have a beautiful view of the ocean."

Maisie turned to look at the beach. The tide had left its daily gifts to beachgoers on the sand, and Maisie let her eyes follow the meandering line of flotsam—driftwood, glistening sugar kelp, a myriad delicate shells and polished rocks. All of a sudden, she wanted to throw her trowel down and run over there, feel the sand under her feet, let the cool water nip her calves. She inhaled; suddenly the salty air tasted like an elixir of happier years.

"Have you gone on a walk this morning?" Vince asked.

Unable to take her eyes off the water, Maisie shook her head. "I haven't, beautiful as it is." She sounded surprised to her own ears. "I couldn't wait to get into the garden, do a bit of good before I leave again. But I might as well not have bothered." She shook her head and pointed at the wheelbarrow, overflowing with compost. "It's only a drop in the bucket."

He chuckled. "And each drop helps. There's no skipping ahead when it comes to gardening."

Maisie tore her gaze off the beach and blinking against the sun, squinted at her neighbor. "So you live in Carriage House then?"

"I bought it five years and three days ago. I just celebrated the anniversary of moving to Beach Cove with a cup of tea and a piece of tiramisu."

"Good choice," Maisie said. After the former owner had passed away, Carriage House had stood empty. Its heiress lived in England. According to the realtor, she'd always planned to visit but never arrived. And when she'd finally decided to sell, the house had sat on the market like a beautiful piece of waxed fruit. Tempting, but inedible.

Because while it bordered on the beach, it was more cottage than house. There were only two rooms and a kitchen with a tiny pantry downstairs, a single bedroom and bathroom upstairs. Yet the sales price had been eye-wateringly high. Ocean-front property didn't come cheap even in Beach Cove, and the house's distant mistress, dreaming of making time for Carriage House herself, had been in no hurry to sell.

Even Robert had shied back from the deal, though they'd considered the cottage as a guest house. After all, at one time it had belonged to the same estate as Beach House. But in the end they'd decided it was too expensive and too far from the house to be practical; they could only just see the gable from the bedroom upstairs. And since there were plenty of rooms in Beach House itself, and the poor ratio of price to square-footage had made neighbors an unlikely problem, the little cottage with all its quaint charm had remained empty.

Maisie returned to the present. "How is the house working for you?" she asked, genuinely interested.

"Very well indeed. And the old orchard behind the house keeps me busy." Vince's eyes were the sort that changed color with mood and light, and the thick eyebrows and heavy lids veiled them even more. Maisie couldn't tell whether his irises were more green or blue as he looked out at the sea. She'd just have to call them hazel, that nondescript catch-all.

Vince didn't appear to notice her scrutiny. "Your tree comes from the orchard, by the way. The scion should grow my favorite heirloom apple. It's, uh, I'm not sure you've heard of it, but it's a Calville Blanc d'Hiver. A little bit sweet, a little bit spicy." The lids of his hazel eyes suddenly lifted, and he winked at Maisie, acknowledging that he was taking her down the rabbit hole of his hobby. She smiled, and he continued. "The apple was first described in the early 1600s in Normandy, France, and was served at the court of the sun king himself." The lids dropped back. "It's still a favorite in Parisian restaurants. Bakes extremely well. I do bake, you know, so this is important."

Maisie laughed. "If my gift is that fancy, I'll ask my housekeeper whether she'd be willing to water it every now and then."

Vince smiled. "I don't think you will regret taking care of it."

She returned to gazing at the ocean. "Mm-hmm."

Then Vince asked, "Since you didn't go yet, would you like to take a walk at the beach?"

Maisie was already inhaling the air to say yes, yes, she wanted to go on a beach walk very much. Because talking more about gardening and French heirloom apples sounded lovely, and she wanted to learn more about the book.

But she couldn't leave. The beach was infamous for swallowing radio waves.

The podcasters were searching the forest. Freddy and Pam were hard at work, sniffing their way up the mountain under the guidance of Sam and Tommy, who'd make sure the dogs hit all the spots Alex liked.

Maisie shook her head. "I have to stay close to the house."

Somehow, Vince picked up on her train of thoughts. "I heard about your son."

"Yeah." Everyone in Beach Cove had heard about her son. That was her identity, not neighbor-with-the-garden. Maisie looked at her hands. They were dirty despite the gardening gloves, the nails rimmed with soil. "They're searching the mountain with dogs today."

"That must be very difficult."

"It is."

"I lost a daughter."

Maisie looked up. "I'm so sorry, Vince."

He looked over her head, back at the cove. "I never get used to it. But—" He sighed, a sound so quiet she almost missed it.

"But?" she prodded gently. Because what came then? What could change the fact that you never recovered?

Vince put his hands behind his back and spoke in an almost apologetic tone. "But the love stays. I still have all my love for my child. When Nora died, I grieved because I desperately wanted to give her more. With all my heart, I wish she could've had more of all this beauty." He paused, taking in the view.

"I know." *Careful.* Already, Vince's last words bounced off her like raindrops off a roof tile. Wishes were treacherous sinkholes. Off-limits.

"A drunk driver took that away from her. She was coming home late at night, and he…" His voice changed, becoming lower and quieter. "You know, she was a very happy person. She was glorious. And here is what I hold on to."

Maisie looked up. His eyebrows were streaked with gray like his hair.

He held her gaze, his eyes kind. "I believe that nothing could have filled my girl with more love than she already carried in her heart."

"I know." Alex was like that, too. He was full of

love. Love for everything, love for life.

Vince gently continued. "And so Nora had everything we get here on earth; a longer life had nothing more significant or more beautiful to give her."

"What about having her own kids?" Maisie whispered.

Vince nodded. "I don't know whether children fill us with more love than we were born with or whether it simply makes us aware of what was already there. I often wonder. Though she would have been a good mother, and I—" He broke off and cleared his throat.

"I'm sorry I asked. I'm so sorry. Forgive me." Maisie's heart hurt for him. "But you know, my son's only missing," she added, the words stumbling out of her mouth. "He isn't… I don't know if people say he's—but there's no evidence that he's…"

Vince rubbed his chin. "That must come with its own heartbreak."

"Yes." Her voice was barely a whisper.

"Would you like me to leave? I didn't mean to intrude on your day or your feelings."

Maisie stopped herself before she could blurt out the first thing on her mind. Swallowing, she made time to form new ones. "Maybe—maybe we could just take a very short walk? Stay close enough to the house so my phone still works?" She hesitated. What was saying too much? "I wouldn't mind company while I wait. For the search party. To call. I don't know if that's…"

He straightened. "How about we save the walk

for a better time, and I'll just wait with you? You can let me know anytime if you want to be alone. I may carry my own feelings on my sleeve, but I don't offend easy."

His face was open, the skin lined with the sorrow and laughter of a lifetime. No, Vincent Grey didn't offend easily. He wasn't fragile. He'd been burned with fire and come out strong and kind, and he wouldn't mind if she suddenly decided she wanted to be alone.

"Would you like a glass of water while I clean up?" She gestured at her dirty clothes. "I wish I could offer you some lemonade or iced tea. But I didn't go shopping since I'm not staying long."

He waved both offer and explanation away. "Maybe I can start digging the hole for your new tree? If it's not presuming too much."

"Oh. Well, that would be great." Planting a tree sounded easy, but digging any sort of hole in the rocky soil of the coast was exhausting work. Maisie's back already hurt from weeding; she was that out of shape.

"Good. If you give me a spade and tell me where you want it, I'll get busy while you wash up." He inclined his head. "Not that you need to, mind. You look enchanting."

Maisie smiled.

Of course she didn't look enchanting. Far from it. But she believed Vince spoke the truth when he said he didn't mind the dirt from gardening. Her new neighbor had the ability to see deeper than that by far.

Chapter 25

Sam wiped the sweat from her brow. The cove always made for a warm climate, but this was ridiculous. The air practically dripped with jungle-like moisture. Insects launched themselves from grasses and leaves, buzzing in and out of her vision. Sam swatted them away, the brush clippers in her hand poking at the air. Gnats. And tiny electric blue bees that wanted the salt on her skin. A yellowjacket kept coming back to check out her yellow T-shirt.

Wearily, Sam eyed the little bit of brush still left between them and the blueberry patch. It wouldn't take long now. She and Tommy had cut most of the brambles and vines, clearing the path.

"You okay?" Sam called out and scratched her neck. Not that long ago she'd made him Goldfish snack bags, and now he was doing most of the work.

Tommy gave her a thumbs-up. "How about you?"

"Hanging in there, kid." She looked over her shoulder. Again, the trees and bushes felt more like a tightening net than a forest.

Or maybe she was just sleep-deprived. The night before her mind had churned, groping through memories for places the dogs could check. Places the kids had liked to go. Berry fields and bonfire spots and teenage hideaways that Alex could possibly have reached by foot.

Places he'd liked. Places he might've gone to end his life even though Maisie didn't believe her son would have chosen to. Sam hacked at a kudzu vine the size of her arm. She didn't believe it either. Nobody did. Unlike Robert with his quiet, repressed nature, Alex had been a child of the sun and the sea. Always laughing, always happy, always kind. She tossed the vine as far as she could. It hit a low branch and flopped to the ground.

Of course, you could never tell. Teens were good at playing their cards close to the chest.

In the end, none of them knew what he'd felt the day he disappeared. How far had his teenage despair gone? Maybe Bonnie's girl really had broken his sweet, inexperienced heart.

"That should do it." Tom brushed by Sam, waving.

Sam let her clippers sink and stepped through the opening he'd hacked. So the clearing was still here; the blueberry bushes had held their own against invading saplings. Sam looked around, remembering.

The dog handlers came rustling down the path and stepped into the clearing. "Where? Here?"

"All around here," Sam said helplessly, spreading her hands at the large field. "I guess."

"Okay." The handlers urged the dogs around the

field, snapping their fingers where they wanted the dogs to sniff.

Sam swayed.

Despite lolling tongues and happy grins, the dogs' goofiness vanished the moment they heard the search command. Freddy was still young and sometimes circled back to his handler as if he had a question, but Pamela, older and more experienced, never took her nose off the task. Her long ears stirred up scents from the forest floor; the folds of her skin channeled them to her sensitive nose. Pam's focus fascinated Sam.

As long as she didn't sit down and started barking.

Just as long as Pam and Freddy didn't find anything to bark about.

The handlers had almost circled the clearing. Sam forced herself to take a breath. Alex wasn't here. They'd checked the field on the second or third day after he'd disappeared; they would've found him.

She glanced at Tommy. He too looked relieved.

Maybe now they could wrap up. Get back home. She wanted to take a shower and wash the sticky day off, shampoo her hair and rinse the search away with the suds.

Her stomach grumbled and she pressed a hand against her midriff.

Tommy had heard it too. "Are you hungry? I have protein bars if you want."

Sam shook her head. "That's just my stomach telling me I'm nervous."

"It's tense, isn't it? I have just one more place to check if that's okay." Tom looked almost embarrassed. "Alex and I found a small...well, cave for lack of a better word. I mean, barely. I'd honestly forgotten all about it. We went only that one time."

"Couldn't sleep last night either?" Sam sighed. "I've been trying to think of the best places to check, too."

"I've been trying to think of places to check every night for ten years now." Tommy shrugged his shoulders. "It's just so unlikely he came up here."

"*Something* out of the ordinary happened," Sam said softly, watching the dogs. "So we might as well check. But then we stop. The podcasters have enough for a story."

Tommy pulled out a protein bar and studied it, then dropped it back into his backpack. "That's the forever question, isn't it," he muttered. "When should we stop looking?"

Sam waved a mosquito away. "You can't spend your life looking, Tommy," she said automatically. "At some point, you have to call it. Don't you think?"

"I just don't know."

Sam didn't even think that herself. If she were the mom, she'd likely do what Maisie had done: give her life to find her son. What else could a parent do?

But the kids... When the first shock wore off, it had become clear that Alex's disappearance wasn't going to be an open-and-shut case for them, either. No. It was ongoing horror that still kept them up at night.

Suddenly, one of the handlers called out. "Ma'am?"

Sam exchanged a glance with Tommy. Then she hurried over to the handler, trampling berry bushes and conifer saplings in her haste, Tommy right behind her.

"Ma'am, Freddy wants to go back in there." The elderly lady in khaki field pants pointed into the brush at the edge of the clearing. She was holding Freddy by his collar. The retriever didn't strain against the hold but stared intently at the undergrowth. Sam followed his stare. Lots of young trees. Trees that could've been knee-high seedlings ten years back.

"Is there something back there? He's set on it," the handler said.

The air frizzled with stress, raising the hair on Sam's neck. She tried to remember what used to be here but couldn't. "Tommy?"

Tommy rubbed his chin. "Wasn't there a big fallen oak here?" He looked around. "I think we used to play on the trunk... Do you remember that? There was a poison ivy vine on it, and all us kids got burned. I think I was ten. Remember?"

"Oh yeah." Dimly, the memory resurfaced. "Ellie and Cate used a plastic bag to pull off the vine so it wouldn't happen again. Turned out the bag had a hole." Now that Tommy had described the scene, images from the past fluttered up like moths. Ellie's burned hand. That's how they'd found out Cate wasn't allergic. Yes. "There was a tree at the end of the clearing; you're right."

Sam turned to the handler, who was still holding Freddy back. "We should check it out."

They started chopping their way through as best they could. Blackberry thorns hooked into Sam's clothes and scratched her skin, leaving itchy claw marks that drew bugs like an open bar. It took time, but eventually, they'd hacked a narrow path from the blueberry field into a smaller, more overgrown opening. At the far side was the old, fallen oak still.

"Go check," the handler said and gave Freddy leash. Pam, who'd finished her round and had joined them, followed eagerly.

Without hesitation, the dogs ran to the fallen oak, sat, and barked. Freddy low and short. Pamela bayed in a keen that rose and fell.

"No." Tommy covered his mouth with his hand.

"Of course not," Sam muttered. Reflexively, she grabbed Tommy's hand as if he were five and she had to keep him from running over and seeing what the dogs had found.

The handlers strode over to the dogs, rewarding them with treats and praise.

"Come on," Tommy said, his voice hoarse.

"Tommy, you stay here," Sam ordered. "I don't want you to—"

Stress pulled on his mouth. "Nice try, Sam. I'm not a kid anymore. *You* stay here. You're old, who knows how your heart's holding up." The joke came out harsh and prickly, a scratchy coping mechanism.

Sam tried to help him out; she tried to chuckle,

but her throat was dry, and it turned into a choked sound instead. Was this it? Had they *found* him? "I'm telling your mom you're rude," she whispered.

"Sorry, ma'am," Tom murmured. "Let's go see, Sam."

Sam couldn't feel her legs, but they walked her over to the small group gathering around the dogs anyway. Jim was already there talking into his cell phone. Ashley stood wide-eyed, one hand on her cheek, the other one holding onto the arm of the sound guy.

"We're taking the dogs back over to get them out of the way." The handler tried to move Pamela, but she was rooted to the spot. Freddy was already trotting off with his owner, proudly carrying a purple rag toy.

"Does this mean there's…" Sam couldn't see anything.

"Yes, ma'am. There are probably human remains here."

Sam swallowed. "Can you see them?"

The woman shook her head. "Not yet. But both dogs marked; I promise there's something here. Here, Pam…" She coaxed the hound away, offering bits of chicken and praise. Jim and Ashley followed.

Sam tried to take a breath. The tension pressed down on her like an unexpected wave. She couldn't think. She—

"Look." Tommy picked up a stick and pointed.

Sam leaned forward. Deep in the long, dried grass of years gone by, something poked out of the ground. Something gray and porous.

"Sam, that's it." Tommy dropped the stick and put his hands on his knees as if he'd run a marathon. "That's where Alex has been all this time. I can't believe it. I can't believe—he's just here."

Sam tore her eyes off the bone. What was visible was small, smaller than her palm and corroded, but she'd seen the dipped curve, knew that once it had been smooth and white and covered in cartilage.

The head of a leg bone. Maybe an arm.

She reached out and put a hand on Tommy's shoulder. "Come on. Come away."

"I need to..." His words trailed off, and he straightened. Sam almost caught her breath. Tommy's eyes were wide with shock, the way they'd looked back when his friend first went missing.

"Come on. Let's get out of here." Sam herded Tommy back to where the podcasters had huddled together. She tapped him on the shoulder, feeling dazed. "Jim. It's him."

Jim, his face pale with either shock or excitement, looked like he was going to throw up. He swallowed. "Are you sure? How can you be sure? I mean —we shouldn't get our hopes up; it could just be a deer."

"It's Alex." Sam inhaled, though the air suddenly seemed tainted with the sweet smell of death. She spat out the air. "But do what you have to do."

"Sir?" Pam's handler had come back. Both dogs were leashed to a birch tree, watching the scene with canine composure. "Don't go back. We should call the police."

The muscles in Jim's neck relaxed. "Yes. We don't want to disturb anything."

The handler turned to Sam and Tommy. "We should also all stay here until somebody comes. Since you know where we are, could you make the call?"

"Yes." Tommy fumbled for his cell phone. "I know the cop that's on the case. She'll come right up; she knows we're here with the dogs today." He walked away, trying to find reception, and the podcasters restlessly traipsed after him.

"Great," the handler said, her voice calm and encouraging. Casually, without making eye contact, she reached out and put a hand on Sam's arm.

The woman's touch, stranger though she was, flowed through Sam like electricity, and it was as if the current zapped the shock that was coursing through Sam. She flinched. But she could feel her legs again. The air was pristine once more, the forest around her alive with birds and bugs. The net lifted.

"Are you all right, ma'am?" The handler took her hand off Sam's arm, as casually as she'd put it there.

Sam blinked hard and rubbed the spot on her arm. It felt hot. As if a mosquito had stung her. "Yes. I'm—I just have to make a call, too," she stuttered.

The handler nodded. "Remember that identification can take a while."

"I know it's him."

The handler glanced at Sam, a quiet smile on her lips. "Mind what you say, my dear."

What was that supposed to mean? "Is there a chance it's not human bones?"

"No, ma'am. The dogs only mark human bones. It's human. But you know—always could be someone else."

"Okay." It wasn't like their forest was strewn with missing persons. "I'll just—I'll just make that call now."

Sam dialed, closed her eyes, and held the phone up to her ear. She heard the handler's footsteps retreating.

"Yes."

"Maisie? Maise, listen…the dogs have found something near the blueberry field, but we don't know yet if—Are you—Yes, probably human, but we can't—Maise, take a breath, sweetheart. Sit down. Is someone with you?"

Vince was with her. They were sitting in the sand on the beach.

Sam tried to swallow the urge to cry, but it vibrated in her voice when she spoke. "Listen, Maisie. I think it's Alex. But we do not *know*. We don't know who it is, or what happened, or anything. We don't even—" She took a shaking breath. "We don't even know what exactly it *is* we found. Tommy's called Sophia at the station. She'll cordon everything off, so don't come up here. I don't want you to—I'll stay. We'll be on the phone the entire time, Maisie. Okay? Are you okay?" It was a rhetorical question, the answer as clear as the cloudless sky.

Maisie was not okay. Nothing was okay.

So Sam started talking, rambling on about the search, talking as calmly as she could, listening to Maisie's breathing. At first it was ragged, panicked, then it deepened into quick, dry sobs. The sobs sounded like empty buckets drawn from a well, a well Sam recognized but whose depth she hadn't fathomed. The rattling, scraping sobs scared her.

Sam stood with the phone pressed to her ear, desperate to soothe a grieving mother as she stared at the old fallen oak that had marked a grave for so long. No wonder. No wonder they hadn't seen him there, half buried under poison ivy and blackberries even before the soft ground claimed him. They'd searched the blueberry patch, calling and shouting his name. And he'd been only yards away, hidden in that slim strip between clearing and forest, no man's land the eye instinctively skipped.

"There they are." Tommy stepped beside her and pointed.

Behind the trees, Sam saw a line of people coming up the trail. They were carrying large backpacks, equipment. Sophia, who had inherited the case, led the small troop.

Sam felt a small rush of gratitude as she described what she saw for Maisie. They hadn't just sent a ranger to check it was really a human bone. Sophia knew what—and who—they'd found, and she came prepared to secure the scene and take charge. She waved, and Sam raised a hand in return.

"Maisie, Sophia's come. I'll go talk to her, okay? Do you want to be on speaker? Okay. Hang on." Sam switched to speaker, put a finger to her lips, and handed it to Tommy. She motioned him to go meet the cops.

Before they got here, she'd go and look again at what was behind the tree trunk. Her stomach swam inside her abdomen, tilting this way and that like an empty barrel. Her body didn't want another look. But once the police took over, Sam wouldn't be able to double-check the image already burned into her retinas. But she needed to make sure.

Because if Maisie had any questions later, Sam owed her an answer.

Chapter 26

Maisie dropped her phone into the sand. She could still hear the voices of the podcasters squawking, the cops, Tommy, everything all mixed up, all meaningless.

It was over.

Everything was over.

The bones—the skeleton curled up behind the old oak tree—were all that was left of her baby. Alex. Alex was dead. He would never come back. The sudden clarity whipped away the cobwebs that for so long had spun a net around her soul, those of doubt and those of hope.

All that sleepless hope, hope hoarded in a decade of searching the internet for John Does, for Facebook pictures, for clues, came falling down on her. The weight crushed the air from her lungs.

"Maisie," Vince said. His voice came from behind rushing water. "Maisie, I'm going to end that call for you."

She didn't move. It didn't matter. Nothing mattered. She'd lost her child. She'd lost the race to find him, the battle of saving him. She'd lost everything.

Now, nothing mattered.

The chatter stopped, and there was only the lapping of waves and the screaming of gulls.

She didn't know how long she sat like that, her eyes unseeing, her heart hollowing deeper with every beat.

"Let's walk back," Vince finally said. "Let's get you a chair and a cup of tea with sugar. Can you come with me? Take my hand."

Tea with sugar. The words were simple enough for Maisie to grasp, and she nodded.

"Come on." Vince took her hand, put an arm around her waist, and pulled her to her feet.

She walked mechanically, one foot in front of the other, sand shifting with every step.

Like life. As if the foundation of life was shifting under her.

When they'd reached the house, Vince sat her on a chair in the sunroom, and Maisie obliged like a little child. He put his hands on the armrests and brought his face to hers, his brow frowning, his gaze going from her left eye to her right and back. "I know it's a foolish question, but I'm going to ask it anyway. Are you all right?"

Maisie nodded. She couldn't grasp the concept of being all right, but years of nodding when someone asked whether she was all right made her nod anyway. "I'm fine. Tea would be—" What was tea to her now? She didn't know.

Vince smiled a sad, warm smile that hooked into Maisie's soul, claiming a tiny spot for itself in the shifting sands. "I'll be right back." He disappeared.

Maisie looked out at the garden, the brown, the green. Blue water. She had to snap back. She had to pull out of it.

There was the spade. The wheelbarrow.

They were safe, and Alex's bones were lying up the mountain near the blueberry patch. She'd been looking in all the wrong places, followed all the wrong clues.

Only her fear had been correct. That he was gone and she couldn't get him back.

"Here." Vince set a steaming mug on the table beside Maisie's chair. "It will help if you will drink it."

Trying to pull herself together, she picked up the mug and sipped. Earl Grey, cream, sugar. She sipped again.

"Would you like me to stay? Or I can leave," he asked. "Whatever you need."

She looked up at her neighbor. "I don't know." Her voice was pale. There was nothing in it.

"Then I'll stay until you do." Vince sat. He put one leg over the other, his tan hands resting on the arms of the chair, his eyes on the ocean. He wasn't afraid of her. He wasn't running away. He'd grieved a child himself. He knew.

"Yes. Thank you." Maisie took another sip. The tea warmed her throat, dulled the razor edge of pain in her chest.

The waves were blue, the sand was yellow, the grass was green, her son was dead.

"What do I do now?" Maisie asked. She let her

mug sink onto her lap.

Vince's eyes were kind. "Now you wait," he said. "It takes time."

"I have time," she responded. "But I don't want it. I don't want time without hope." A tear slid down her cheek. And another one. She didn't mean to cry, didn't feel like she was, but the drops kept falling. Calm and fast, dripping off her cheeks, running down her jaw, dripping on her hands.

Vince sighed. "No, we don't want it, not under those circumstances. We want our babies back with every fiber of our being, don't we."

"I love him so much." The tears fell faster.

"That's a good thing," her neighbor murmured. "Love is good. It keeps. It's the only thing that keeps."

Maisie swallowed a breath and set her cup on the floor. "Do you think he did it himself?" Once spoken, the words rung in her mind like a gong that wouldn't stop, sending tremor after tremor after tremor.

Vince ran a hand over his cheek. For the first time, he looked old. "I don't know. I didn't know your son. What do you think?"

Maisie didn't know.

Robert had.

Finally, Vince broke the quiet. "What happens next? What did Mrs. Bowers say?"

It took Maisie a while to return to the present. She cleared her throat, noting that the tears had stopped dripping. "The police are going to… They're investigating. They have to make a proper identification." She took a breath. "It should be quick; they have his dental records. I heard Tommy say they found a backpack."

Vince shook his head. "I'm so very sorry, Maisie." From his pocket, he pulled a handkerchief and handed it to her.

Maisie wiped her cheeks with its lavender softness. The sweet scent made new tears blur her vision, and she pressed the handkerchief to her mouth.

"Don't stop your tears. I'm sure your son deserves them. That too takes time. Everything takes its time," Vince murmured.

Maisie squeezed her eyelids shut. Already, they started to swell and burn. The anesthetic of the first shock was wearing off. What came next? "I can't do this, Vince."

She'd never said this before. She'd pulled up her big girl pants and done it, and done some more, pushed and pushed harder to find Alex. She'd done everything in her power.

But this?

She truly couldn't do this. She was done trying, and she was caving in to the grief that hollowed her. She could feel her body curling forward.

"Those roses over there need water," Vince said suddenly. "I believe a pair of secateurs could do a lot of good, too. Do you happen to have any?"

"In the garage," she said, her voice brittle.

"May I?"

She nodded.

When Vince returned, he held two pairs of secateurs and gardening gloves. "Come with me, Maisie. Let's get those roses straightened out."

Maisie looked at the shears he was offering. What did he want?

"Come cut roses with me," he repeated. "We still have all the love left, ours and theirs, and we can still do some good in this world. Let's start with your garden."

Maisie rose from her chair, slipped on the gloves, gripped the secateurs. "Shouldn't I call the police? Should I call Sam back?"

"You already know the end of the story, my dear," Vince said gently. "The details will come in time."

Maisie took a breath. She *needed* the details.

"Cut roses with me," Vince repeated. "Cut roses while you tell me about your son."

He led Maisie out of the sunroom and down the steps, to the rose bushes that stood neglected and forgotten.

"What color are they when they bloom?" he asked.

"Yellow. They're yellow roses." Her breathing was shallow. Did she have to call the police?

"Did Alex like roses?"

The vases... "He did. He liked roses. He never said it, but he would always let me know when it was time to change the cut roses."

Vincent clipped a brown twig. "What else did he like?"

"Oh. So much."

She knew what he was doing. But prompted, a part of her brain jumped to the things that Alex had liked, sorting through memories to turn them into stories, something she could say. "He liked his friends."

"A man who grew up on the coast and liked his friends and yellow roses." Vince smiled. "I very much wished I'd known him."

"Maisie?"

She looked up, blinking to clear her vision.

"Maisie. Sweetheart."

Ellie and Cate came down the patio steps, their arms already lifted.

"Sam told us." Ellie pulled her into a hug, and Cate joined.

The arrival of her friends loosened another coil in Maisie, and she started crying in earnest. Not the unfelt tears from earlier, but real tears erupting from her eyes like lava.

And then she lost track. She was led away from the roses and into her bedroom, she was laid on the bed, curled up, and cried herself to sleep, a friend on each side.

Alex was gone.

No amount of asking questions, following up on details, or cutting roses could make it better.

Chapter 27

The afternoon sun eyed the large magnolia in the driveway, drawing the pattern of its branches on the red door of Beach House. Maisie never locked it, not even now. Ellie knocked and let herself in. "Hello?"

"Hi." Cate, a bundle of papers in her arms, came out of the kitchen.

"How is she?" Ellie set her large tote bag on the floor. Carefully, so as not to upset the contents.

"Good, I think." Cate shifted the papers to free an arm and gripped Ellie's hand gratefully. "She's been working in the garden."

It'd been three days since the police took Alex's bones off the mountain, two since they'd been officially identified. The day after, Maisie had thrown herself into gardening. She didn't talk much, but she seemed okay. Calm. Present.

The podcasters had left, and Cate, Sam, and Ellie took turns staying in the old house so Maisie wasn't alone. Ellie slipped off her denim jacket and tossed it on the chair. "Gardening is good."

Cate gave her a tired smile. "Only she's been at it since five in the morning and hasn't let up."

"Good enough for now?" Ellie lifted her bag. "I brought lobsters. Maybe that'll cheer her up."

Cate grabbed her purse from the sideboard. "Nice. Well, Maisie's just come in to pull a splinter. Wish I could stay, but I have to get dinner ready for Allen and the kids. Have fun with your little friends."

Ellie grinned. "I always do."

"Bye, Maise!" Cate called toward the kitchen. "I'll see you tomorrow."

"Bye, Cate," Maisie's voice came back. "Thanks for the company."

"You bet, darling." Cate hitched her papers higher and left.

"Hey." Ellie went into the kitchen and placed her tote on the island.

Maisie was too skinny and there were blue shadows under her eyes, but she smiled and laid down the forceps she'd been holding. "Hi, Ellie." Maisie shook her hand. "Big splinter from the rose bush."

"Ouch." Ellie went to her friend and put her hands on her shoulders, turning her this way and that for a better look. "You seem okay. Tired and sad, but not despondent."

"I'm trying."

"Good girl." Ellie kissed her on the cheek—she was neither a hugger nor a kisser, but sometimes it felt good—and stepped back again. "Listen, no more gardening for you. I hear you're going crazy out there. We don't want crazy."

"There's just so much to be done." Maisie shook her head. "The more I do, the more I notice. You have no idea."

"No, probably not. Ha." Ellie didn't have a green thumb. There were a couple of spider plants on the mantle in her house and some living stones lined up on the bathroom windowsill, but that was it for her house plants. Her yard was left to do what it liked as long as she could access the faded-blue Adirondack chair in the middle. Dale forever threatened to hire landscapers, but so far, Ellie had managed to weasel out of organizing her green chaos. She liked it.

"I need your help, Maisie." Ellie untied the leather strap of her bag and gingerly reached inside.

"What's that?"

One by one, Ellie pulled out the three lobsters she'd bought from Bonnie the week before and put them on the island. "Lobsters."

"Did you wrap them in seaweed?"

"It keeps them moist." The iodine scent of kelp and seawater filled the kitchen. Ellie looked up and saw Maisie smile. It was the first since Alex had been found.

Ellie smiled back, busy keeping the lobsters from scuttling off the kitchen island. "I had them cooled down, but they're waking up now. We better do this quickly. Could you grab that one?" She nodded at Garnet Boy and picked up the two others herself.

"Oh, Ellie." The smile almost reached Maisie's eyes. "How's your market doing these days?"

"I know. But just look at them. Dale's fixated on

eating these gorgeous creatures."

"Ells, you're a fishmonger." Maisie lifted the big lobster, its jointed legs crawling the air. "Shouldn't you be *selling* your wares?"

Ellie headed toward the patio door. "I should, but I don't want to. It's hardly going to make a difference one way or the other."

"I'm surprised your business has survived this long."

"Me, too. Hey—just in case Dale asks you, we've eaten these bad boys tonight."

Maisie looked surprised, following her out the sunroom. "You think he might follow up with me on what happened to them?"

Ellie tried not to sound guilty. "It's become a weird thing between us. I don't think he would actually call. But, just in case. Because that's what I'm going to tell him if he asks me." She left the sunroom, then led the way across the lawn to the stairs down to the beach.

"And why don't you want to eat them, Ellie?"

"They belong to the sea, not to us. And listen, the entire boiling water thing? I can't stand the thought of it. I've always tried to tell myself it's just the way it is, but you know what?" They climbed down to the beach, their feet sinking into the loose sand.

"I really don't."

"I don't want to try anymore. I choose to save lobsters. Putting them back in the sea makes me feel a lot better than eating them."

"Okay. I don't like the boiling water thing myself.

Nobody does."

The sun was drifting toward the bay, and both sky and water shimmered gold and purple. The beach was almost deserted; only one lone person stood far off on a dune, hair fluttering in the breeze. Ellie squinted at them but couldn't make out who it was in the fading red light.

Not Dale, anyway.

Ellie stopped. "Will you look at that." She'd lived here all her life. She'd seen the sun go down over the water a thousand times, and still the spectacle took her breath. "How beautiful." Even the lobsters wriggling in her hands seemed to quiet and dip their antennae as if bowing to Mother Sea.

Maisie made an exasperated sound. "Uh, Ells, I need to put this thing down. It's doing the tail-whip thing."

"Okay, come here." Ellie went down to the waterline. "Um, hold this one too for a minute."

"Aah, I don't want to." But Maisie took the proffered lobster; both her prisoners waved their great claws at the ocean, ready to go home.

"I just need to..." Ellie slipped off the bands that bound his claws.

"Careful, they're snappy," Maisie said.

"All good." Before the lobster could realize he was once again able to pinch fingers, Ellie had set him into the shallow water and let go. "Godspeed!" she called after him. "Go hide better than last time!"

The lobster sat for a moment in a confused rush of oxygen, then scuttled off toward deep rocks, sweet kelp, and safety.

"Here, do this one quick, or he's going to jump in all by himself."

"Gimme." Ellie took the second lobster and freed him, and last, Garnet Boy. "Have lots of babies!" she called after them.

Maisie chuckled. "Some fishmonger you are."

Ellie wrapped her arms around herself. "So? Makes me happy."

"Good."

Ellie leaned against Maisie's shoulder, her eyes on the glimmering water, the wind lifting her hair and mingling it with that of her beach sister. "Do you think you could be happy again sometime, Maise?"

Maisie put an arm around Ellie, holding her. "I don't know. I feel empty. There's nothing, only one moment after the other. I can't tell at all what I'll be."

"What happens next? Did they tell you?"

"There's an autopsy. Sophia promised it'd be soon. She's also going to let me know what's on his phone. She said they might be able to recover some messages."

"Oh man." Ellie sighed. Alex's waterproof backpack had been found under the fallen oak; it'd been safeguarded from the elements by layers of leaves and vegetation and the great trunk that hid it. His cell phone had been zipped into an inside pouch. "No wonder you garden all day. I'd go crazy waiting for that call."

"I *am* going crazy." Maisie sounded surprised. "It's burned me out. I already know how the story ends, but whatever is on that phone—Ells, if it's bad —I don't know how I'll bear it."

"I hear you." Ellie didn't try to reassure Maisie. The story wasn't over, closure still elusive. They put on brave faces, but there was only a wafer-thin layer of pretense between their usual routines and actual horror. Grading, gardening, releasing lobsters back into the sea—underneath flowed the great anxiety of finding out what Alex had gone through before he died.

How Maisie bore it, Ellie had no idea. She only knew that they'd all agreed not to let her out of sight, in case the thin layer lifted for even a moment. Maisie put up with them, probably because she had no energy left to protest her guard.

They stood arm in arm, looking out over the sea.

"I thought I'd be so happy in my fifties," Maisie said quietly. "I was looking forward to having my garden, and the beach, and you girls. More time to travel with Robert, Alex in college…"

"I know." Ellie's fall to reality was nothing like Maisie's, but she too had imagined herself in a better spot. She'd figured she'd grow closer to Dale; reclaim the connection they'd had when they first got married. That Tommy would find someone, that she could get her shop to turn a comfortable profit. But it wasn't like that; Tommy had no time or inclination to date or move out. Her market had become too small and expensive to compete with supermarket seafood counters. And Dale…

"Should we go in?" Ellie asked as the last of the

gold in the sky turned a tarnished bronze.

"Yep."

They turned and made their way back through the shifting sand, the soft swell of waves, and the secret life of lobsters whispering behind them.

Maisie was walking ahead, her shoulders hunched.

Compassion welled up in Ellie's heart. Never mind her petty complaints. She had Tommy and all his future ahead of her. She could try harder to recover the slipping connection with her husband. She still had all the cards in her hand, and that in itself was great good luck.

Climbing the steps in the wake of Maisie's grief, Ellie made a vow. She'd do more. Try harder. Take life by the horns and make it happen. She could start with her business. She'd have that dreaded conversation with Dale, negotiate the money to expand her store. It would make the profit Dale had always looked for. They'd both be happier, and a tighter connection between them would follow. Then she'd find Tommy a nice place in the village and help him move. He'd be looking for company soon enough if he was on his own.

Yes, she was lucky. She could make her dreams happen, and she'd not waste any more precious time.

Chapter 28

Maisie glanced at the patio, which was bathed in the light of late morning. The girls—all three of them—had abandoned their gardening tasks and were lounging on the wicker chairs, lemonade tumblers in their hands and sunglasses on their noses.

"Yes, I can talk." She stepped behind a small dogwood tree that had already sprouted its leaves. It hid her pretty well, and she wanted privacy for this call.

"I just got the go-ahead to call." Sophia, usually so professional, sounded nervous. Her voice was higher than usual. "Do you want to come to the station?"

Maisie swallowed. There was no way she could bear the tension of waiting. "Tell me now," she said. "Is it bad?"

"Oh Maisie, I don't know how to answer that. I mean..."

Maisie grabbed a branch. The rough bark was real, something to hold on to. "Go ahead. Tell me what you've got."

"Okay. He exchanged a few texts with his friends, the times and contents confirming their testimonies. Nothing we didn't know about. But then—" Sophia cleared her throat and inhaled audibly. "But then he tried to text you. A few times. The messages didn't go through. Reception in Beach Cove was even worse back then than it's now."

"Oh." Maisie exhaled shakily. He'd texted her.

"Do you have someone with you, Maisie?" Sophia sounded choked up.

"Yes. Read me the texts."

"It's from your son for you, Maisie. I don't want to read them out loud. That doesn't feel right. But I'll stay on the line with you. I'm sending them to you now."

Maisie's cell phone vibrated as Sophia's email landed in her inbox. With shaking fingers, she tapped on it.

There was no introduction from Sophia, no explanation.

Only her son's last words.

Mom, I took walk because really upset. No worries food ate huge bag of chips. Going up cliff need some quiet and alone. Love you see you later

Mom, I'm by blueberry place. Super thirsty from chips and is hot lol Lucky found wild grapes, check photo. Sour but juicy ate a bunch. Be back dinner

Mom, I'm sick. Can you ask Dad get me?

Did you get my texts? I'm really sick stomach

Mom, I wish you'd get my texts. Prob not going thru. I'm by old oak stomach cramps and throwing up. I'm dizzy. Don't be mad if I don't make it dinner I come when can

I love you, Mom. I love Dad. I love you. See you soon I hope

And that was it.

Sophia's soft words broke through the haze. "Maisie?"

Maisie's voice trembled, but she marshaled it. "Did you get the photo of the grapes he ate?"

"Sending it now."

Maisie's phone vibrated again, and she opened the jpg attached to the email.

Yes. There they were. Dangling from the hand of her son was a cluster of little dark berries framed by lobed leaves.

"Oh sweetheart," she whispered, tears starting to blur the image. "Those aren't wild grapes, my love."

"Maisie?"

"Hmm."

Sophia's voice was as soft as spring rain. "I think we can settle the cause of death. We sent the image to poison control. It looks like Alex ate a number of Canadian moonseed berries, thinking they were wild grapes."

Maisie nodded, but it took her a moment to form words. "Yes, that's Canadian Moonseed. I didn't know it grows up in the forest."

"One of the patrol officers is into plants. He went up there and found moonseed vines all around the clearing. I'm sorry." She cleared her throat. "Uh, the pathologist said it could've been fast."

"Yes."

"So the medical examiner is going to put that

down as cause. And then... Maisie, I think we are done with our part. We're ready to release his remains." Sophia couldn't keep her voice even and stopped.

She'd known Alex, too. He'd been on the top of her list for years, too.

"Thanks, Sophia. Thank you." Without waiting for an answer, Maisie ended the call.

She had gotten the answer.

It'd been an accident. He'd eaten poisonous berries. Lots of them because he was thirsty from his chips and full of glee at his find.

He'd suffered, hoping she'd come and help him. But when she didn't, he'd wanted her to know that he loved her.

I love you.

"I love you too, my sweet child," Maisie whispered. "I wish you'd brought some water that day. Or come home instead of taking a walk. I wish you were still here with me."

She waited until she could see where her feet stepped. Then she went to the patio and sat.

Ellie, Cate, and Sam fell silent. One by one, they stood.

"Maisie? Did you get a call?" Sam finally asked.

Maisie nodded. "He ate moonseed berries. He thought they were grapes." She held up her phone with the email still open. "He tried to text me." She handed the phone to Sam, who read and handed the phone on to Ellie, who handed it on to Cate.

"It was an accident." Ellie put a hand on her

heart, tears in her eyes. "Now we know...we know."

Maisie put her face in her hands. "I wish I could have gotten the text. I wish I could've..."

Sam rubbed a hand over Maisie's shoulders. She too sounded teary. "That's the thing with accidents; there are a thousand ways it could've gone better. You did what you could, sister. Best mom. You are, Maisie. You're the best mom Alex could've had."

"You want a cup of tea, Maisie?" Cate asked quietly. She looked sick.

Maisie took a breath that hitched in all the wrong places. There was so much in those few lines Alex had written her. She'd need years with those lines, but she didn't have to start right now. She could take her time.

Because she had time now, real time. The urgency of finding her son, of releasing him from whatever hell he was suffering was over, lost the evening he'd disappeared. Already, it was starting to flake off her like tiny chips of old paint.

She took a new breath, testing the air, shedding weight. "There's a bottle of wine in the fridge." She cleared her throat and tried again. "Let's get some glasses and sit on the beach. I want to see the water."

"On it." Ellie ran inside and got wine and glasses, and Cate found the beach blanket and Sam took Maisie's arm, and Cate said she'd run back to get some cheese because she had to drive later, and then they were on the beach.

Sitting side-by-side on the blue blanket, a glass of chilled white wine in their hand, their arms wrapped over each other's shoulders and waists as if they were twelve, not in their fifties.

The noon sun made the water sparkle; the seagulls screamed their song of fish and krill and wave.

"Here's to my baby boy." Maisie, hand shaking, lifted her glass to the cove that she loved and that her son had loved. He was gone, but all his love was still here.

The women raised their glasses. "To Alex," they said in unison.

The golden wine was cold as grief and sweet as sorrow, and they drank it together.

I love you, Mom.

I love you too, my darling.

Chapter 29

"Maisie?"

Cate set down her shopping bags and closed the front door behind her. The entrance hall of Beach House really was the pinnacle of sophistication. Ellie liked the sunroom, and Sam liked the big kitchen best. But the marble and mahogany, the graceful, wide staircase framed by those windows... It was something else.

"In here, Cate," Maisie's voice came from the kitchen.

Cate nodded to herself; Maisie sounded good. Strong. Well, stronger than the day before anyway. She wasn't the old Maisie, perfectionist, über-happy. That was over. But she was still perfect in her struggle to heal as best she could.

Alex's funeral had been two days ago.

Cate's eyes filled with tears again, and she swallowed. "I'll be there in a moment, just need to sort through this." She wasn't going to let Maisie see her cry. She rubbed her hand over her eyes and exhaled slowly and quietly, giving the images in her head time to resolve.

Maisie had invited only a handful of people. Other than Sam, Ellie, and Cate, there'd only been Robert's mother and his sister. Two skinny women, one in her eighties, one in her sixties. They were the only remaining family Maisie had, but they'd stayed only for the interment. The second it was over, a navy Bentley had whisked them away again.

Maisie didn't talk about Robert's family, but it was clear that they vaguely blamed her for his passing. From what little Cate knew about them, Robert's family wasn't caring. To them, compassion was like an expense, necessary only as prescribed by society.

Cate checked her face in the mirror. Too plump. Too sad.

The lack of family hadn't mattered. With Maisie's blessing, Sam had put the date of Alex's funeral into the Starfish Report. And Beach Cove had responded. Men, women, kids, even babies in carriages had crowded the tiny cemetery on Church Hill. Alex had lived all his short life in this town, had gone to school and church and community events here, had played baseball and football on the local teams, had volunteered for their causes. He'd always been part of the town, one of the kids. But when he'd disappeared, he'd become everyone's child and everyone's brother.

There wasn't an adult soul in Beach Cove that hadn't taken part in a search, feared for his safety, and hoped for his return. All of Beach Cove grieved for his death, and they all needed closure. A hand touching the casket, a coming-together to confirm that yes, this was real. Their son had come home at last, and they poured out their love with flowers, handshakes, and the wish to say so much more than they could.

Okay. Cate blinked and checked the mirror again. The red in her eyes was almost gone; she didn't look like she'd been crying, just like she was tired. Which she was.

"Have you eaten?" Rallying, Cate carried her bags to the kitchen. "Ellie was selling mussels, so I bought some. They're clean; all we'd have to do is cook them."

"There you are. I thought you'd left again." Maisie, dressed in a soft white shirt and cuffed jeans, greeted her with a smile. "Perfect timing, I was just thinking about dinner. You know, I'm starting to feel guilty. I haven't been to the market once since I got here."

"No worries, Maisie. We're glad we can pitch in." Cate put the nets holding the mussels in the sink. There were a lot of them. "Is it okay if Claire and Emily eat with us tonight? Allen isn't home, and the girls seemed a little lost this morning."

"You don't have to ask. They are welcome anytime. But also Cate, if you're needed at home... I'm fine. Well, not fine. But I'm okay. You've—" Maisie stopped, and Cate looked up, surprised.

"You've been great, you three," Maisie said, her voice choked up. "I know it's been hard on you to get me through this, and I didn't exactly deserve it after all these years of being out of touch. But I'll take care of myself now, I promise." She cleared her throat.

"What's this, Maise? No worries."

Maisie shook her head as if Cate had made the understatement of the year. "I don't want to be a burden."

"Aww, you aren't a burden. I'm glad I get to come over here. I'm just so glad to be able to hang out again, you know? And honestly, it's nice to be in Beach House. Being at home just makes me think about all the chores I have to do." She chuckled.

Maisie tilted her head. "Really?"

Cate nodded. But instead of trying to explain how she couldn't relax in her own house—the fate of any working mother—she ripped open the nets and started rinsing the mussels.

"You know what they do in France?" Maisie said, peering over her shoulder. "Oh, those are spectacular. Look at the size." She picked up a mussel to admire it. "Leave it to Ellie! Where does she get these from?"

"Bonnie's catch," Cate replied, pleased at the change of topic. "Ellie says she buys all her best seafood from Bonnie."

Maisie's throat moved, but when she spoke, her voice sounded the same as before. "So do you know what we ate with mussels in France?"

"Crusty brown bread with garlic butter?" Cate shook a sourdough loaf from its paper wrap. Still warm from the oven, the comforting smell of fresh bread filled the room.

"That's definitely what *we're* having." Maisie inhaled. "But back then, we had the mussels with French fries."

"French fries, huh? That's weird."

"But *so* good. Hot and crispy."

"I get it." Cate's stomach grumbled embarrassingly loud. "I'm the last one to turn down a nice French fry."

Maisie smiled. "Me too. How about a glass of wine while we cook? I'm not an expert, but I remember Robert liked Vouvray with seafood."

While they steamed their dinner in a broth with garlic and bay leaf, cut the bread, and mixed a crock of garlic butter, they sampled the Vouvray. Cate had never heard of it, but Robert had had style, and the wine was perfect for the moment.

Claire and Emily joined them after soccer practice was over, and Maisie dug up a clean towel so Claire could shower before they ate. After her second glass, Emily decided they needed a salad to stay healthy and called Tommy to ask if he could come and bring one.

Minutes later, Tommy arrived and brought his mother, a huge bowl of bacon frisée salad, two more bags of mussels washed and ready to cook, a pan of sizzling hot, deliciously salty French fries, and another tray of garlic bread.

Claire joined them again, a towel turban wrapped around her head, and started to put Robert's records on the turntable in the sunroom. After a few tries, Claire settled on Maria Callas. Arias floated onto the patio and garden, the notes weaving themselves into the rushing of waves and the whistling of sandpipers.

Maisie stood, watching their little group.

Cate smiled at her through the steam rising from the stockpot. Tom and Emily were sampling garlic breads and arguing over which one was better. Ellie had given up her unsuccessful search for salad tongs and was spooning Tom's salad-for-twenty into a china serving bowl. Claire's turban had fallen off, and the girl, hair dripping like a mermaid, was dancing from kitchen to patio and back with plates and silverware for the table, humming along to the music.

Catching her eye, Maisie smiled back. "We'll need another bottle or two," she declared. "Now that the kids are here. And maybe something sweet for dessert. I'll see what's in the basement."

"Sounds good to me."

Maisie disappeared. Ellie, dropping all pretense at being fancy, lifted Tommy's plastic bowl and let the salad gracelessly slide into the serving bowl. She scooped the spill off the counter and tossed it in the trash. "Maisie seems good, no?"

"Mm-hmm. Could you hand me the platter there? This batch is done." Using a slotted spoon, Cate started to scoop mussels from the broth.

Ellie inhaled the fragrance and sighed. "*I'm* good. I like being here. I missed Beach House. I missed Maisie."

Cate topped off the platter. "Same."

Ellie handed over the new tray and lowered her

voice to a whisper. "Did she say anything about leaving? She's already stayed a *lot* longer than she figured when she first came. I mean of course she has with everything that's happened. But what now?"

Cate didn't want to think about Maisie leaving. She shook her head. "I'm not sure I want to bring it up with her. I don't want her to leave. Beach House is… It's a little bit like the center of everything, isn't it?" She couldn't express it better than that. Beach House was beautiful, and everyone liked being in a beautiful house. But it was something else too; it was the spirit of the place. All of them had nice enough houses, yet none had replaced the role Beach House had played for their group. Sure they visited each other sometimes. But only here did they all seem equally comfortable.

"I know what you mean, Cate. I've seen much more of you and Sam since Maisie came back. I forgot how often we used to hang out. Obviously it's been unusual circumstances." Ellie's large eyes were thoughtful. "Do you think we'll drift apart again when Maisie leaves?"

Cate lowered new mussels into the broth and put the lid on the pot. They each had their own lives. Work, kids, husbands… Before Maisie returned, Cate had figured it was their schedules that kept them too busy to hang out. But suddenly, they were making time for each other. "I don't know, Ellie. Maybe. It seems so natural with Maisie here, doesn't it? If we have to, you know, *decide* that we will meet more often, it just becomes this item on our to-do lists. I don't mean…ugh." She chuckled. "Sorry, that came out wrong."

"No, I know exactly what you mean. With Maisie gone, the flow is missing. Not sure why, but I feel it too."

Cate put down her slotted spoon, and they each grabbed one of the heavy stoneware platters to carry outside. On the patio, the long teak table was already brimming with the china and crystal, food and flowers that Maisie and Claire had arranged, and it took some jostling to make space for the main course.

The air was salty, La Traviata wept to the peeping of the sandpipers, and a string of fairy lights Emily and Tommy had rigged around the pergola twinkled in the fading light. It threw Cate back to when all the kids had been happy, healthy, and chubby-cheeked, running around in their sun-faded swimsuits. Back then even the husbands had often joined in, taking turns in procuring fragrant, and probably illegal, after-dinner cigars.

"Done and done." Ellie looked out at the sea that waited deep and blue for the sun's good-night kiss. "Pretty, isn't she?"

"She?"

"The sea."

"The sea's a girl?" Coming back to the moment, Cate smiled. Leave it to Ellie to have an opinion on the Atlantic's gender.

"A girl?" Ellie's eyebrows rose. "The sea's a *queen*. Let's go get our wine glasses."

"I think you've had enough already, what with your queens and all." Cate chuckled. She felt safe and warm and happy.

Ellie was already turning back. "I haven't even finished my first glass, sister."

Cate followed her inside. "I met someone," she said without thinking.

Ellie grabbed her glass from the counter. "Wait—what? What do you mean, you *met* someone?"

Cate laughed at her big eyes. As if she, frumpy teacher that she was, was going to reveal a torrid affair. "Only the new pharmacist in town. Alan needed something, and I'd already been to the market and almost back at the car, so I didn't want to go back."

"Understandable," Ellie muttered.

"But I was near the old pharmacy, and I knew it had opened again, so that's where I went."

"Right." Ellie grinned. "That makes sense."

The fuzzy way Cate was telling her story, her need to share how she came to meet the pharmacist was silly. It made Ellie laugh. Cate cleared her throat. "So I went inside, and he was there," she concluded lamely.

"Right." Ellie's blue eyes were definitely laughing, and there was a glimmer in them that Cate had to squelch. Right away.

But to her surprise, she didn't *want* to. Cate picked up her glass, swirling the Vouvray. Wasn't *going* to. Why shouldn't she make a fool out of herself for once? She was under no obligation to be boring at all times. At least not with Ellie and not in this kitchen. Cate took a swig from her glass, feeling rakish.

"He was very—odd." She giggled, surprising herself. This was her second glass already. She looked at Ellie.

"How's that?"

"He gave me a tour of the pharmacy."

Ellie leaned forward. "There's nothing to tour. There's only the one room."

"Yes, but he showed me where the paper tissues were, and the..." Suddenly, Cate couldn't remember what he'd shown her. She could only remember the expression on his face.

"He said..." She leaned closer to Ellie, almost whispering now. Emily and Claire didn't need to hear this. "He said it'd be unethical to sell me a face mask because I looked perfect already." She straightened and took another sip of wine, watching Ellie's face. She felt like giggling but stopped herself because Ellie wasn't responding. Cate shouldn't have told her; she'd been laying it on too thick. Being cute didn't feel right. She wasn't cute. Cate cleared her throat. "I guess it's just his spiel. Bet he says the same thing to every woman coming to the pharmacy."

Ellie glanced at her. "I'm a woman and he didn't say it to me. He only said 'good morning' and 'are you ready to check out?' and 'thank you' when he handed me my change."

"Oh. Well." Cate's stomach squirmed. Had Calvin really given her special treatment? "Still, it was just a silly thing he did for attention."

Ellie laughed, low and quiet. "Oh Cate, you sound like a schoolteacher."

"That might be because—"

Ellie waved her to stop. "I know, I know. Listen, did you like him?"

"Calvin?"

"*Calvin*? Is that his name? Because he didn't mention it to me."

Cate set down her glass and put a hand on her stomach. "Obviously that's his name. Why would I mention some other man's name all of a sudden?" More squirming; an entire can of worms. She should drink some water. And eat something to soak up the alcohol.

"Uh-huh." Ellie smiled. "Cate, I *like* that you like him. Go for it. You need a little bit of fun."

Cate stared at Ellie, stricken. What did she mean by fun? Go for what? An *affair*?

"Are you two coming? The mussels are going to get cold." Maisie stood in the patio door, waving them to join the rest.

Cate hadn't noticed, but the rest of the group was already gathered on the patio. She'd been so looking forward to the feast, but now her appetite was gone. She stepped outside and took a breath. The air smelled of beach, of garlic and bay leaf.

Cate inhaled again. Well, her appetite wasn't *gone*. Maybe it was a little muffled.

They sat, and Cate soon found that she could block out any thoughts of the pharmacist. She had a good husband and daughters that needed her, and it was only her general midlife crisis that made her susceptible to Calvin's nonsensical flattery. Aging people made stupid mistakes out of boredom, but she was smart. She could do better. She wasn't throwing it all away for a silly compliment and a laugh.

They ate the mussels and sopped up the broth, had Tom's fries and bacon frisée and more wine while early Viburnum flowers glowed in the dark and the cove murmured long after Maria Callas had sung her last aria. At some point, Maisie dug out candles and set them on the table, and Claire wrought another chain of fairy lights around them.

When the main course was done and everyone leaned back, Maisie magicked up a tray of cocoa-dusted tiramisu. It turned out that Mr. Grey had created this symphony in marsala-and-mascarpone but begged off joining them for dinner. Cate eyed the creamy desert guiltily.

A small piece only.

"I'll make some mocha," Maisie said busily. "And brandy for those who like. Emily, would you mind helping clear the table and bring out dessert plates?"

"Sure." Emily jumped up, and her sister followed suit without having to be asked.

Cate smiled. She was so proud of her girls. Smart and beautiful and strong.

"Hey, I can help." Tommy got to his feet as well. "I clear tables for work." He smiled in his good-humored way.

Cate didn't miss the look he gave her oldest.

She tilted her head. She must've been mistaken. Now her pathetic middle-aged brain made her see things.

Averting her gaze, Cate looked at Ellie, who was sitting opposite. Arms comfortably crossed, Ellie's own eyes were on Cate. The glimmer was back in her eyes; Cate could see it even in the flickering light of the candles.

She set down her wine glass, picked up her water, and took a long, thirsty drink.

Tomorrow, she'd call Allen at the conference center. Talk to him. Be a little fun, a little seductive. Try, anyway. Maybe she could make mussels again when he got back home, and they'd have a nice dinner together.

She hadn't tried hard enough lately. Well, for a while. She hadn't cared to try for a while.

Chapter 30

Sam put the last book on the shelf, cut the last carton box flat for stacking, and only then allowed herself to check the phone. It was well past eleven. Dark outside, too. Sam stretched, trying to unknot her back and neck after lifting books all day. It'd taken most of the day and a good chunk of the evening, but she'd finally gotten the new books priced, sorted, and shelved.

Sam glanced at her handiwork, admiring the neat rows of unfamiliar spines gracing the shelves. The old books would love the new additions…hopefully. With a sigh, she swiped the screen on her phone, revealing a slew of messages she'd missed.

Looked like she'd missed out on dinner at Maisie's. Maisie, Ells, Cate, and sweetly, even little Claire had texted Sam to join them.

Sam smiled; it didn't happen often that she got a bunch of invitations. She'd missed the dinner, which was a bummer. It'd been fun, no doubt. But it was heartwarming to know she'd been missed herself.

It was almost like before. Before Alex took a walk; before the sky broke and fell on their heads. But Maisie was going to leave them soon. Sam hadn't heard Maisie mention it, but she could feel it in her bones. It was a feeling like an open suitcase, ready and waiting but not yet packed.

She'd text the girls back tomorrow. Maybe she'd invite them to the bookstore to admire her new books. But really, to eat cheese and drink wine. And talk.

Because they talked again... She'd missed talking with the girls. It was different than talking to Larry. It was like Sam had a brain for talking to her husband and another brain entirely for her friends. The two brains were as different from each other as men were different from women. One by itself left her unbalanced.

Maisie's return had shifted Sam's world back toward balance. The girls coming together had.

Larry wasn't an easy person at the best of times, but lately he'd seemed even stranger than usual.

Sam tapped on a text she'd gotten from him. He was busy working and would sleep in the office, if at all, and not to wait for him.

Point proven...

What are you working on? Sam texted him. Why, she didn't know. She didn't even expect a response back.

But her thumb had barely slipped off the keyboard when he replied.

new stuff weird am tired sleep soon don't disturb

Sam clucked her tongue at the tone and tucked the phone away. Larry could be mysterious if it suited him. She was too tired to engage in his shenanigans anyway.

She might call him tomorrow… After she'd slept, had at least three mugs of straight black coffee, and maybe eaten some scrambled eggs. Probably he'd unearthed an old manuscript that had sucked him in. With Larry, every new old manuscript was the most important thing he'd ever come across. No doubt he'd talk about it in excruciating detail when they'd meet again.

Sam picked up her purse from the counter. Then she left the store, stepping into the cool air outside. She locked the door and stood for a moment, looking at the cobalt sky. She often felt it stretch like a dome above, but on this clear night, she could almost see the sky curve around the edges of the universe. At its center, like a navel, the moon was waxing, big enough to cast a silver sheen on the world.

"Sam Burrow. On your left. Don't scare."

Sam startled and wheeled around. "Who's that?"

"Bonnie."

A shadow pushed away from the doorway of the former candy apple store.

Sam took a breath to quiet the anxious flutter of her heart. "What are you doing there, Bonnie?"

Bonnie didn't respond. Instead, she shook a cigarette from the pack, then a flash of fire as she lit up. A throaty exhale and smoke reached Sam's nostrils.

"I'm taking a walk."

Sam nodded. Strange time for walking up and down Main, or for hiding in the shadows of the candy apple store. But who was she to judge? She'd just been staring for who knew how long at the moon herself. Trying to be casual, Sam glanced down the street. There was no one else.

"No worries." Bonnie chuckled, a sound that was new to Sam. Beach Cove was small, and the locals knew each other well enough. Sam had heard most people chuckle or laugh. Not Bonnie, though.

Sam grabbed the strap of her purse as if it were a safety line. "I'm not worried." But there was an edge of unrest in her chest that called the words out as a lie. Again she looked over her shoulder. "You're not here for me, are you?"

The red dot of Bonnie's cigarette glowed, then faded. Another puff of smoke reached Sam.

"No, I'm just taking a walk. I often do. But you—you're out late."

Sam shrugged. The tone of Bonnie's voice suggested that the town was hers at night. Sam resisted the urge to explain herself.

"Did you work this late?" The red dot again.

Sam didn't want a late-night conversation, least of all with Bonnie. "Yes," she heard herself say nevertheless. "I got a load of new books I needed to sort and put on the shelves." That was enough—enough to get away.

Yet her feet didn't walk.

"New books? I thought you sold old books. Says so on the window."

"That's right. They're new *old* books if that makes sense." Sam laughed the laugh of an embarrassed teenager, high and breathy as if air was in short supply.

"How old?"

Sam shrugged. She didn't want to appear snooty, too stuck-up to talk books with an insomniac fisherwoman. "It varies. Some are very old. Hundreds of years sometimes."

The red dot glowed and then plummeted. Sam heard Bonnie grind out the butt with her boot.

"I heard you had a witch in your family," Bonnie said.

Sam felt her eyebrows shoot to her hairline. What sort of time was it to bring up something like that? "Listen, Bonnie, it's late," she started.

"I know."

"I'd better ..." Sam pointed at her car parked at the curb.

"I might come by someday," Bonnie muttered. "Look at your books."

"Oh." Sam started to feel dizzy. "Sure. Of course."

"Okay." Bonnie's moon-silvered form stepped to the side.

"Good night," Sam murmured and now she was able to walk. She forced herself not to clutch her purse.

"Hey," Bonnie said as Sam passed her.

Sam took another step before she turned. "Yes?"

"The woman who lost her boy— you're friends."

"Yes. We are friends." Sam let go of her purse and wrapped her arms around herself.

"Is she all right?"

"I don't—Um, I think so."

"Because my daughter was his—I don't know. Girlfriend, I guess."

"I know." Sam felt a stab of sympathy. She turned to face Bonnie more fully. "Did the police tell you what happened?"

There was a moment of silence. "I read it in the Starfish."

"I'm sorry, Bonnie. If I'd known the police didn't get in touch, I'd have told you." Bonnie had felt the need to send Brandie away to protect her from accusations and unfair fallout. Sam frowned. The woman had missed raising her own child because of Alex's disappearance, and no one had even told her he'd been found? No one had bothered to share that all suspicion had been lifted off her daughter?

"Is the mother doing okay? Is Maisie okay?" Bonnie asked again. She sounded more distant as if she'd walked farther away. But she was still standing in the same spot she'd been all along.

No wonder she sounded distant. Anyone would understand if Bonnie held a grudge. Instead, she was asking how the other mother was holding up.

"It's hard to tell," Sam hedged. Who knew how Maisie was doing? If Sam had it right, Maisie herself didn't know how she was doing. Judging from the fact that she was gardening and cooking for her friends, things she used to do in happier times—sure, she was doing better. But where on the scale was "better"? Had "better" reached the level of "okay" yet? Sam shrugged lightly. "I think she'll be okay. She eats and sleeps and has her friends over." She stopped herself. There was no reason to go into detail.

Bonnie nodded. "I'm going to leave now."

"Oh. Okay. Goodnight." Sam dropped her arms. "I have to get home myself."

Bonnie turned and simply walked away.

"All right, that was weird," Sam muttered. Very softly, in case the fisherwoman had good ears. Her hands trembled as she fumbled for her car keys. Finally she found them and quickly slipped into the driver's seat, locked the doors, and switched off the little overhead light. And then Sam took a deep breath.

There wasn't a thing Bonnie had said to make her feel this weird. She'd been nice. Asking after the books and Maisie. Right? She *had* been nice, hadn't she?

Then why was Sam's gut in all sorts of coils and knots? Sam shifted, scanning the dark, empty street. She shouldn't have worked so late. She was tired; her stomach was off. Her sixth sense was off—and she felt like she'd done everything wrong just now.

She started the car and pulled away from the curb, trying to settle into more mundane thoughts. So now she'd reached the age when she couldn't pull late nights anymore. She had to eat more fruit and vegetables. Maybe start taking a multivitamin. Broccoli made good soup. Maybe she'd clean all the junk from her cabinets tomorrow, go shopping for real food. Maybe she'd get some salmon at Ellie's.

Maybe Bonnie was going to drop off some freakishly nice fishes at Ellie's.

No. Stop it, you're being weird. Paranoid.

Sam swallowed the wrong way and coughed, low key but unable to stop until she felt empty inside.

When she pulled into her driveway, she unbuckled and then sat in her car, watching her lovely, rambling old Victorian. The windows were dark. Made sense, since Larry wasn't home. But the old glass panes, originals still, shone in the dark as they reflected moonlight like mirrors. Sam pulled out her phone and dialed Larry's number.

"Yes?"

She straightened, pleasantly surprised that he'd answered. "Hi."

"What's up?" He sounded distracted.

"I just wanted a familiar voice," Sam said after a moment.

"Hi there." Paper rustled.

"Give me a little bit more than that." She opened her door and stepped out.

"Sam, I'm really busy. Why are you—"

His distracted pause was long enough for her to reach her front door and push the key into the lock. "Why am I what, Larry?"

"What? Oh. Why are you even awake?"

Sam pushed the door shut behind her with a foot and flicked on the light. "Is that a joke? I'm never not awake at this time."

"What's the time—ah. I thought it was later."

"What are you working on, Larry?"

"Something new."

"Byzantine?"

"Maybe?"

Sam rolled her eyes at the dark corridor and felt for the light switch. "Well, thanks for talking to me." Larry was in one of his most unbalanced work moods. Putting up with that was part of being married to a researcher. Or this particular researcher anyway; the other faculty spouses never quite seemed to understand what she was complaining about.

"Not a problem. Call me anytime, babe." He spoke slowly. Clearly, he was reading something.

"Yeah. Goodnight." Sam ended the call.

It hadn't been a fruitful conversation. But at this moment, the familiarity of playing second fiddle to her husband's work reassured Sam. She went to the kitchen and flicked on the lights there, too. Then she poured herself a glass of pinot from the fridge and sat at the kitchen table.

Definitely back to normal. A little bit of Larry and a lot of pinot was a winning combination.

The house was silent; the night was silent. Sam loved this time. She loved having the house to herself if she was perfectly honest. She could take a hot bath, curl up in front of the TV and watch all the bad reality shows without getting a comment... There were lots of delicious possibilities when you had a house to yourself at night.

Sam smiled at her reflection in the dark window. Now that was relaxing, she felt good. Not only good.

Great. Better than usual. More aware.

Suddenly hungry, Sam fixed herself a plate with olives, tapas cheese and crackers, refilled her glass, and carried it to the upstairs bathroom with her claw-footed bathtub. She ate while she waited for the tub to fill with hot water and bubbles, then poured a few drops each of lavender and eucalyptus oil into it, undressed, and let herself sink into the water. This was the best.

Sipping her wine, Sam wallowed, safe, happy, and alone, until she grew bored. Then she got out, dried off, and brushed her teeth. Her bed was glorious, the flannel sheets hugged her cozily. She watched trashy television about men searching for Bigfoot in all the wrong places until her eyes wouldn't stay open any longer.

Sam's last thoughts went to Maisie and the open suitcase.

In the morning, they should all take a walk at the beach. Make sure they got it in before Maisie left.

Chapter 31

"Thank you." Maisie closed the trunk of the white Acura, trying to breathe around the lump in her throat. It was solid, made from gratitude, grief, and a hundred conflicted feelings. Sam, Ellie, and Cate stood in a semicircle around her, blinking at her, the noon sun, their tears.

Maisie smiled through her own haze at the three women. Each one had in their way shaped her life with their friendship.

Ellie, short, impulsive, dark and sweet like a rainier cherry, stepped forward. She opened her arms. "I hope you'll stay in touch this time," she whispered into Maisie's ear as they embraced. "Don't cut me out again."

"I couldn't if I tried. I'm not like that anymore," Maisie mumbled into Ellie's ear.

"No, I guess not." Ellie let her go, and Cate took her place.

"Don't do anything I wouldn't do," Cate said. "I'll be checking."

"Got it. Hey...hang in there, Cate." Maisie pulled her closer. Cate's lack of self-love niggled at Maisie;

she'd make sure to be there for her. Phone, text, email, online—there were plenty of ways to stay in touch.

Cate made a stifled sound, either a sob or a chuckle. "I've got it good, but what do you have in New York City? Other than your work, I mean?"

Maisie stepped back. "My work is so important, Cate. I can help families that go through the panic I experienced myself. I know where to start and what to do."

Cate wrapped her arms around herself. "But why not just run it online or from here? It's your organization, isn't it? You should be able to do what you want."

An image of a mother crying in her arms, a dad sobbing into his hands, of Angela running back and forth with files, cups of water, paper tissues flashed in front of Maisie's eyes. "People have to see, sometimes touch, to understand there is help. For some, it can be all they have to keep going." Maisie shook her head. "Beach Cove has no public transportation; not even reliable internet. People can't get here, and even if they do, there's nowhere to stay. And it'd be a logistic nightmare to organize national searches and support services from here."

"But you'll come visit?"

Maisie nodded. "Coming back has been—" The lump lodged lower in her throat, choking her.

Coming back had been everything. She'd found her son; she'd gotten the answers. She wasn't a victim of fear and guilt anymore; she was a survivor who'd lived. A survivor who could visit the grave of her son, could lay her hands on the marble and know Alex was home and at rest. Know also that when her own time came, she'd lay beside her son, her headstone forever telling him she loved him.

Cate rubbed a hand over her face. "Don't cry, Maisie, or I'm going to start."

Maisie inhaled the salty air and shook her head. "Sam?"

Without hesitation, Sam came to hug Maisie. "I'm bummed I slept in," she muttered. "You might've told us you were going to leave today. I meant to drag everyone on a beach walk beforehand."

"It's okay," Maisie let her go. "I'll visit. We'll go then."

"When?" Sam narrowed her eyes, all suspicion.

"I'm not sure—August?"

"August? That's a long way off." Sam exchange glances with Ellie and Cate.

"It's a long drive," Maisie murmured, already hearing Angela's tired protest in her mind. "Six, seven hours. I can't do it too often."

"Drive-schmive." Cate pulled her cardigan closer around herself. "You can say if you need time to sort things out. We'll miss you one way or the other, but you promised to let us in on your feelings."

Maisie blew out a breath. "It is a long drive, Cate. But maybe you're right." She tried to sort through the gaggle of thoughts in her head. "It really is because of work. I have my share to shoulder. But you're right; I also need time to sort things—"

Maisie stopped and stared at the house. Had the curtain moved? But no, it hung flat and still. She sighed; she needed to decide what she would do with the house. She'd held on to it so Alex could find his way back there. But he didn't need it anymore, and there was no point in letting it fall to ruin. The garden, the house, the beach—it all was there to be enjoyed. Not be a memorial to a time gone by.

She should sell. Not this moment and maybe not the next. But soon.

Maisie climbed into her car and buckled in.

Her friends were looking at her, all three ditching work to see her off. Maisie blew them a kiss and closed the door.

Over the rim of her paper coffee cup, Maisie scanned the bistro tables scattered around Bryant Park. People chatted or sat silently, stretching their faces toward the mid-morning sun. Others read books or swiped on their phones. In best NYC form, nobody looked back, and nobody took notice.

Since her return from Maine, the city seemed more crowded, urban anonymity more toxic, her apartment drearier than before.

Maisie still dreamed of Alex. But the dreams had changed. She wasn't searching anymore, nor playing out scenarios of what could've happened. Even in her dreams, Maisie knew where her son was. Sometimes, Alex would see her and turn to walk away. Often he was sad. Occasionally he smiled. Either way, Maisie always tried to catch up with him, but even though her feet drummed the ground, she couldn't. It wasn't because she wasn't moving; she was running as fast as she could. But the ground under Alex's feet rotated to a different rhythm than her own, swallowing her progress.

Only twice there was a fortunate alignment of their worlds, a temporary resonance of speeds. Both times, Alex stopped and reached for her, and she caught him in her arms. There was nothing that needed to be said. Maisie held her son and kissed his cool, sweet forehead. Then she rested her face on his hair the way she'd done when he'd been a toddler sitting on her lap and breathed in his scent. It never lasted long before their worlds slipped apart again and carried him away.

Maisie was grateful. She didn't know what caused the rhythms of their dreams to fall in step. She wasn't going to try to find out, either. Just in case it would jinx her chances of holding her child again.

She shifted the hot paper cup in her hand. There they were, sitting by the fountain, facing the library, their backs to her. Jim and Ashley. Heads together, phones in hand.

Maisie wound her way through strolling tourists and speed-walking New Yorkers.

"Hi," she said.

The podcasters stood to shake her hand. "So good

to see you, Mrs. J," Jim said. For once he looked well slept and apple cheeked. His face was younger than she remembered.

Maisie smiled. "It's good to see you too, Jim. And you, Ashley."

"Sit down?" Ashley pulled an empty chair closer.

"Yes." Maisie sat. "I'm so glad you two could make time."

"Of course. We meant to get in touch anyway, let you know what's happening with your episode." Ashley set her ubiquitous phone on the table.

"I'd like to know."

Ashley cleared her throat. "The crew finished doing their magic, so we're ready to put it on air. Whenever you give us the green light."

"Yes. You have it. All green." Maisie wanted to say something more appreciative. But for her, the search was over. She didn't want to relive it. Though the kids certainly deserved the credit, the five-star ratings and sponsor offers that kept them going. To help others by drawing awareness to their missing souls.

"And..." Jim hesitated. "We're sort of making it into a five-part episode." He looked for her consent, and Maisie nodded. Sure. His shoulders relaxed. "Thanks. There's too much story to cram it all in one episode."

"You have permission to do whatever you want. I know you'll stick to the facts."

"Of course," Ashley said. "I can send you the files before they air if you'd like to sign off first."

"Oh, I won't listen to them. I don't want to live through it again."

"Of course," Ashley said again. "We'll do Alex justice. I promise."

Maisie sighed. "And then it's over. Because you two found him."

"Yes," Jim said, a satisfied expression on his face. "I'm glad we decided on the dogs. It was a close call; we almost weren't going to."

"I'm glad too." Maisie blew out a tense breath. "Listen, I know I've said thanks before, but I want to thank you properly. What you did means everything. Thank you."

"I'm so glad we could help." Jim blushed.

"What comes next for you?" Maisie wanted to know.

Ashley looked wistfully at the fountain. "We'll move on to the next case. Searching for missing people is where it's at for us. What are you going to do next yourself, Mrs. J?"

"I'm continuing my work, help families search for their missing loved ones."

Ashley smiled. "Can we end the episode with that statement?"

"Sure."

"I suppose that's one good thing to come out of it," Jim said. "You can use your experience to help others. I'm sure they need you."

"They do need help."

Beach Cove had changed her. A slow and private grief had taken the place of racing fear. She'd self-medicated that fear with endless work; her everlasting search had been a drug to cope with the need to find her own son. A rope to find her way through a nightmare labyrinth.

But there was another rope, one she'd been unable to reach before her return to Beach Cove. A rope of friendship and grace that had led her not through the labyrinth, but out of it. Because friendship didn't lose itself. It was always—

"You know what?" Maisie set her cup down suddenly, spilling coffee. "I think I'm more needed in Beach Cove than here."

"Oh. Well... You did seem to have a lot of friends in Beach Cove," Ashley remarked. "They must miss you."

"They do miss me," Maisie said. Robert's death hadn't cut the ties the way she'd feared. She'd never been lost. She'd been trying to survive. But she was healing. She was healing, and she was ready to take her place again.

"They do miss me," Maisie repeated again. "More than I realized. And I miss them. I really—"

"Do you have to go?" Jim asked, eyebrows rising in surprise.

Maisie noticed that she'd half-risen from her seat. She sat back down. "No. Not right this second."

He straightened. "Can I ask you a question to wrap up? Like, officially?"

Maisie coughed a groan away. "Sure. Ask away."

Jim tapped his phone and set it on the table between them, then solemnly looked at her. "Mrs.

Jameson, you are back at work already. How are you feeling?"

"Better." Maisie put a hand to her heart. "I'm feeling better."

"Because you found closure?" There was a smile in Jim's voice.

"Yes. But it's not the only thing I found."

A small boy, maybe five years old, ran into a swarm of pigeons. They took off, wings beating the air.

"What else did you find?"

"Strange as it sounds, I seem to be finding bits and pieces of myself again. I've found my friends. And I think I found my place."

"What place is that?"

Maisie stood, picking up her cup. It wasn't quite noon yet—the things she needed to do herself, like packing her bag and arranging things with the concierge, she could finish quickly.

"Well, it's Beach Cove," she said. "I'm going back. I'm going back tonight."

To her house, her garden, the beach, and the sea.

To her friends.

Maisie turned to the young woman. "Ashley, would you mind walking with me? I want a word."

Chapter 32

"You think she means…what?" Sam let her phone sink.

Ellie shrugged, frowning again at the text Maisie had sent a few hours ago.

Coming back.

Ellie let her phone sink and squinted into the dark. Beach House's sunroom was lit cozily, but out there, night had fallen. "It's late. Are we sure she's coming here? Tonight?"

"We have to assume, since it's a group text to the three of us." Sam tucked her phone away. "And she's not answering her phone because she's driving. Ergo, she's coming here, tonight." Her foot drummed a nervous rhythm on the floor. "I *think*."

"Everything's fine," Cate muttered. "Nothing bad has happened."

"How do we know?" Ellie turned to her. "We can't reach her. Maybe she's gone off the deep end."

Cate closed her book. "I'm not a mathematician, but statistically, we're due a break. She's fine. Maybe a little confused or something. But she's coming back, so that's good. This is good."

"It's dark." Ellie glanced at the clock. "Almost eleven." She scratched her chin. "If she left from New York City and headed straight for Beach House, she should've gotten here already." Ellie groaned.

Cate studied her mildly from across the room. "All of Connecticut is one crazy traffic jam. Go home if you like; there's no need for us to sit here like hens waiting to lay eggs."

Ellie let her head fall into her neck. "I have to talk with Dale about expanding the store, and I was finally going to do it tonight. It'll be a *lot* of money, but it's that or going bust. I'm worried he's fed up subsidizing me. I don't want to ask him."

Cate came to sit beside Ellie. "If Dale can't help, you could get a loan. You're good for it, aren't you?"

"We do have a chunk in savings. It's just—money talks are the worst, aren't they?"

"Are they?" Sam piped up. "I don't mind talking money with Larry. Why shouldn't you bring it up with Dale? It's your money as well as his. It's an investment too; you're not asking for a favor or to throw it out the window."

Ellie huffed, impatient with herself. Why couldn't she be more like Sam? "You're right. It should be fine. It's just, um, Dale's been so busy lately. He's always working."

Cate clucked her tongue. Ellie smiled at her, grateful for the sympathy.

Sam shrugged. "Larry practically lives in his office. So they're working on their careers. You work on yours. I've never met a better fishmonger. You have the freshest fish in town."

"Thank you. I like being a fishmonger. It's weird, but it is what it is." Ellie had come to terms with her odd passion. Fish were like beings from a different world with their shimmering grace and otherworldly faces. Plus, they paired well with wine.

"It's not weird. You're like a marine artist. Fish is your medium."

"Aww. Thank you." A small, insecure part of her was glad that there wasn't a trace of sarcasm in Sam's voice.

"You should go for it. Have that talk with Dale. Did you run some numbers to show him?" Cate inquired.

Ellie smiled. "Run what numbers?" It was hard to resist teasing Cate who'd never run a business, and even harder not to deflect the issue.

"Oh I don't know." Cate didn't let Ellie get to her any more than she'd let a student fluster her. "*Numbers*. If you have a business, that's what you do. Run numbers."

Sam chuckled. "Gotta hand that one to Cate, Ells."

"Yeah," Ellie relented. "I've run the numbers. It'll take three or four years, but it'll pay for itself and then some. The problem is getting Dale to *look* at the numbers. He's so busy I'm worried he'll—"

Sam held up a hand. "Kids, I hear something! I hear tires on gravel!"

Rattan crackled as they stood, and Cate's book clattered to the floor.

Ellie's heart sped up. "Cross your fingers it's her,

and she's in one piece."

They got to the front door just as it opened.

"Surprise!" Cate pulled the door open wider.

On the doorstep stood Maisie, eyes wide, her hand with the key suspended in the air. "You're all here! I didn't mean—Ah, forget it! Hi!"

"We waited all afternoon for you." Ellie put a hand to her throat. Her pulse was beating fast under her fingers. "Come in. We didn't know what was going on after we got your cryptic text." She closed the door behind her friend.

"It wasn't cryptic! I said I was coming, didn't I?" Maisie spread her arms as if she were an exhibit in court.

Ellie shook her head. "We were hoping that's what you *meant* to say. More words would've been good. Next time spell it all out for us, girl. Or, you know, throw in a call."

"Oh. Sorry! I was rushing around to get things sorted. Like, *really* rushing around."

Sam pointed at the large canvas tote in Maisie's hand. "So have you come to stay for a while?" There was a threatening tone in her voice. Ellie grinned.

Maisie let the tote plop onto the floor. "Yep."

"Oh." Sam's fair eyebrows dropped back to where they belonged. "Good. Whoa. Okay. Good. Honestly, you came back a lot sooner than I figured."

They stood around Maisie, staring. Or maybe they weren't staring, but Ellie at least felt like they were. No one had said it, but of course they all were worried about the same thing.

What if Maisie had come to sell Beach House?

Cate stretched her neck as if she was hard of hearing. "Maisie, have you come back to stay *for good*?"

Maisie inhaled. "Yep."

Ellie tilted her head. "Yep you've come to *stay for good*? You're moving back to Beach Cove?"

"Stop asking," Maisie said happily. "Yes. I'm moving back in." She pointed to her bag. "I sort of already did. I'm not even going back; I can have a moving company pack up my stuff and bring it." She looked around, then reached out and flicked on the chandelier. She squinted at it as if she didn't have three friends, struggling to keep up, circling her silently. "Dusty, isn't it?"

"Focus, Maisie," Sam said sternly. "We're not talking about the chandelier right now."

"Oh. Okay. Well…" Maisie stopped frowning at the ceiling. "I can't do without you, ladies. I missed my house, and I'm addicted to the sea."

"Well now," Sam muttered irreverently. "We *told* you."

Maisie smiled. "I guess I wasn't listening, Sam."

"Yeah." Sam grinned a little sheepishly. "I mean, don't."

"I've been driving seven hours straight. The traffic in Connecticut was a mess." Maisie lifted on tiptoes so she could peer over Ellie's head out the window. "What do you say to a quick swim and a picnic at the beach? It's warm enough."

"*Now?*" Ellie shook her head no.

"I brought three different sorts of quiche, wine, and my swimsuit." Maisie pointed at the tote.

"Maise. It's almost midnight. We're old women," Cate said, her voice as incredulous as Ellie felt.

"Sounds about right. Who's with me?"

A giggle escaped Ellie. Every moment that ticked by seemed lighter, fizzier, and more hopeful. They were all together again? Growing old together? "We're good for the picnic," she heard herself say. "But I read the sharks come to the beaches at night."

"Nonsense with the sharks," Sam declared bossily. "Nobody's going swimming, but only because it's too dark and the water is too cold. Maise, midnight snack only. Deal with it. Let's go get plates."

Cate hooked her arm under Maisie's. "Good to have you back, Maisie. I agree with no swimming, though."

Ellie grinned and picked up the tote. "Yeah, no swimming. But it's true about the sharks. Sam just isn't *informed*."

Maisie dropped her keys on the sideboard. "Let's go to the beach, ladies."

Note to the Reader

Dear Reader – I hope you enjoyed this first book in the Beach Cove series. You can read more about the secrets of Beach Cove and what happens next with Maisie, Ellie, Cate, and Sam in Beach Cove Inn.

Stay in touch at subscribepage.com/nelliebrooks and be the first to know about new releases, sales, and promos. You can also find me on Facebook if you look for Nellie's Reader Group, or at www.nelliebrooks.com

I'd love to hear from you. Email me anytime at Nellie@nelliebrooks.com

As always, thank you for reading and reviewing.

I truly appreciate my readers.

Books By This Author

Beach Cove Inn

Life has finally returned to normal in the small town of Beach Cove. Ellie's ready to grow her business when a startling letter turns her world upside down.

Living alone in her rambling house by the sea, Maisie struggles with the ghosts of her past - and with figuring out her enigmatic new neighbor.

Sam does her best to support her friends when she receives an unexpected inheritance. Meanwhile, her husband forces her to make a tough decision.

Cate, too, has to make a decision – only hers is a secret. Riddled with doubt, she tries to take charge of her heart.

Follow the women of Beach Cove as they figure out together when to let go and when to fight for love, relationships, and respect.

Made in the USA
Coppell, TX
07 June 2022

78547195R00192